The Glimmer Saga
#3

The Throne of Glimm

D E McCluskey

THE FINAL PART OF YOUR ADVENTURE... ENJOY

D E McCluskey

ISBN 978-1-914381-06-5

Dammaged Production
www.dammaged.com

For Tony Higginson

What this guy has forgotten about books
We can only hope to learn…

Part One:

1.

THE WOMEN WERE the lynchpins of the whole society. They were the ones who tended to the children. They prepared the meals for the men. They were the hunters *and* the gatherers. They chopped the wood that was needed to cook the food, to keep them warm through the cold nights, and to heat the water for bathing.

The women built the homes where they slept and sheltered from the elements; they built the fences that kept them safe from the wildlife and the savage tribes of the forest. They also built the meeting places where the men would gather to talk.

They even designed and built the places of worship.

It was true that their way of life would have collapsed years ago had the women not taken the lead and made the decision to become their world builders.

In all this time, all the men had done was make the decision to grow their beards and hair long and to bleach them so they appeared grey, no matter what age they were. For some reason, this was deemed important as they pondered the meanings of life and communed with nature. They had long ago stopped wearing normal clothing; they now donned themselves in tunics that covered them from their necks to their feet. They bathed maybe once a week, whether they needed it or not, and would sometimes go long periods without speaking, even to each other.

Most of their time was spent in the worship and the study of the teachings of The Great Lord Glimm. They were devoted to his learnings and to understanding his magical practices, his works, and the mysteries of nature.

The women were mostly ignored.

They were seen by the men as a necessity and, sometimes, a distraction. They were just there to raise the children, living their lives marginalised from the importance of understanding the world and how it worked.

What the men failed to understand, or had conveniently forgotten, was that the women were powerful magicians. Stronger and more gifted, in many ways, than they were.

They worshipped the same God, The Great Lord Glimm, but where the men had dedicated their lives to understanding the forces that affected the world they lived in, both light and dark, the woman developed different skills. The men had these skills too, but they didn't offer them as much reverence as the women did.

One of these skills was foresight.

The women were aware of the failings of their menfolk.

The birth rate within the settlement had dropped at an alarming rate, dwindling almost by half within the last hundred years or so, as the men dedicated their time to worship at the Temple of Glimm. The family units became fractured and, in some cases, split entirely. The very little physical contact meant fewer births.

The women, more in-tune with the spiritual aspects of life, could see the errors of this way of life and had decided something needed to be done. They knew the menfolk were undertaking important work, but there were priorities, and they required acknowledgment.

Zadamare was the wife of the current Elder Glimm of the village. This position elevated her to the mantle of matron within the underground covenant the women had formed, the one they called the Sisterhood.

The society had started nearly five centuries earlier, when the women with the strongest magic running through their blood banded together to cast spells and work their magic for the good of the settlement, and for their men. They saved the village during arid times; they fattened the animals for slaughter; they became strong. The bond between the women had become tight, so tight that the Sisterhood still thrived all these years later.

They would gather in an underground chamber; they had spilled their own magic to keep it hidden from the men. They knew if the menfolk found out about the Sisterhood, they would try to destroy their work, and the Sisters could not allow that to happen.

'I have called you here today as I fear a crisis in how we survive is coming to pass,' Zadamare said as she addressed the throng of women before her. They were gathered in their temple, nearly two hundred women sitting silently in rapture, listening to what their elder had to say. 'We have foreseen this crisis; we know it will eventually destroy our way of life. If left unchecked, it will mark the end of our civilisation. This cannot, and will not, be allowed to continue. Steps must be made to ensure it doesn't pass.'

'What is this crisis you talk of, Zadamare?' one of the women asked. 'I have not seen anything dark in the futures of the village.'

Zadamare looked upon the woman who had asked the question. Her smile was gentle, but her eyes told of fear. 'It is a crisis of apathy, my dear. Our menfolk are apathetic to the ways of nature. Oh, they profess to love nature, and have a longing to control it, but it has blinded them to the ways of the world. They ignore our touch; they refuse our advances. As we gather, our numbers dwindle. Last year we recorded four-hundred-and-twelve healthy births. One-hundred-and-ninety-seven of them were male, the rest female. This number is just short of three quarters of the numbers birthed the previous year.'

'Is there a trend to this?' the same woman asked. 'Pray tell.'

'Unfortunately, yes. Our men prefer to spend their time in the temple instead of preserving our linage. I believe that for the sake of the village, and of the Sisterhood, it's time we took this matter into our own hands.'

'What do you suggest we do?' another woman asked. 'We cannot fascinate our menfolk into mating with us, they are too strong in their own magic for that.'

'You are right, but we have to preserve our genes. We need to put our essence back into nature, create our own bloodlines.'

A murmur rippled through the gathered women. 'How do you propose we do this without the menfolk?' the woman asked, her brow creasing.

'I suggest we procreate with the wild men of the woods.'

A gasp echoed around the room. Zadamare was nodding as she regarded her flock. She had expected an adverse reaction, but maybe not as much horror.

'The wild men of the woods?' another woman asked breathlessly. 'But they are savage, feral. They are liable to rape us, kill us, and perhaps even eat us.'

'Not if they are under our influence,' Zadamare replied.

This caused more consternation. The women shifted in their seats; whispers filled the air.

'Are you talking of polluting the gene pool?'

Once the question was asked, the room fell silent and Zadamare felt the glare of two hundred pairs of eyes boring into her. She paused. She knew the answer, and it wasn't one these women would take lightly. *There is no way of softening this,* she thought.

'Yes, that is exactly what I'm talking about.' She paused then, waiting for the outrage in the room to subside. It took a while, but when it did, she continued. 'I do not want our ways to end like I fear they are about to. I want the Sisterhood to continue for the ages to come. But it needs to continue with our essence entwined within it.'

There was another period of consternation. The noise in the room elevated, and Zadamare found herself unable to be heard above the hubbub. 'This is not an issue,' she continued again after the noise died down. Her voice brought silence back to the room. 'We need to breed, otherwise we will die, and our ways will disappear with us. If we take the wild men as mates and build upon our understanding of extending our afterlife, then we will be able to guide our progeny from beyond the grave. Whatever we lose in the wild men's genes, we will make up for in the extensions of our wisdom.'

'Is that even possible?' a voice from the crowd asked, breaking the silence of the congregation.

'I know our men have been working on this for some time now. I have access to their scrolls. We can use our own skills, tack them onto what has already been discovered. I do not foresee any problems for us.'

'Is this something we should be doing? If we are dying out, is it not nature's whim?' another voice asked.

'Do you want everything the Sisterhood has built over the last millennia to be lost in the annals of time? We have an opportunity here. An opportunity to thrive, to educate our children, to usher forth a new generation based on *our* historical learnings. I see *this* as our natural progression. We keep our lineage, and we preserve our ways. In our children's darkest hours, we can be their guiding light.'

Zadamare could tell by some of the looks in the crowd that she was making sense, though others may need time, and persuasion, to make the change.

'All in favour, please stand.' She had been expecting a small percentage of the women to agree with her, but when she saw how many of them rose from their seats, it took away her breath. It was an easy majority. Most of the others were older women, way past child-bearing days. She knew they could be persuaded in time.

She smiled her careful smile again and raised her arms. 'From this day forwards, I propose the Sisterhood should be known as The Sisterhood of the Purple. We are the merging of the red and the blue. Both ends of the spectrum. Our men work backwards and forwards between both elements, but they do not see the middle ground. They are blind to the Purple. I do not put this forward to rub the men's noses in their failures but to learn from them, for the future of the Sisterhood of the Purple and to offer our unborn children the knowledge of those failures when they worship at the Throne of Glimm.'

A chorus of approval ripped through the chamber.

'It is decided then,' Zadamare shouted over the cheers. 'We should meet again at the cycle of the moon. We need to prepare our blood to facilitate the lengthening of our consciences. In the meantime, I urge you to seek out the wild men in the woods. Use every whim you must to dull their savagery, to heighten their sensuality. Do not stick to one man. We need to re-populate. We will keep records on who is related to who, but we need children. Strong, healthy new children. Multiple births to multiple partners.'

Again, there was agreement from the room.

'Oh, and ladies. You need to remember to have fun. The wild men of the forest can be very … pleasurable.' As she spoke, she rubbed her belly, insinuating that there was already something lying within her womb.

The women, laughing, flocked to lay their hands on her, as was their tradition.

2.

FIFTEEN YEARS AFTER the decision to mate with the wild men of the forest had been made, the settlement was a different place. The narrow streets were littered with children. Many of them sported wilder looks than others, these were usually males. The females had taken to wearing shrouds of purple and tended to carry themselves with more purpose.

Zadamare had carried two more children from her unions with the wild men, one more from the one she carried in her belly all those years ago when she offered her solution. Her husband, the Elder of the Glimm, had not noticed that his wife, who he had not had relations with in a long while, had begotten the children. He didn't notice when the second child was born and was even further removed when the third one came along.

The women taught both sexes with equality. Again, this went unnoticed by the men. This was until the day the boys reached their twelfth birthday. Only then were they deemed old enough to join the Glimm, before then, they were largely ignored.

If a boy didn't show initiative in the probational years of the Glimm, they were cast out of the village as, again, was their custom. The men wanted to keep only the sharpest minds in their ranks.

The rejected boys, much to the sorrow and chagrin of the women, were cast from the settlement and into the forest to fend for themselves, where they would usually fall foul of the wild men. Many were killed, and often eaten, as was *their* way.

However, since the change, the boys who were cast out were learned in the ways of science, mathematics, crafts, and defence. These boys were equipped to deal with life outside the village, and when they were eventually pursued by the wild men, they were able to evade them. Eventually, these boys formed alliances with the tribes. They began to educate them. This advancement led to the boys becoming elevated into positions of power within the primitive tribes. They were advisors, doctors, and leaders within the communities. It was under the guidance of these boys that the two largest tribes split from the lesser tribes and took refuge in locations that were defendable, that had access to clean, fresh water, better hunting grounds, and fertile lands.

These tribes eventually became known as the great kingdoms of Azuria and Carnelia.

Of course, this wouldn't be for another three or four hundred years hence, but the seeds of the nations were sown from the changes and the sacrifices of the Sisterhood of the Purple.

~~~~

Zadamare was dying. The ravages of time had caught up with her physicality. The late additions to her family, a boy and a girl, both sired by wild men, had eaten her up inside, and for the ten years after her last child, ill health had been a constant companion.

As she lay on the bed in the home she had built, Rose, another of the Sisterhood of the Purple, sat next to her, attending to her needs. Zadamare's head was constantly moist, despite the coolness in the air, and Rose had been mopping her brow continually. She had also been feeding her herbs, hoping to relieve her pains and aches, but both sisters knew nothing could halt the inevitable.

'Rose, are you still there?' the sickly woman whispered in the darkness of the room, her voice barely more than a dry rasp. Rose could hear the rattle in her throat, the one that came from her chest. The foreteller of death.

'I'm here, sister. Is there anything you require?' the handmaiden asked.

'Roberre,' she whispered. 'Please, fetch Roberre …'

Rose knew where Zadamare's husband would be, even in this late hour. 'I will attend to it, my sister. Please stay strong until I return.'

Rose left the dying woman and travelled across the village, towards the huge structure a while away from their dwelling. She knew the Glimm would be in attendance, worshipping or studying.
~~~~

'Roberre, you must attend immediately,' Rose shouted breathlessly across the great temple. Her voice echoed through the chamber. 'It's Zadamare, she will not see out the night.'

The unexpected voice in the night surprised several of the Glimm who were worshiping at the temple. Rose suspected, by the vacant looks on their faces, that they had been sleeping rather than praying.

Roberre was at the altar. He stood as he recognised the woman in the purple shroud who had interrupted their worship. 'Rose, my child,' he soothed. 'Whatever could cause you to interrupt prayers at this time of the night?' he asked. She could see the sleepiness in his eyes and the white line where drool had dried in his beard.

'It's Zadamare. I fear she will not make it through the night. I have a deep worry that she may not make it through the current hour.' She took a moment to collect herself and take a few breaths. 'Her fever, it gets worse by the minute, and the darkness from the bleeding inside her is spreading. You must attend, Roberre, she calls for you.'

Roberre nodded and looked deep in thought. 'Attend I will,' he whispered finally.

Rose's shoulders dropped as she exhaled, content with his answer.

'I will finish up here first, of course. Then I will meditate on the issue. The Great Lord Glimm provides solutions to all problems. We will be strong!'

'But …' she stuttered, not fully understanding his reply.

'No buts, my child,' he soothed. 'I will attend. Now, you must leave this place. We can't have female distractions this close to a spiritual breakthrough.'

Before she knew any different, Rose found herself ushered out of the temple, back into the cool of the night. She spared a glance at the dense wooden door that had just closed on her and, with a heavy heart, turned back towards the village from whence she came.

~~~~

As Rose entered into the communal hall, she was greeted by several Sisters of the Purple. They all wore the same purple robes, and all were sporting the same concerned expressions. They looked to her, and she shook her head. The small gesture told them all they needed to know, confirming their fears.
~~~~

Roberre was not coming.

Rose was ushered into the small chamber, lit only by a single flickering candle, where Zadamare's bed stood in the centre of the room. She reached out, taking the hand of the frail woman. She was surprised by how cold her fingers were, especially as she could see the sheen of sweat glistening on her brow. Her grasp also surprised the younger woman. It was strong, and it was forceful.

'Roberre?' she whispered, the rattle in her voice prominent now.

Rose swallowed before gripping Zadamare's hands tighter.

'He's … He will be attending, Zadamare. He is meditating in the throne room. He did say he would pray for you, and he instructed me to send you his undying love.'

The dying woman saw through the lie.

A thin smile spread across her damp face. She closed her eyes gently, then opened them a few moments later. 'It is not his fault, Rose. Do not judge him harshly. They are all too far gone. They have tapped the power of the Glimm, harnessed the power of nature, controlled the magics, both light and dark. You mustn't expect a man who has done all of that to remember to love the people who have loved him.'

Although the speech was sad, Zadamare was smiling. She laughed a little. As she did, pink spittle sprayed from her mouth. Rose picked up a small cloth and wiped the blood away.

'Allow me my children, would you?' she asked, squeezing Rose's hand again.

'Of course. One moment.' Rose left the room and returned not a moment later with five younger people. The eldest boys were twins, they were in their early twenties and already sporting the robes and grey beards of the Glimm. These two had been the product of love between her and Roberre and had already been accepted into the Glimm. One had a shock of red streaking through his hair, the other had blue. Zadamare smiled as her gaze fell upon them.

'My twins, as polar opposite of each other you are, the more similar you are.' It was obvious to everyone in the room that even the act of speaking was hurting the frail woman. The boys leaned in and kissed their mother. There were tears in their eyes.

The girl was fifteen and was wearing the robes of the Sisterhood of the Purple. She looked sad, but there were no tears. There was a knowing glint as she regarded her mother. 'Goodnight, dear mother,' she whispered as she planted a soft kiss on the old woman's forehead.

Zadamare blinked slowly in acknowledgement of the girl's smile. 'I will see you soon,' she whispered to her daughter, gripping her hand.

The two youngest were a girl of twelve and a boy of only ten years old. They, like their older sister, were the product of couplings with the wild men. Zadamare had known the boy would never make it into the Glimm, there too much of his father in him. But knowing this, she had made arrangements for his training in the ways of science and the stars. This would give him a head start when he was eventually captured by the wild men. The girl was already headstrong and had taken it upon herself to begin the teachings of the Purple.

All five children loved her, and each other, and all were united in their grief of losing their mother.

The tears of the youngest were flowing as he flung himself onto the bed. The twins leaned in to prevent him from hurting their mother, such was the love and the sorrow he held.

'I am not afraid to pass over to the Great Lord Glimm,' she announced when the children had all embraced her. 'In fact, I rather look forward to it.'

The women from outside began to make their way into the room, and Zadamare took the time to look them all in their eyes. 'Look for me, my children. We have laboured hard to learn the ways of the Purple. We have extended our lives beyond that of the physical. Now it is my time to put our magic to the test. I will return, and I will attend whatever the needs of any of our lineage. My time here is over, all that is left to do is say goodbye and tell you that I have loved every one of you.'

Zadamare closed her eyes.

This time, they did not reopen.

3.

ROBERRE DID ATTEND his wife. But only at the very last.

The Elder of the Glimm presided over his wife's funeral, where he delivered the eulogy.

'I am deeply saddened by the passing of my loving wife,' he said in hushed tones.

The congregation consisted of many men with long white beards and many women wearing purple shrouds. These were interspersed with small children running between the pews, most of them tall with a wild look about them.

'She passed at a time when we, the Glimm, are on the verge of a major breakthrough in procuring the elements required to prolong life, maybe indefinitely.'

The members of the Sisterhood looked at each other. Long had they had an inkling, via their own magics, that the men had begun to move away from the natural order of things to dabble in other arts *they* were already well-versed in.

But most of those present were more shocked that he managed to turn a loving eulogy for Zadamare, their sister, into something about the Glimm and their achievements.

As the service ended and everyone left the temple, there was a wider chasm between the men and the woman than before they had entered.

~~~~

A little more than a week had passed since the funeral before the women of the village started noticing strange occurrences. At first, the events seemed trivial. If any of them were performing a function or undertaking a task and the tool they required for that task was not present,
~~~~

when they turned back to the toolbox after having looked for it, it would be there, in a place where it hadn't been moments earlier.

If they were to attend a service or a meeting, when they arrived at the hall, the candles would already be lit and the wine would have been poured.

On one occasion, one of the sisters had been travelling back from the watering hole, carrying two large pitchers of water. She disturbed a snake that had been lazing in the long grass. It rose, its mouth wide, poised to attack. Without warning, it launched itself at least twenty yards away from where the woman was standing, as if some force had picked up the animal and thrown it clear of the hapless woman.

Accidents had been prevented, torn clothing had been stitched, children had been rocked to sleep at night.

Even though all the events had seemed for the good, it caused concern for the Sisterhood.

The men of The Glimm were unaware of any phenomenon.

The Sisterhood were under the impression that the village was either haunted or maybe even cursed. They had mentioned it to the menfolk on numerous occasions but were either shunned or ridiculed by them. Notions had been whispered that the spirits were cursing them for their dalliances with the wild men of the forest. Others thought it was a portent, a sign from the Great Lord Glimm himself that the end of days were nigh.

One night, the Sisterhood was meeting in their communal room; it was a cold, miserable night, and the rain had not stopped falling all day. They were crammed into the large chamber, keeping each other as warm as they could. Most of the talk was regarding the strange occurrences.

'I believe we may need the guidance of the menfolk with this issue,' Rose addressed the group. 'I don't feel safe in the village anymore. Even in the main hall.'

Several women in the crowd voiced their agreement.

'Whenever I enter a darkened room, I feel someone in there with me, watching my every move,' one of the women said to the crowed room. 'Even when I light candles, I feel the presence remains. It is, it seems, not afraid of the light. I know the things this presence has done give me no reason to fear it, but fear it I do.'

As the women of the room were voicing their agreement, an explosion of lightning illuminated the night sky. It was closely followed by a monumental rumble of thunder. A cold wind blew in through the windows, instantly soaking the curtains. All eyes were on the billowing fabric, so no one noticed the hovering figure that floated above the congregation.

The figure was unmistakably female and was dressed from head to toe in purple robes. Her face regarded the women below her with a gentle smile.

A few moments later, she was noticed. Her presence was greeted with shrieks and screams. Several women bolted for the door, while others fell to their knees and began to openly pray to the Great Lord Glimm.

With a flick of her hands, the doors to the meeting room closed and locked just as the fleeing women reached them. There they stood, crying, banging on the wood, demanding to be let free from the demon visitation.

All of this seemed to amuse the vision. She lifted her hand, and the wind causing the curtains to billow ceased. The rain stopped. She then turned her risen hands towards the congregation. Most of them shied away from the gesture, as if they expected death itself to traverse from the finger and strike them down.

'Oh mighty spirit …' It was Rose who had the courage to stand up and address the visitation. '…please, do us no ill. We are worthy servants of the Glimm; we call ourselves the Sisterhood of Purple. We represent the middle ground between the red and the blue. We do not walk the path of darkness. We shun evil and wickedness …'

The spirit began to laugh.

Rose winced; the sound scared her more than the sight of the woman herself. As she turned from the shimmering woman, she stopped. *I recognise that laugh,* she thought.

'My sisters …' the vision said.

The kindly lilt to her voice caused the majority of the Sisterhood to stop their crying and praying. Those at the door stopped banging and turned to look at her.

'Do you not recognise your own sister? Was I so forgettable in life?' the woman asked.

'Zadamare?' Rose whispered.

She nodded and smiled. 'It is I,' she replied.

'By the Great Lord Glimm,' Rose whispered, a smile transforming her face. 'It is you. It worked?'

'Why would you even question it, sister?'

Rose was laughing now. 'I cannot lie, Zadamare. I did question it, a lot of us did. Hence our surprise at seeing you now.'

'It was not as simple a transition as I anticipated. It took me a while to traverse the corridors of death, but I now have it under my control. However, I can only reveal myself to you, to the members of the Sisterhood. I tried to contact Roberre, but he would either not be distracted from their work or simply could not see me.'

'Is it you who has been helping us? Watching over us?' Rose asked.

'Yes,' Zadamare replied. 'I no longer have the desire to be seen by anyone other than you, my sisters. I believe we will all be reunited in death.'

There was much rejoicing as this news was digested. Death, it seemed, was no longer a barrier to be feared.

'Do not allow this news to make you blasé with your life. It is a gift that should be cherished. I propose the Sisterhood of the Purple devote their time to helping other sisters and our own lineage. We should use it for the times when our sisters are in danger and in fear of their lives, or others' lives. Are we agreed?'

The agreement was felt throughout the great hall.

Part Two:

1.

Two thousand years later

CASS SLEPT. SHE woke, and then slept again.

There was very little else she could do. Her body was broken. Her muscles ached, and her bones felt swollen, sore, and useless. She was sure there was a fire in her veins that was spreading through her whole body. She had been this way for what felt like an eternity, although in reality, she knew it could only have been a couple of days. Ever since she had been carried away, out of the tunnels, and deposited in this dirty, dank prison.

She had been stripped and wrapped in rough cloth rags that chaffed her skin, flesh that was already painful to the touch.

They had also taken her glimmer.

She closed her eyes. Despite the unadulterated agony and the rags cutting into her distressed skin, she slept again.

Before she did, she prayed she wouldn't dream.

2.

ENDELLION WAS SITTING in a comfortable chair within her chambers in the castle of Carnelia. Ever since her men had returned from their routing of the Ferals and the Rebels, she had been in good spirits. Cassandra was imprisoned in her dungeon, and the Glimmer that she possessed was now in Endellion's possession. There was very little now that could hold her back.

Ultimate power was within her grasp.

Another smile, the latest in a long line of wide smiles, crept over her face as she pondered on whether or not to kill Cassandra. She had outlived her usefulness. Initially, she had kept her around as she didn't know if she needed her alive to keep her image alive, but that dilemma was moot now. She was custodian of both Glimmers. The girl was now just a thorn in her side, an inconvenience that could be snuffed out at any time.

'What tickles you so, my queen?' Alexander asked as he walked into the living quarters.

She looked at him and beamed. Her smile was infectious, and Alexander caught it with his own grin, which was in danger of splitting his head in two. 'My good and brave knight,' she said softly, even though she felt like she wanted to scream, to yell, to dance. 'I'm tickled because now we have everything that I, or we, ever wanted from life. Everything is within our grasp, and I can only feel things getting better.'

Alexander's smile widened, and he nodded as he turned away.

'Brother, why don't you take the rest of the day off? You've had a busy few days, and I think a boy of your age needs to blow off steam. Maybe you should seek out some of your friends and play. I have errands of a … personal nature to attend to.'

'Play, my queen?' the boy asked. His eyes widened; there was a vulnerability within in them that Endellion liked. It was this that kept him under her thrall without having to resort to murder. 'A knight of the realm does not *play*. My place is by your side.'

Endellion rolled her eyes. *I have created a monster,* she thought. 'Well, Alex, that is as may be, but seeing as I am your queen, *and* your older sister, do I really need to command you to take some rest?'

The boy recoiled as if he had been slapped.

'No, I didn't think so. Now, go before I throw you into the dungeons for your insolence,' she laughed. But her smile was only skin deep.

Alexander stretched his arms as he attempted to stifle the yawn that was rising within him. 'If you insist, my queen,' he said through gritted teeth. 'I will take my leave.'

At last, she thought, still smiling. 'I do. And further to that, I insist you do not return until morning. I have ample guards to keep me safe. Mayhap I'll have a quest for you tomorrow,' she teased.

The boy's face lit up. 'You will?' he asked.

She smiled again, but it was only the pretence of joviality. *How long must I keep up this game?* she thought. 'Maybe. Now go, leave me alone, my knight.'

Alexander clicked his heels and bowed low. 'Till the morning then, Your Majesty,' he offered before turning and leaving the room.

As the chamber doors closed behind him, she sighed. 'Thank Glimm for small mercies,' she whispered. She got up and popped her head outside the door and saw her handmaiden sitting at her station. The young girl was making shy eyes at the guard who was also stationed outside her room. 'Maiden, to me,' she ordered.

The young girl snapped out of her daydream and stood to attention at the queen's bequest. 'Y-yes, ma'am?' she stuttered.

Endellion looked at her with Cassandra's face and grinned inwardly. She enjoyed the power at her disposal, being the Queen of Carnelia and Azuria. 'I'll be taking some much-needed relaxation for the rest of the day. Any affairs of state will be dealt with by the council. I want you to inform them of this. If I go, it's likely I won't get out again for another five days. I have no head for politics today.'

The maiden swallowed as her eyes widened. 'Y-yes, ma'am,' she stuttered.

Endellion looked at her; she was disgusted at the girl's weakness. *Is that all she can say?* she hissed in her head. The girl repulsed her, she reminded her of herself when she was younger: weak, fragile, nervous. 'I'm not to be disturbed by anyone. Do you understand that? Not even if the sky is falling down.' Endellion's face softened and she smiled at her little joke. *If I scare her too much,* she thought, *the message will not get through and my plans for the day will be ruined.* 'Do you hear me?'

'Yes, ma'am,' the girl said again.

Endellion almost laughed at her response.

'Will you also do me a favour? There seems to be an infestation around the castle for the last few days. Have you noticed the butterflies? They seem to be everywhere.'

The maiden looked around the room at the pretty beasts fluttering around in the musty light.

'Ever since I got back, they seem to be everywhere,' Endellion continued.

'I think they're rather pretty,' the maiden replied without thinking who she was talking to.

Endellion's face changed. 'I didn't ask for your opinion on them. I want you to look into where the diseased, horrid beasts are coming from and have them destroyed.'

The girl instantly dropped her head. 'Yes, ma'am,' she whispered.

Endellion raged internally. Externally, she smiled. She wanted to reach out and grab the girl's hair, she wanted to pull it, to bash her head against the walls and the doors. But she didn't; she couldn't.

'Run now, child,' she said instead.

The girl bowed, and with one last look around the room at the fluttering butterflies, she left.

Once she was alone, Endellion re-entered her chambers. She breathed deep, countering the rage that had been building up inside her. She relaxed herself, then reached into the folds of her gown and wrapped her fingers around the reassuring weight residing within. She grasped her orb and closed her eyes. Her appearance began to shimmy, and the beautiful youthfulness of Cassandra began to melt away. It was replaced with the once beautiful but now haggard appearance of the real Endellion. Once the transformation was complete, she steadied herself on the wooden dresser against the wall. The dizziness passed, and all traces of

Cassandra—the dark hair with the blue tinge, the bright, youthful eyes—were gone. She smiled. This time, it was genuine.

She removed the Glimmer from her pocket and watched as the orb pulsed a dim red. She always felt better after looking into the ball.

'Today, I grasp my destiny,' she whispered. 'My vengeance will be complete. I hold both Glimmers in my grasp. Even the Great Lord Glimm himself will bow to me. I will reign supreme. Nature itself will bend to my will.'

The old woman cackled as she hurried to the small, hidden door in the wall. She opened it and bowed low to enter. This narrow route would take her to a deserted corridor in the castle; from there, she could make her way anywhere she wanted, and no one would recognise the form of Endellion.

She revelled in the power at her whim.

3.

BERNARD WAS LYING in a makeshift bed. His head was on a pillow that was stained brown and yellow from the blood and sweat the young prince had expelled since the bloody and violent battle with the mutant fireflies. Robert Ambric was in a seat beside the bed. His clothes and hands were dirty from battle, and there was blood too; some of it was his, but most of it belonged to others, including the fireflies.

He had been administering as much first aid as he knew on his young ward, but field triage had not been one of the more advanced areas of his training. He knew the boy was slipping, he could see it in the discolouration of his skin, hear it in the shallowness of his breathing; but there was precious little he could do about it. He had seen people die before, many times, a large number by his own hand. It was never pretty, and it was never entertaining.

The wound the boy had received from the firefly did not look too bad, but the blue tendrils of infection that were running from it, spreading through his chest, gave away the fact that that the poison administered by the sting was running deep.

'Sir Ambric …'

The thin, reedy voice startled him out of his reverie, and he turned towards the boy. He was surprised to see his eyes open; he was even more surprised to see him with a hand reaching out towards him.

'Sir Ambric …' the scratchy voice said again. 'To me,' it commanded.

Ambric leaned in close, taking the offered hand, and this time, he wasn't surprised to feel it was cold. 'It's no longer sir,' he whispered. He didn't know why he was whispering, but it seemed like the respectful thing to do in this hospital tent. 'Bernard, you must learn to call me Robert.'

A thin smile spread across the boy's bluish lips. Although there was very little humour in it, the amusement was there somewhere. 'That is something I will never do,' he whispered, culminating in a light but painful bout of coughs.

Ambric's smile was full as he gripped the boy's ice-like hand tighter. 'What can I do for you, my friend?'

'Cassandra? Please, tell me what happed to Cassandra.'

Ambric's smile fell instantly and was replaced with a bitter look, as if he had sucked on a particularly sour fruit. 'Are you sure it was Cassandra who you were with?' he asked. 'You know that her and the witch share the same face?'

Bernard offered him a weak smile. 'I am aware,' he replied.

'I saw the girl with Cassandra's face alight a firefly and was away. I may be old, but there is nothing wrong with my eyesight.' He watched as another thin smile spread across the boy's pained lips. 'Bernard?' he asked, his wild eyes staring down at the weakened prince. 'Why do you smile when I tell you a story of potential betrayal so close to you?'

Bernard coughed; his face winced, but his smile was resilient, and it returned. 'It is because you have fallen into the same trap that Carnelia and Azuria did.'

Ambric cocked his head as he regarded the boy.

'That was Cassandra you saw aboard the firefly,' Bernard finished.

'My Prince, I have seen the transformation up close between the queen and the witch. I cannot say which witch was which.'

Bernard lifted his hand again towards the older man. He responded by grasping it. The youth began another coughing fit, this one seeming worse than the others, and one that didn't look likely to pass anytime soon. Ambric was ready to find a nurse to administer to him when he noticed something funny about the coughs. They were more like laughs.

Bernard was laughing at Ambric's small, unintended, joke. 'That I do not doubt, my friend,' he croaked between chuffs.

'So, how could you tell the difference between them?' Ambric asked, his attention piqued by the boy's education in the witchcraft he had witnessed.

'Did she say anything before she was taken?' the boy whispered.

Ambric pouted, remembering a confusing name the girl had shouted. 'Aye, she did. She mentioned a name.'

The boy smiled; it was a pained smile. 'Was that name Anthony, per chance?'

Ambric's brow creased. 'It was.'

'That was the name of her beloved advisor in Azuria. It was also the code word she was to use when she returned to the compound so the soldiers knew it was her. That was Cassandra you saw being taken, not the witch. She told me all about the Glimmers.'

'The orb she produced when you removed the head of the soldier masquerading as her?'

'The very one. It has magical properties. It gives the custodian powers beyond that of natural bounds. Powers that neither you nor I would believe possible.'

'So, she is in possession of a Glimmer?' Ambric asked. He wanted to believe what his ex-prince was telling him, but he was having difficulties believing Glimmers could be in play in the battles between Carnelia and Azuria.

'As is Endellion,' Bernard continued in a whisper. The relaying of this information was tiring him. 'The girl you saw with me was indeed Cassandra. The one who controls the fireflies is Endellion. It is how she has been able to dupe the nations into war.'

Ambric's gaiety at watching his friend become more animated dissolved. 'I have had dealings with Endellion. It was many years ago. She was, at one time, very close to your father. A great injustice was done to her, and she was forced into exile from Carnelia. Your grandfather was enraged by her, for some reason, and she was expelled. That was when she was a young girl.' Ambric's head dropped as the memory of what had occurred came back to haunt him. 'She was ritually humiliated. I believe it was something to do with how your grandfather was killed. No one ever solved the mystery of how he came to die, although I remember talk in the taverns of something called a Glimmer. I scoffed at the thought of it. Glimmers were old stories told by nursemaids to get the children to sleep.'

'Well, it turns out those tales were true,' Bernard wheezed.

Ambric sat back, a thoughtful look washing over his features as his eyes passed Bernard, squinting as he searched his own memories. 'There were two of them,' he mused. 'One red and one blue. Both equal in power, if the memory serves.'

'Cassandra is in possession of the blue one. It was given to her by her brother, Alexander, on the mission to Carnelia after her mother was abducted and murdered.'

'The murder they blamed us for?' Ambric asked.

Bernard winced again as he nodded. 'There was compelling evidence,' he whispered. 'Cass informed me Endellion has the other one, the red one. If what I believe is true, and Cass was truly taken during the battle of the fireflies, then there is a good chance that the witch has them both by now.'

Ambric's face dropped. 'Even though they were children's tales, they spoke a deep truth. The story went on to tell that if any one person were to be in possession of *both* Glimmers, that person would be virtually indestructible. They would have limitless power,' he whispered. He looked towards the boy on the bed and saw his covers rising and descending slowly as shallow breaths rattled in his chest. A faint snore issued from him. Ambric stood from the bedside and made his way to the door.

'Matthew, to me,' he ordered to the guard stationed outside the tent. 'Tell me, solider, how healthy are our medical supplies?'

The soldier looked at him. Ambric could see the man wanted to lie to him. He knew he wanted to tell him their supplies were plentiful, enough to nurse the prince back to health, along with the rest of the men. But he couldn't. All he did was close his eyes and shake his head. 'They were not great before the battle,' he admitted. 'After the last run in, with those … things, I would think we'd be lucky to see the end of the week; some say maybe the end of today.'

Ambric looked around at the other beds around them. He noticed several patients were sporting dirty yet colourful bandages on their arms, legs, and heads. He saw they were ripped and torn tunics.

'We're going to need to move Bernard back to Outpost Three. The medical facilities there are far superior to here.'

Matthew looked at his superior officer. 'That is as may be, sir. But we have precious resource to attend his needs *here*, I can only imagine what care he would require on the road.' The soldier moved closer to Ambric and lowered his voice. 'I have been watching the progress of those veins. The black ones. Now, I am a million miles away from being a doctor, Sir Ambric, but they look bad. Very bad.'

Ambric flashed a look at the soldier. He opened his mouth to reprimand him for his impudence but stopped. He knew the man was telling the truth. He closed his eyes, raised his head, and exhaled deeply. 'Matthew, I'm going to put you in charge of this team. I need to leave for a small while. I want you to break camp, but I want you to do it slowly. Small chunks at a time. Prioritise the sick and wounded, include Bernard as soon as you can. Do not offer him any privilege due to his status, he will reject it if he is able. But get this compound as clean as you can.'

'Aye, Sir Ambric, I think I can take care of that. Pray, indulge me, where are you going?'

'I have some Azurian favours I need to cash in,' he replied with a wink. 'I'll meet you back in Outpost Three in one week.' He placed his hand on the soldier's shoulder and squeezed. 'Glimm speed to you, Matthew,' he said at last.

'And to you, Sir Ambric.'

Ambric nodded; as he walked away, he turned back towards the soldier. 'Matthew, just one more thing,' he said.

'Your name, it is Sir Ambric,' Matthew replied, snapping back to attention.

'Can you please just call me Robert?'

'Never,' was the soldier's reply. It was accompanied with a large grin.

4.

ENDELLION WAS IN her element as she made her way through the busy courtyards and thoroughfares of the castle completely unmolested. If she had been even remotely interested in the commoners' opinions of Queen Cassandra's rule, it would have been the perfect opportunity to eavesdrop on the drinkers in the taverns and the washerwomen in the cleaning shops. As it was, she was only interested in herself and her mission. However, she was enjoying the trip down memory lane this journey was affording her.

Her mind was focused almost exclusively on the two objects she was carrying in secret folds of her dress. Both had the same weight, the exact same feel, and they both had the same smooth reassurance about them. She was safe in the knowledge that the one thing she had worked for, for what felt like her entire life, was about to come to fruition.

Her vengeance had been taken on the people who had wronged her, and now she would take her rightful place as the most powerful leader this world had ever seen.

I will no longer stand in the shadows of The Great Lord Glimm, she thought. *He will gaze upon me as an equal, no longer a subordinate.*

Her mind was lost in the whirl of euphoria that unlimited power could bring when she turned a corner and found herself in a darkened location. It was a location she knew. She knew it led to the old tunnels, the ones that would lead her underground, ultimately towards the locale of the ancient Carnelian tribal centre where the original red Glimmer had been offered to the leaders of the time.

As she made her way along the corridor, she was bothered by a cloud of butterflies fluttering around her head. She swiped at them to shoo them and noticed something strange about them. They were bigger than the ones that had infested her chambers in the castle.

She tutted and continued, trying her best to ignoring the flying pests. It was difficult due to their number. Huffing, not allowing them to ruin her good mood, she continued towards her destination.

After almost an hour of wandering in the darkness, she saw the light at the end of her tunnel. The air began to smell fresher, and a breeze stroked her face, cooling the sweat that was coating her skin. She emerged into a large primitive room. The walls were adorned with old drawings, and there were several benches placed around. In the centre was what she was looking for.

It was the throne of the tribal elders.

She sat herself down in the chair, wriggling, unable to find comfort in the primitive design. After a few moments, she gave up her fidgeting and decided to get down to the business at hand.

The reason why she was here in this mystical place.

The pesky butterflies were still flicking around her head, although there seemed to be fewer of them now. Shaking her head to rid herself of their nuisance, she reached into the folds of her gown and produced the two orbs.

She had no control over the smile that cracked through her old, weathered face as her eyes shone with a greedy glow, devouring the image of both Glimmers together; both in her possession. *All I need is the location of the Throne of Glimm, and unlimited power will be all mine.*

The orbs were both pulsing dimly. To her, it looked like they slumbered, resting, waiting for their powers to be unleashed. Her smile spread further as she held them both up high and closed her eyes.

They began to glow deeper; one red and one blue.

~~~~

When she opened her eyes, she was no longer in the dimly lit, primitive structure. She awoke in the darkness of the Throne of Glimm. The room around her was pitched in an almost impenetrable gloom; the only thing that she could see other than the men with the white hair and the long beards was the altar behind them. The two skeletons of the long-deceased brothers were still in situ.

None of the men looked happy to see her.

She didn't care. She knew they were at her command; it was all she needed.
~~~~

'I don't know if any of you dead men have noticed, but I am now the custodian of both Glimmers,' she scoffed. 'I no longer have to listen to your inane drivel and your patronising tones. You will all bow to me.'

'But, my lady—' one of the men uttered from the darkness.

'Don't you *my lady* me,' she snapped. 'None of you have ever *wanted* to help me, and I know you have only ever done it grudgingly.'

'You will get no argument from us on that respect,' another said. 'The Glimmers are to be used for good, not for ill. They should not be used for personal vendettas or greed. You have tainted us with those three elements.'

Endellion laughed aloud. It was a cold sound, and it echoed through the empty surroundings. 'Well, you must be so disappointed then,' she mocked. As suddenly as her laughter started, it stopped, and she glared at the men surrounding the altar. 'Now,' she spat. 'I will take my Glimmers to the Throne of Glimm, and I will accept the powers that are beholden to me. I will grasp immortality, and the world will bow to me for an eternity.'

At the mention of the Throne of Glimm, the old men, as one, stepped back from the woman in their midst. Their collective expressions spoke of concern. They jabbered quietly to each other.

A word the witch had spoken struck fear into their collective core.

Immortality!

She smiled as they squirmed. With both Glimmers at her command, she could do whatever she wanted. There would be no one, no force strong enough to stop her. It would be a dark time for the Glimm; it would be a dark time for everyone.

Endellion enjoyed their discomfort; it was what she came here for. She wanted these condescending old men to struggle with the knowledge of her power. Her only wish was that they were not only in spirit form. She wanted to strike them, to cause them physical pain. But she was happy in the knowledge that what she wanted from them now would cause them more pain than any physical strike. It would darken their souls more than she already had.

'Give me the black rain,' she ordered.

The men stopped talking amongst themselves and, one by one, turned to look at her. The fear and loathing on their faces amused her.

'I want the black rain, and I want it now,' she whispered. Her voice was soft, seductive, even alluring, but the darkness in her eyes spoke of malice and the havoc she was about wreak on the world in her immortal reign.

'My lady,' one of the men replied, his head bowed low. 'You have already made use of such an abomination. Would it not be prudent to—'

'Don't talk to me of prudence, you worm!' she shouted, the violence in her voice echoing once again from whatever walls were in this place. The same violence shocked the men with its venom. 'Give me the black rain,' she demanded, her voice back to silky levels.

One of the men stepped forward, again his head was bent low. The others watched with horror. They grabbed at his tunic, attempting in vain to stop him from doing what he was about to do.

'So be it,' he whispered.

~~~~

When Endellion opened her eyes, she was back in the ancient throne room. The smile she wore in the other realm followed her into this one. 'Now, to finish off the Rebels and Ferals in one swoop,' she cackled in the gloom of the underground chamber.
~~~~

5.

THE CARAVAN OF wounded had been travelling for three days. The journey was slow, as they needed to stop many times to rebandage wounds, to hydrate the sick, and because they had to keep to the back roads between outposts. Some of the trails had not been used in earnest since the last wars between the two kingdoms, hundreds of years before.

Matthew was well travelled in these paths, and he knew how treacherous they could be. He had briefed the guards and scouts who were accompanying this troupe to keep them safe from bandits and from Azurian ambush. He had told them that even though they were escorting Bernard, there was to be no special treatment of him over the other injured. He had, however, been keeping a close eye on the prince and was dismayed that it looked to him, in his less than expert opinion, that the infection from his wound was getting worse.

A rider sidled up next to him, breaking him from his thoughts. 'Sir, we've had word from one of the advanced scouts. They've sighted Outpost Three and are pleased to report that there is a Carnelian Sigel in the gatehouse. I believe we still hold it.'

'Excellent news, Commander. Now, let us make camp for the night. I don't want to see the sick and wounded stressed any further than they already are,' he commanded.

'Of course, sir,' the soldier responded before riding off to the head of the expedition with the order to make camp.

~~~~

Later that night, Matthew was beside the bed of Bernard. The young man looked tired, and sicker than he had before they had left the tunnels.
~~~~

His face was devoid of the pink glow a few days ride should produce. His eyes were rheumy, and his brow, moist.

'So, there is good news about the compound. It seems the Azurian guard have forgotten about it, or they deem it unimportant enough to allow us to keep hold of it. Either way, we now have a base of operations to launch any offensives we seem fit.'

Bernard coughed after Matthew's report was over. It was as if the very act of listening brought him nearer to death with every word.

He had wanted to keep the prince informed, but he also wanted him to take his rest. 'Would you like some water, my prince?' he asked.

Bernard attempted to sit himself up in the bed. A task that seemed beyond him. 'Are you aware that the kingdom of Carnelia no longer exists, Matthew?' the boy asked when the exertions of sitting up had calmed down.

'I am,' the soldier replied as he handed over a flask filled with freshly drawn water.

'Then, you will be aware I no longer have hold over any lands. Therefore, I will never be king, and hence, I am no longer your prince,' he said, gratefully accepting the flask and drinking deeply from it.

'That's as may be,' Matthew replied, taking the flask away before he drank too deeply and made himself sick. They both knew that the strains of vomiting would tear open the already infected wound in his chest. 'But I am merely a soldier and in need of a flag to follow. Otherwise, things don't make sense to me.' He laughed as he spoke and was uplifted to see a small pained but enthusiastic smile on Bernard's face. 'You will be my prince until the day we re-enter the walls of Carnelia, when you don the crown that is your birth right and take your righteous place on the throne. That day, you will cease to be my prince, and I will call you King.'

Bernard laughed again. The sound was more akin to that of a dry wheeze. The small elation Matthew had taken from the boy's smile disappeared in an instant as he helped him with his pillows.

'According to our scouts, we should be at the outpost by midday tomorrow. There's a well-stocked infirmary there, and there is a trained medical team. We'll have you back on your feet in no time,' Matthew said as he fussed over his prince. He shook the flask Bernard had drank from and signalled to a soldier outside to fetch more water. With a furtive glance inside the room, the soldier accepted his small mission with a smile and a salute.

'I think both of us know there's no medicine in that compound that will heal me of this ailment,' the boy whispered.

Matthew's face screwed up tight as he listened to the words issuing from his prince. 'I know not of what you're talking about. Of course, the medicines at the compound will help you. They'll help all the wounded, and our forces will be strong again. You'll be strong. The new regime will need that strength, and your wisdom.'

This caused Bernard to laugh again, which rapidly turned into a coughing fit, and Matthew wished he could call a nurse, for fear of the boy ripping his field-sutures. 'I am, by no means, wise, Matthew. Although you are kind to say so. It wasn't so long ago that my folly, chasing a wild boar, got two of our party killed.'

'That was before the world turned, my liege. You've grown from the petulant boy you were, into a great and revered leader.'

Bernard never smiled at this compliment; all he did was look Matthew in the eye.

Just then, the soldier returned with the flask of water. Matthew received it before shooing the lingering soldier out of the make-shift ward.

'I'm dying, Matthew. I know this, and by the look on your face, you do too. You are as loyal a man as Ambric, and a good friend, but I must show you this.' He began to unlace the medical tunic he was wearing.

Matthew turned away.

'Matthew, you must see this,' Bernard whispered as he opened the top.

The wound was deep, and the skin around it was an ugly, dull yellow. Black tendrils were running from it as the infection in his veins carried whatever poison the fireflies had injected him with around his body.

'It would please me very much to die in Carnelia, but that no longer seems an option. So, I would ask you to get me to Outpost Three, and there, I will relieve you of your burden.'

'My liege, I could never—'

'Hush, man. Do not attempt to molly me as a child. I'm dying, and I need to do it on Carnelian soil. Outpost Three is the closest we have to that. But, Matthew, I need you to be my witness.'

'Your witness to what, my lord?'

'Come closer,' he requested. Matthew complied. 'I have no heirs, I have no kingdom, but apparently, the Carnelian people still look to me. Therefore, I need to assess my right of ascension. I name Sir Robert Ambric to lead the people of Carnelia after my passing. Do you hear me, Matthew Gardine?'

Matthew dropped his head in reverence. He knew he had just been witness to the passing of kings. It was an honour to him. 'I hear you, my liege. I hear you well.'

Bernard relaxed then, deeper into the bed and pillows. His eyes began to close, and he suddenly looked many years older than he was. 'Please, leave me now. I think I will sleep the rest of the night.'

'By your leave, sire,' Matthew whispered as he stood and bowed low.

The soldier turned and left the tent without another word.

Just before the canvass flap closed, three large blue butterflies fluttered into the tent and began to frolic around the lamp that had been set up next to the bed. Matthew looked at them and smiled. *Strange,* he thought. *Is it not late in the season for butterflies?*

He shook his head and closed the flap.

As he did, one of the beautiful insects fluttered away from the other two and came to rest on the chest of the sleeping prince.

~~~~

In her dark cell beneath the castle of Carnelia, Cassandra slept. There was a small smile on her pained face.
~~~~

6.

THE GLOOM AND the darkness of the corridors and passageways Alexander found himself drawn to terrified him. He had heard stories from the boys when he was in school and from some of the knights when he was in the mess. Tales of beasts and ghosts. Werewolves and vampires were said to stalk the old underground chambers. There was even a story of the undead being sealed into a chamber, that their wails and screams could sometimes be heard in the dead of the night, shrieking and crying to be fed. According to these tales, the food they desired was the flesh of unsuspecting humans lost within the walls of the castle.

The tales scared him.

He had always been afraid of the dark, ever since he was young. This fear had been enhanced by the atrocities his sister had made him witness since their mother was murdered.

The fireflies were a case in point.

After he watched them tear the men limb from limb, he revered them and loathed them in equal measure. Their awesome power to help his sister was negated by their destructiveness. Yes, they did his bidding, but when he rode them, he could feel their insect coldness and their strength beneath him. He knew it would only take one word from his sister and they would no longer serve him, would, with no remorse, tear him to pieces like they did the Carnelians.

Because of his fear, he felt the need to push himself to whatever limits he could. Tonight, that meant patrolling the halls and corridors that he feared the most. The ones he thought were haunted.

'I'm a brave Knight of Azuria. I am not afraid! I am a brave knight of Azuria. I am not afraid.' This was the mantra he whispered as he stalked, as silently as he could, along the dark, lonely corridors.

He had been having trouble sleeping recently. It was the same reoccurring dream over and over again. In it, there was an old woman. She would summon him to some dungeon or other—he didn't know for certain it was a dungeon; all he knew was that it was dark and as cold as one. There was an altar in the centre of the room, and on the altar were the skeletal remains of two long-dead men.

Sometimes he recognised the old woman, other times he didn't, but even when she was at her most unrecognisable, there was still a semblance of familiarity to her; that was what unnerved him most.

When he got to the dungeon, or whatever it was, the old woman would suddenly burst into a bright red light. This light would be countered by a blue one. The bold blue light would come from a corner of the large room, but he was always too far away to identify its source. The two lights would merge, and an eerie purple glow would hang in the room. In the shadows of this light, there were eyes, and they were watching him.

It was at this point he would usually wake up with a start, and always covered in a slick, cold sweat. He knew it wasn't the worst dream in the world, there were no monsters, no ghosts, no falling down impossibly deep, dark chasms, but it was still unsettling in every way imaginable. The old woman rattled him every time. Even though it was a dream, he knew her face, and he felt if he passed her in the courtyard, he would recognise her instantly. But he couldn't put his finger on who she was or even why she was so familiar.

There *were* nicer points to the dream.

The blue glow, for instance.

There was something nostalgic about it. It elicited a warm memory that soothed him before it merged and became purple. It reminded him of Cass, on the morning she left to find their mother.

This thought, although nice, was also unsettling. It was nothing to do with the dream, just the realisation that he was growing to resent his sister, his queen.

This was not a nice thing for him to admit, even to himself. It was especially not a good thing for a Captain of the Royal Guard to admit. But she had changed. He didn't know if it was the weight of being queen and the responsibilities that came with it, but it had gotten worse since the battle in the tunnels.

Here I am, a captain at the age of fourteen, he thought, *stalking the corridors of the castle.* 'Why am I here?' he shouted into the darkness. He disliked the muffled way his voice bounced off the walls, but he knew it was only the acoustics, and he knew, deep down, there were no ghosts, werewolves, or ghouls down here to hear him.

He was alone, and he liked it that way.

He took another deep breath, ready to shout the question again, when a noise caught him mid-breath.

He stopped and listened.

His heart pounded, making him sick to his stomach. It also throbbed in his ears, and he could have sworn he could feel it in his arms and legs too.

The noise came again.

It sounded like a door opening and then closing somewhere ahead of him.

That meant he wasn't alone down here after all.

Who could it be, and what was their business down here?

Suddenly, he wasn't so sure about his conviction of no monsters, and he wanted nothing more than to push himself against the wall and disappear.

He snuffed out his lantern and slunk into a small recess. He knew it wasn't going to offer him complete protection from whoever, or whatever, it was down here, but it was something for the boy—who suddenly felt a lot smaller than he was—to do.

A dim light illuminated the corridor, coming from the direction he had been headed. It shone from the walls; its cold whiteness cast everything into shadows. He breathed deep and held it as long as he could. He didn't want anything to give away his presence.

The source of the light became a silhouette. He didn't know if it was to his relief or if it furthered his horror to see that the source of the light was human.

As it got closer, he could make out it was a woman, an older woman. As she made her way slowly along the corridor, her profile began to reveal itself to him.

It was an old woman … *It's* THE *old woman,* he thought as he pushed himself closer into the wall. *What is she doing down here? Who is she?*

The woman stopped, and he watched as she cocked her head like she was listening for something. She put down her lamp and rummaged around in the folds of her skirts, then took something out of an unseen pocket and held it in the air.

'Light,' she commanded. Her voice sounded old, but there was power in it.

The corridor bloomed into a bright red light.

Instantly, his dream was broken. *Red light.* He gulped.

'Prince Alexander, what are you doing down here?' the old woman asked.

He didn't like the fact that she knew his name. *But then, I'm the prince, a lot of people know my name!* 'I-I couldn't sleep,' he stuttered eventually, wondering why he was answering the old hag.

'Oh, you couldn't sleep, eh? Why don't you come over here and tell me all about it?' she said, grinning the worst smile Alexander had ever seen in the whole fourteen years of his life.

'I … I need to speak to the queen,' he said, turning to run down the corridor that was still dimly lit by the hag's red light.

'Stop,' she commanded.

He couldn't believe that he complied with this order, but he did. His legs stopped moving, even though his brain was commanding them to continue. A panic rose from deep in his stomach. He could feel it rolling, like a ball traversing through his body. He didn't want to turn back and look at the old hag, the same one who had been plaguing his dreams. However, his body had other ideas.

He turned towards her, slowly, fighting the movement with every fibre of his being, but he couldn't stop himself. She should have been at least twenty yards further down the corridor, but she was now, inexplicably, right behind him.

Is she a wraith? he thought as he jumped, remembering the soldiers' tales of the things that stalked these corridors. He wished he had never tried to prove himself now. *Never again. In the name of the Glimm, if I survive this night, I will never try to prove myself down here again.*

'Where are you going, boy?' she whispered in his ear. Her breath stank of age and neglect.

He didn't want to reply but was compelled to do so, as if an unknown force was making him. 'I … I want to see my sister. Queen Cassandra,' he replied quietly.

The old woman cocked her head again, and the hideous grin returned. 'But, Alexander, I am your sister. I am your Queen Cassandra.'

His eyes narrowed.

'Look upon my face, boy. You've seen me before. I was in your home. I was at the outpost; in fact, I've been everywhere your beloved sister has been. That is because … I am her!'

'You're not. What are you talking about? My sister is young, she's beautiful. You're a … a …'

'An old woman?' she finished for him. 'Oh yes, I am an old woman. A bitter and twisted old witch. I killed your sister. I murdered her two years ago, then ruined two kingdoms in her name. You've been following me around like a lost puppy dog for almost two years, and I hate you. It amused me when I showed you all those atrocities and involved you in my war crimes. It was testament to your ignorance and your stupidity. Tell me, Alexander, would you really follow someone so blindly, so stupidly, and for what? Some mindless fireflies? For some misplaced glory?'

Tears were welling in his eyes. He hated crying; it was a sign of his weakness. 'Leave me alone,' he blubbered. 'Leave me alone, you—' he paused as a sob caught him mid-word. 'Murderer,' he finished.

The old woman smiled again. 'Oh, child, I am worse than that. Much worse. You don't need to worry yourself, though, as I need you to finish my mission. I won't be killing you just yet.'

'I would sooner die right now than help you.'

The woman smiled again. She raised the red orb she was holding in her hand and placed it on his forehead.

He flinched, afraid it might burn him.

It didn't.

It surprised him by feeling cool against his clammy skin. The ball flashed, an intense red light that blinded him momentarily.

He felt disgusted that he had allowed her to do it, that he was too scared to stop her, to fight her.

There was another flash. This one looked to be of the purest red he had ever seen in his life, but he didn't understand how he could have seen it; it must have been in his mind, as his eyes were closed. Eventually, he opened them and was relieved to see his sister standing before him. He smiled at her. 'Cass, I've been looking for you,' he gushed.

‘Well, I’d say you’ve found me,’ the young, beautiful Cassandra replied.

‘Where have you been? I thought I saw someone down here.’ His face creased as he tried to remember who he had seen, who he had been talking to only a few moments ago. The memory was gone; he didn’t even know if he *had* been talking to someone.

‘I've been taking care of some business,’ she replied, grasping his hand.

For a moment, he was repulsed by her touch. Her skin felt old, cold to the touch, and moist. But then, almost as quickly as the revulsion had risen, it passed.

‘Why don’t you escort your sister to her chambers? I have a busy day ahead of me tomorrow, and I need my sleep.’

He smiled as she picked up the lamp that was at her feet and allowed its dim light to illuminate the gloomy corridor before them.

7.

AMBRIC WAS IN the doorway of the small shack that served as the guard's hut for the south-east entrance to Azuria. It was a little-used doorway into the city but had always been the main headquarters to the elite troops of the Kingdom. He was soaking wet, covered in mud, and grinning. He had never been happier than when he was out in the elements, sneaking into places, and generally causing mayhem.

'Well, well, well. You have some balls coming here, I'll give you that,' a large, gruff man laughed as he regarded the dishevelled man before him. He was dressed in the garb of the Azurian guard and was a mountain of a man. His shoulders were wide, and his arms were akin to tree trunks. He had once been a man of muscle, but in his advancing age, it was slowly turning, relaxing, although Ambric knew he was still a formidable foe.

'I had nowhere else to go, brother,' Ambric replied. There was a smile on his lips, but his eyes didn't reflect the humour. They were busy assessing his surroundings, looking for contingencies if this meeting didn't go as planned.

The large man sneered. His eyes narrowed as his lip curled. 'I'm not your brother, old man. We are far from kin. Enemies is what we are. Do you not remember?'

Ambric's smile didn't falter as he looked the bigger man in the eyes. 'Aye, I remember, Carlos. We have been enemies all our lives, if my memory serves. Enemies within allies …'

'We're no longer allies, Robert. You don't wear the coat of arms of Azuria. You don't wear the coat of arms of anyone, not any force I recognise anyway.'

'This is true. I no longer run alongside a banner. That was torn from me. I am now a rebel.'

Carlos gripped the thick leather belt that ran around his considerable girth. The smirk on his face fell, leaving behind curious eyes, ones that never left the smaller man. It was as if he knew what Ambric was capable of and didn't want to give him any opportunity to prove it. 'I know, and for that reason alone, I should kill you where you stand.'

Ambric lifted his hands in the air, showing Carlos he was unarmed.

The bigger man's expert eyes roamed over his body, seeking the notches and niches where smaller weapons could, and probably were, hidden. 'I've heard tales of you killing my clansmen, Robert. Why would you come here this night?'

'I kill out of necessity only,' Ambric answered. 'A necessity that you and your clansmen brought about. You sacked my kingdom on a whim.'

'You killed our queen,' Carlos countered as if keeping tally.

'I'm glad you mentioned that, as it's kind of why I'm here. May I come in out of the cold?' Ambric asked.

The big man looked behind him towards the group of men who were keeping sentry with him on this wet night. Each looked fit and dangerous. Ambric was aware of their training and was also aware of their orders regarding the Rebels, the Ferals too.

'Come in, but know this, any sudden movements and I will not be held responsible for my men's actions.' Carlos stepped back, giving Ambric all the room he needed to escape the night.

'I'm not here for trouble,' Ambric replied.

'That's a relief,' the big man laughed, then his face turned serious again. 'So, what are you here for?' he asked, throwing Ambric a towel.

He caught it and dried his face. He nodded his thanks to the five men and indicated to Carlos that he wanted to speak in private. The bigger man pointed towards a small door at the back of the room. Ambric, keeping his well-trained eyes looking for escape routes, nodded and entered the room behind. The big man closed the door behind him, trapping him inside. Ambric knew Carlos's weaknesses and would be ready in an instant to kill the man, and the five outside if he needed to, but the reason he was here was too important to ruin with petty differences.

'You have been duped,' he began. 'The queen you follow is nothing more than a witch, a witch with a vendetta against both kingdoms.'

Carlos laughed. 'What? Ambric, I expected better than this from you. Do you expect me to believe something like that?'

Ambric's face remained stoic. 'Have you ever known me to joke about anything as grave as this?'

Carlos stopped laughing and eyed his counterpart. 'I have never known you to joke about anything.'

'Then why would I start now?'

'What would you have me do with this information?' There was still a smirk on the bigger man's face.

'I need your help in exposing her.'

Carlos nodded, still smiling.

'You'll help me then?' Ambrose asked, cutting through the awkwardness between the two soldiers.

'I never said that. I want to know what you want.'

'I no longer have access to a library,' Ambric began.

Carlos scoffed. 'A library? You want books? Have you grown so frail that you need to read about past glories?'

'Old? I'll show you who has grown old, fatty,' Ambric laughed as he poked at the bigger man, diffusing the building tension between them.

Carlos laughed again and grabbed at the enormous girth of his stomach. 'Who would have thought, the us two, getting old and fat, eh? We were destined to die in the heat of battle.'

'There is still plenty of time for that,' Ambric agreed.

'We were so competitive back in the day.'

'You were,' Ambric laughed. 'You had to be because I was so much better than you.'

'Are you hungry, brother?' Carlos asked.

Ambric nodded. 'Cold, wet, and hungry.'

'Come with me. We'll get you dry clothes and some broth. How long have you been on the road?'

'A few days, nothing to someone of our ilk,' Ambric replied. 'I am serious, though, my old friend, about the witch. If I get access to your library, I hope I can prove it.'

'What has happened to you?' he asked playfully. 'Tales of witches and magic, duping kingdoms into killing each other?'

Ambric bowed to his old friend. 'I humbly thank you, my brother in arms, for not killing me on sight and for listening to what I have to say.'

Carlos eyed him again. 'I did think about it, seriously, I did,' he laughed. 'I still am!'

8.

THE BUTTERFLIES WERE everywhere, swooping and fluttering through the air, turning it blue with every beat of their wings. They were of varying sizes. Some were small, not even the size of Bernard's hand, others, like the one he was sat astride now, were huge. Bigger than the fastest horses they had at their disposal.

As the great beast swooped through the air, Bernard laughed and whooped; he cheered his courser on as it chased and frolicked with a second beast that was a little faster than his.

Cassandra was astride that one. Her blue gown was thin, and as her butterfly danced through the air, the breeze caused the silk to cling to her every curve. It caressed her skin and ran its fingers though her long, dark hair.

He drank heavily from the beautiful sight before him.

He could not keep his eyes off her. She was everything to him.

She turned and laughed as she sped away. He marvelled that it was *the* single most fantastic sight he had ever seen. He instructed his butterfly to catch hers and lunge at it, which it did. However, Cassandra was a superior rider, and she easily dodged his playful attack.

As she raced into the clouds around them, he noticed his beast beginning to labour. He also noticed that the clouds had begun to darken, becoming bloated and threatening. The air itself had gotten cold.

His chest began to feel tight.

He raised a hand to see where the pain was coming from, but it hurt to touch.

Cassandra's voice called to him. It was faint but unmistakably her. 'Bernard,' she called. 'Are you OK, my love?'

He couldn't answer. All the breath that had been in his body was now lost. He was struggling to breathe. That was when his courser began to falter. His stomach felt the change in its pitch as it angled its flight towards the ground. He began to cough as the agony in his chest expanded in waves. The day grew darker still as the pregnant clouds amassed around him the closer he got to the ground. He looked to see where Cassandra was. As he saw her swooping behind him, the pain in his chest exploded. His hands no longer worked. He watched his fingers rebel against his will, letting go of his butterfly. He felt the sensation of falling.

He landed on soft ground. He rolled over and looked towards the sky. It was now the obsidian of night. The clouds were impenetrable; full darkness had fallen.

'Bernard?'

It was Cassandra's voice. It was close.

The closer her voice, the worse the pain in his chest became. He looked and saw that she had dismounted her butterfly and was running towards him. 'Bernard,' she called.

He raised his arms, beckoning her. He needed her to help him with his pain, when suddenly, she started to change. Her face melted away, like a candle in the heat, and her body began to crumble. She became a running mound of earth and clay.

'Cassandra,' he croaked. The agony in his chest had become all encompassing. It refused him air to replenish what he had exhaled during his fall.

He was suffocating.

Another face appeared where Cassandra's had been. It was old and haggard, but even through his pain and shock, he could see it had once been beautiful, stunning even.

But no more.

Another explosion in his chest coincided with something dripping onto his face. As he struggled to sit up, he felt an oily splash sink into his flesh. It sickened him. He could feel it eating through his skin like a malevolent force, intelligent and vicious. More fell, covering him in the dark oily liquid.

Rage!

Anger!

Pure, unadulterated hate surged through him.

The torture in his chest was overshadowed by these new sensations. He bared his teeth as a low growl issued from somewhere deep within him.

As the haggard old woman's face leaned over him, instinct took over. He reared up, surprisingly fast, considering his wound and the pain. His teeth tore into the flesh of the crone's neck, cutting through the meat and the muscle. As her warm, salty blood gushed into his mouth, she laughed. 'Do it, Bernard,' she whispered.

He did as he was told.

He turned her head in a parody of a passionate embrace, placing his mouth over hers, and bit.

Her lips came off between his teeth, as did the tip of her tongue. The urge to chew them, to swallow them, was too much for him to resist.

She continued to laugh.

Her taste was electrifying. It made the pain in his chest go away. All he wanted to do was to bite and tear and eat the old woman.

And so, he did!

~~~~

A hand on his shoulder roused him. He opened his eyes and was surprised to see the face of his friend Matthew looking down at him, his hands holding his face gently.

'Bernard, you're dreaming; you need to wake up.'

The voice soothed him, and he relaxed, the vile dream slipping from his mind. The rage that had built up inside him subsided, but the agony in his chest intensified.

'I'm sorry I woke you,' Matthew said. 'But you were clawing and snapping.'

'Something bad is going to happen … today,' Bernard gasped.

'What?' Matthew asked.

'I don't know what, but it will happen.' His eyes were wide and wild. He was scrambling to get out of bed, but the effort was too much for his weakened state.

Matthew soothed him, gently resisting his efforts to get from the confines of his blanket. 'It's your imagination,' he chided. 'You've had a bad dream. Nothing more.'
~~~~

Bernard lay back in the bed and looked up at his friend. ‘What time do we break camp?’ he asked.

‘We’ll be on the road within the hour.’

‘Good, we need to do it with haste. I have a very bad feeling.’

9.

CASSANDRA AWOKE WITH a start. She sat up in her bed and instantly regretted it. Her head spun, taking the rest of the room with it, but they didn't tell her stomach. The dull ache that had been a constant resident in her head since the battle was boosted by her sudden movement, and it took the chance to raise its potency a couple of notches. She was covered in sweat, and for an instant, she didn't know why.

Then it came to her.

My dream, she thought.

She had been riding a giant butterfly, playing with Bernard, but somehow, he had fallen off and the sky had turned black.

She shook her head, attempting to clear the unpleasant memory, but all she managed to do was make herself feel more nauseous than she already did. Gently, she laid her head on her threadbare bed and regarded the small room. The only human she had encountered since her capture had been Endellion. *If you can call her human,* she thought with a wry grin. Everything else had been attended to by the fireflies.

They were monstrous things. Their black, emotionless yet intelligent eyes pierced into her soul every time they came to feed her or to change her waste bucket. She shivered at the thought of them. *How did I find myself in another of Endellion's prisons?* she thought.

Against her better judgment, she continued her attempt to get out of the bed. She knew she had to, she needed to keep up her strength, but her body screamed in agony. Torturous waves coursed through every limb, every organ, from her toes to her head. Her veins, her nerves, felt like conduits for molten lava to surge through her.

Her innards were fit to burst.

Not for the first time, she questioned her request from the Glimm, even though she knew it had been necessary if her plan was to work.

'Guard,' she croaked through the bars of her cell. 'Bring me food.'

A firefly hovered around the corner of the dimly lit corridor where her cell was located. It carried a tray laden with half a loaf of bread and a pitcher of water. She regarded the meal, and her heart sank. *It's probably all I could keep down anyway,* she thought as a cramp from deep inside her sent hot spears through her body.

She accepted the meal and crouched into the corner, gasping as her limbs burned with every movement.

As she picked up her bread, her thoughts went—as they did almost every waking moment—to Bernard. She hoped, prayed, he had survived the battle.

Then, in a flash of inspiration, she understood her dream.

She pushed the meal away and closed her eyes.

A pained smile crept over her features.

10.

ENDELLION HAD SENT most of her servants away for the day and had left word with the rest of the staff that she and her brother were not to be disturbed during their *meditation* period. She had everyone removed from the throne room too and ordered the door to be locked. The only people allowed in or out were her and her brother. Since their encounter in the underground corridor, Alexander had been under her thrall. As he had seen her in her true form, she found it prudent to have him in this state for the foreseeable future, until she needed him otherwise.

She was sitting on the throne while he sat in the corner, smiling vacantly into thin air. Her eyes were fixated on the Glimmers in her hands, pulsing their dim glow; one red, one blue.

She tore her eyes away from their light and looked around the room. *Everything here is mine,* she thought.

She then closed her eyes, and the Glimmers began to pulse.

~~~~

She opened her eyes in the darkness of the throne room, surrounded by the old men with the white hair and beards. 'Hello, old men,' she greeted with faux joviality. 'I do hope you have seen fit to grant me my request.'

The men stared at her, their faces paler than usual as they shifted and twitched nervously at the sound of her voice.

She laughed. 'You do not have the right to refuse me, Glimm,' the last word spoken as if she were chastising a naughty dog. She raised her eyebrows and crossed her arms, an amused look in her eyes. 'I want my
~~~~

black rain, and I want it now.' She knew they were trapped, bound to obey her. They had no choice *but* grant her request.

'Yes, my lady,' one of them muttered.

His head was bent low, and Endellion struggled to hear him. 'What did you say?' she asked. 'Can you speak a little louder, please?'

The old man raised his head and looked at her. His eyes were blazing, and he was physically shaking. 'I said, yes, my lady.' It was his turn to spit his words.

The rest of the men stared at her. No one else moved.

She shrugged and leaned forwards as if she were a bored schoolteacher addressing an unruly class. 'Well, do it then,' she ordered.

The Glimm slowly began to form a circle, grasping each other's hands. A rush of wind whipped through the throne room, ruffling Endellion's hair. She held her hands out to her sides, allowing the wind to caress her body. Adrenaline surged through her, and every inch of her body felt alive, tingling with power.

Her skin flashed purple for the merest of moments before the wind died almost as quickly as it had risen.

'It is done,' the Glimm said, his voice quiet and soft.

'Excellent.' Endellion laughed.

~~~

She opened her eyes and was back in the Carnelian throne room. Alexander was still smiling into thin air, and the Glimmers in her hands were still glowing. She stood, raising the orbs into the air.

'Black rain,' she whispered. 'Obey me!'

The same wind that had caressed her body in the Throne of Glimm beat against her now. Her long hair blew backwards as the orbs began to pulsate at a rapid speed. Red and blue light spilt into the hands holding them. Endellion's eyes were wide; her smile was manic. As she closed her eyes, visions of Outpost Three filled her head. 'Go to where I command thee. Pour your chaos down upon the unsuspecting heads within.'

The wind continued for a moment longer before dying; at the same time, the pulsating of the orbs began to slow. Soon, they were back to their dull glow, mere decorative orbs again.
~~~

Endellion placed them on the seat of the throne behind her. Her work was done, for now.

'What's just happened, sister?' Alexander asked, his voice dreamy, as if from far away.

'Nothing … and everything, my dear Alex. Nothing and everything.'

'Oh,' he replied with a giggle, then returned to staring at whatever it was that had caught his attention in the corner of the room.

11.

THE CORRECT SIGNALS were flown from the caravan as they headed towards Outpost Three. These signals allowed the men inside to know that the approaching party was friends and not foes and were to be treated accordingly. With an almighty squeal of metal resisting metal, the drawbridge was lowered, and the portcullis was raised. The dishevelled company of Ferals and Rebels limped into the compound. The healthy men were escorting, and in some cases carrying, the sick and wounded from the battle with the fireflies.

As they entered the courtyard, the guards tasked with defending the compound had their arrows trained on them the whole time, not wanting to be caught by the same ruse they had used when taking this compound in the first place.

'Guard of the watch,' Matthew shouted as he reached the centre of the courtyard. 'To me,' he ordered.

A large, flustered man, his barrel chest heaving as he buttoned up his jacket, ran from one of the rooms on the perimeter of the yard. 'I am the guard of the watch,' he panted, checking his trousers. 'Speak the password!'

Matthew grabbed him by the lapels on his jacket and dragged the red-faced man closer to him. As he did, the bowmen on the wall, with their arrows trained on the newcomers, flinched. An air of unease lay heavy among the men.

'Charis, you fool,' Matthew shouted in the face of the bigger man. 'Do you not think it's a bit late for a password to be spoken when the men are already in the centre of the castle?'

'I have my men with their weapons trained on you at this very moment,' he retorted. Looking around him, indicating the archers.

'And every last one of them are hesitant to shoot, thinking they'll be killing kin!' Matthew said as he let go of the man's lapels.

'But the signals ...'

Matthew shook his head. 'We need to talk about the security of this stronghold. But, before we do that, we have King Bernard with us, and he needs urgent medical attention. Do you have anyone at this facility who can help?'

Charis fixed his tunic and looked around at the men on the wall. He signalled them to stand down. 'We don't have the best facilities—' he started.

'But they do have me,' came a female voice from somewhere behind Matthew. A petite woman strolled towards him, dressed in the garb of a medical practitioner. Her dark hair was tied back, and she was wiping her hands on a towel. When they were dry, she offered one of them out towards him. 'I'm Linda. I'm a trained and fully qualified midwife, but I also know my way around men's parts too,' she offered.

This caused a few sniggers and wolf whistles around the walls.

She smiled, shaking her head as she took the jibes with good humour.

Matthew took her hand and was impressed with the strength of the grip the small woman offered. 'Excuse me for asking, but if you're a midwife, then tell me why you run with the Rebels and Ferals?'

'I don't. I'm Azurian. I was stationed here before the conflict. When I said I know my way around the men's parts too, I meant it. I'm a qualified field surgeon. I go where I'm needed. When your men took this place, I offered to stay. I have no allegiance to either kingdom.'

Matthew cocked his head and smiled. 'Why, then, did you offer your services as midwife before field-surgeon?'

Linda smiled back before walking past him towards where the sick lay on their mobile beds. 'I take it these are your wounded?' she replied.

Matthew looked at his men and smiled. 'Well, it looks like you've passed your first test.' There was a murmur of laughter from around the courtyard.

She looked at him, her eyebrows raised but with humour on her lips. 'We need to get these men and women to the infirmary straight away,' she ordered, snapping into a professional tone in the wink of an eye.

'This is just the first volley of them,' Matthew offered. 'There'll be another three caravans coming in. We took heavy casualties in the last battle.'

'Where's the king?' Charis asked, whispering into Matthew's ear.

'He's in there with the rest of the wounded. I'm afraid he's in a bad way,' he confided.

'Linda is the best we have. I'll make sure she has access to him, twenty-four hours a day.'

Matthew grabbed the big man by the arm as he turned away. He shook his head. 'Don't,' he whispered.

Charis looked at him as if he had been speaking a different language.

'Bernard would not sit still for that. If he knew he was getting preferential treatment over someone who needed it more than he, there would be hell to pay.'

Linda saw the two men whispering and made her way towards them. 'What are you two gassing about? I'm supposed to be the gossiping midwife?' she asked. 'If you tell me it's just men's business, I'll pack my bags and leave today, dropping you both deep in the—'

'I was asking where the king was,' Charis interrupted.

She turned to Matthew and offered him a look.

Matthew understood the silent question. 'He's in with the others. He'll not accept preferential treatment,' he offered.

'Then we will agree on something because I'll not offer him preferential treatment. However, in your opinion, is there anyone in the company, man or woman, who is in need of my services more than this king of yours?'

Matthew shook his head. 'There's not, ma'am. But do us all a favour, make it look like he is not the priority, please.'

Linda winked at him as she walked off.

Matthew found himself blushing. He looked towards Charis, who was watching Linda walk off, or rather, appreciating Linda walking off.

'Commander?' Matthew cleared his throat, getting his attention.

Charis snapped from his trance and turned towards him.

'I think we should have that conversation about security. Don't you?' he said, pointing towards a door in the wall on the perimeter of the yard.

12.

CASANDRA WAS COWERING in the corner of her cell. The light of the day had travelled over half the floor; it was her only indication of the passing of time. She was resting in a shaded corner where the light never touched. The moss and damp that crawled the walls were testament to this fact. She was oblivious of any external factors influencing her environment, as her hands were currently covering her eyes and face. Her body shook as if she were in terrible pain. She was mumbling something.

It was a mantra.

She whispered the same incomprehensible phrase over and over again. Tremors wracked her thin body as if doing so caused her immeasurable pain, yet still she persisted. A shadow passed in front of the sunlight streaming in from the barred windows. It was only small, and it went unnoticed by the stricken girl. This shadow was quickly joined by another, and then another. Before long, there was a kaleidoscope of shadows fluttering around the room.

They were butterflies. Their dark blue wings were casting the odd shadows on her prison walls. She took no notice of them. Her hands still covered her eyes and most of her face, while her body continued to shake uncontrollably.

Another shadow passed by. This one was larger than the others, much larger. It passed her window again; this time its shadow touched Cassandra, and the tremors wracking her small frame stopped.

She removed her hands from her face, allowing her bloodshot eyes to regard the window. Something she saw there caused her sweat-lined features to twitch, and a ghost of a smile haunted her dry, cracked lips.

A blue wing fluttered past.

It was the same colour as the smaller ones that still fluttered about her cell, but it was bigger, much bigger.

It's from my dream, she thought, her smile widening, drawing blood from in-between the cracks of her lips. With an effort, she eased herself up from the floor and, on shaky legs, made her way to the window. Gripping the cold, rusted bars, she regarded the day.

Her heart sang at what she witnessed.

The butterfly fluttering outside her window was enormous. Easily the same size, or maybe even bigger, than the dreaded fireflies that had brought her to this prison.

She fell back onto her bed and laughed.

The laugh soon turned into a cough, but it didn't knock the mirth from her face.

13.

LINDA WAS MAKING her rounds. Enough tents had been set up in the courtyard to contain the sick and wounded who had been brought into the compound by Matthew and the other caravans that had arrived over the course of the day. As she made her way towards the tent that contained Bernard, the one with guards stationed outside, she shook her head. *If he knew they were there, he wouldn't be happy,* she thought, pushing the canvas flap, entering the gloom and the stink of the sickly room. It was dark inside due to the hour in the day. When the sun had passed over the courtyard, it put the rest of it into the shade. She had marvelled on numerous occasions that whoever had the foresight to build this compound hadn't taken enjoying the sun on their face into consideration.

'So, you're the King of Carnelia then?' she asked, sounding chirpier than she felt. One look at the sickly young man on the bed told her everything about his condition. Mostly about how long he had left in this world. Her instincts told her it was not long.

The boy, as that was what he was, a boy, smiled at her. The smile almost broke her heart. 'Some people would call me that.' He coughed. 'Mostly Carnelians, though. I'm guessing by the blue streak in your hair that you won't be calling me King Bernard anytime soon?'

She smiled at him. 'I've never been one for calling anyone king,' she said with a laugh. 'Or queen, for that matter.'

She leaned over and put her hand on his brow. He flinched at her touch before easing he head back into his stained pillow. 'So, apart from the obvious, what seems to be the problem, King?' she asked.

He smiled again, although this one was only a phantom of the first. 'I think I might have picked up a scratch or two in battle, nurse. I'm sure it's nothing you haven't seen before. You should be able to get me back on my feet in no time.'

The coughing fit that accompanied this joke removed the humour from his face.

Without any preamble, she pulled back the covers and opened the top of his tunic. The bandage that covered the wound on his chest was dirty; it also appeared to be made from the torn jacket of a soldier. As she peeled it away to get a better look at what she was dealing with, the boy winced.

The wound was ugly.

It was circular, as if he had been stabbed with something cone shaped. It was infected and festering. The skin around it was puffy and yellow, and black lines of poison stemmed from it and went around his body.

She took note. 'As you say, my king, just a scratch. However, I'm going to need some fresh bandages. I believe the owner of that sleeve you have patching you up may need it back at some point. We'll have you back wielding a sword before you know it.'

Bernard smiled, but she could tell by the look in his eyes he knew his fate; knew it and accepted it.

'I've got a feeling it's going to rain,' she said conversationally, as she washed her hands in the small basin by the door. 'The sky was lighter when I came in. A lot lighter, actually.'

As if on cue, a wind whipped from out of nowhere and wafted the canvass flaps of the tent wide open for a moment, causing her dark, blue tinged, hair to blow in the breeze. She looked out and upwards at the sky. It was black, *Unnaturally black*, she thought.

Then she caught sight of Matthew across the way.

He noticed her and smiled.

She smiled back.

You fool, she chastised herself. *Keep your mind on the job at hand. No time for funny business, there is a war on.* She gave him a wave, and to her delight, he waved back.

~~~~
~~~~

He didn't know why he did it, but he waved at Linda. It seemed like the natural thing to do. The contents of his stomach shifted as he did. He rolled his eyes at this folly and happened to look up into the sky.

The dark sky.

Or was it a black sky?

Where have I seen that sky before? he asked himself.

Charis, the guard of the watch, was standing next to him, babbling on about something or other, but Matthew's attention had shifted. A bad feeling was eating its way through him. His stomach churned, much akin to the maelstrom in the black clouds above. He looked towards the courtyard, where there were at least fifty soldiers and a good contingency of the refugees they had brought with them milling around.

Most of them were looking into the strange sky.

Charis noticed Matthew was no long taking any notice of him, and he followed his superior's gaze. His face changed from mild confusion to one of abstract horror. 'Matthew, I've seen this before,' he whispered.

'So have I, but I'm stumped if I know where.'

It clicked then in both men's heads at the same time.

Matthew burst out into the yard.

'Get out of the courtyard!' he shouted at the top of his voice. 'Everyone, out of the courtyard, now! That is a direct order!'

He saw Linda and rushed towards her.

'Charis,' he shouted back at the guard of the watch. 'Gather the civilians and the men, right away. Get yourselves to a secure location and lock yourselves in.'

The guard of the watch didn't hesitate and ran out into the courtyard to round up all who were looking up into the turbulent sky.

Part Three:

1.

FIVE HUNDRED YEARS or so had passed since the death, and the reappearance, of Zadamare. In that time, things had reached almost critical levels between the Sisterhood of the Purple and the Glimm. The number of men being initiated into the order of the Glimm was dwindling due to the dilution of the bloodline from the womenfolk mating with the wild men of the forest.

During the time of Zadamare, the Glimm had conceived the idea of making orbs that they could infuse with their magics, in the case of an emergency. This would ensure their studies and the levels of magics they had achieved would not be lost.

The orbs, as it happened, had been a good idea.

By now, the numbers had been reduced to a mere handful of old men. A low-level panic had been simmering within them for a few years, but no one had given any thought to the cause of the problem; they had been far too engrossed in their own importance. No one had noticed the males over the last few generations had been getting physically stronger, more aggressive, and less gifted than the previous ones. Now, there was much lamenting regarding the lack of respect given to their longevity and the neglect they had offered their wives. There were no longer any wives left, and no wives meant no sons.

No sons meant the extinction of their ways.

They had, however, noticed the rise of the primitive cultures around them. The wild men of the forest had begun to build settlements using complex tools and organise themselves within hierarchical societal structures.

What the Glimm, with their infinite knowledge and insights into life after death, had missed was that after nearly five hundred years of interbreeding with the wild men, the Sisterhood of the Purple had become stronger than either of them could have ever foreseen.

The Sisterhood had decided to disassociate their society from the dying Glimm. They had removed themselves from the villages and set up their own communities out of their view and the view of the burgeoning societies that the wild men had been developing. They were strong in numbers, strong in will, and even stronger in magic. Over the years, they had studied and perfected the art of prolonged life, but they didn't want to progress in the same direction as the Glimm. To them, the Glimm were fools who squandered what the Great Lord Glimm had given them. The Sisterhood chose to be selective and secretive with their powers.

'We will look after our own,' Zadamare would preach in the many visitations she bestowed upon her sisters. 'When a sister dies, they will be given the option to continue to serve the Sisterhood or to pass over and embrace what the next world has to offer.' Many of the Sisterhood had passed over, but a great number had chosen to stay in the ethereal world and help the next—and growing—generations. 'When a Sister is in trouble, we will show ourselves and guide them through their dilemmas. Anyone who puts a sister in danger will feel the wrath of the Purple.'

This always came with a murmur of approval from the gatherings.

'I foresee the end to the Glimm in this world. They have been wasteful in their duties, and now they're too old to reproduce. This generation will be their last.'

'What can we do to help them?' a voice asked from the crowd.

'I do not know, my child,' was Zadamare's candid answer. 'We must be strong. We must give them the support they require, but at the same time, we must work to continue our own line. The wild men of the forest are no longer wild. Their civilisations are strong, and they are growing. We must interact with them, for they are the future, our future. We must integrate, twist our history into theirs, after all they are our descendants.'

Once again, there was a roar of approval.

'Go then,' Zadamare ordered. 'Reproduce, embrace the future. Forge ahead with new generations of the Purple. Together, we can fashion and shape kingdoms.'

2.

THROUGHOUT THE AGES, as the great kingdoms were built, through the ups and the downs, though great wars, triumphs, and disasters, there were always stories of women in purple shrouds who would help people in difficult situations.

They had become ghost stories. Tales told to children as wintertime fire warmers or campfire tales. They were intended to scare the youngsters, to the amusement of the older children who had been scared by the exact same tales years before.

People had reported being led to safety by purple ghosts, or oppressors had suddenly found themselves at the business end of a broadsword, falling from high towers, or hanging from bridges.

When war came, the Sisterhood had taken a back seat.

There were too many of their numbers involved in the killing and atrocities that inevitably came with it. But there were still sightings of purple wraiths helping and, occasionally, seeking their vengeance and wrath.

~~~~

It was getting dark. Philip knew he shouldn't have galloped away from the hunt party as he had, but when the scent of kill was on him, he always had trouble keeping his spirits down. No one could have stopped him, even if they had wanted to. He was one of the best huntsmen in the Kingdom of Azuria. He was also the king.

His horse, one he had forged a relationship with from a very early age, was speeding through the undergrowth. He knew it was dangerous for his courser, but she seemed to be driving herself instead of the other way around. He decided that no matter how close the wild boar was, it
~~~~

wasn't worth hobbling his favourite steed in the process of bagging, so he pulled on the reins, and she slowed to a trot. She was still skittery, and he could feel her rapid breath and nervous shivering beneath the saddle. He pulled back, instructing her to come to a stop. He patted her flank, reassuring her that everything was fine. She whinnied in response, but he could tell she was not happy.

'What is it, girl, eh?' he whispered into her ear.

Normally, this would reassure her, but not today. Today, it seemed there was no placating her.

Suddenly, she reared up on her hind legs, whickering loudly.

He fought with the reins, struggling to stop himself from being thrown.

Once she was back on all fours, he leaned forwards again, patting her neck and whispering. 'Easy now. Come on, easy now,' he soothed. 'What's spooked you, eh?'

Philip was an experience and skilled rider and had been riding this same horse for many years, but he was struggling to calm her today. He backed her away from the small clearing they had found themselves in. The further they got, the calmer she became. He looked around for whatever could be spooking the normally stoic beast, but all he could see were trees, plants, and bushes. There was nothing else.

'Come on, girl,' he whispered as he pulled the reins. 'Let's get back, eh?'

Something moved in his peripheral vision. It was there one moment and gone the next. He whipped his head around to where he thought he'd seen it, but there was nothing there.

Nothing but trees and bush.

Now it was his turn to be spooked. As he turned his horse in a circle, the breath coming from both their noses created plumes of steam in the air.

Whatever was in the bushes moved again.

The horse whinnied beneath him and snorted. He pulled the reins, turning her around so he could get a better look at the forest around them.

There was still nothing to see.

'Come on, girl, let's get away from here,' he whispered.

That was when it hit him.

It came from nowhere, knocking him off his horse. The animal screamed; he had never heard the beast scream before, but that was exactly what it did. As he lay in the tall grass of the clearing, he watched the tragic scene of his beloved childhood friend falling, narrowly missing him. As she fell, something flew off her. He didn't get a good enough look at it as it was masked by the bulk of the stricken horse.

Bessie was shuddering as she lay on her side. Her back legs were kicking, and she was issuing the cruellest noise he had ever heard in his life. He crawled over and wrapped his hands around her neck. He wanted to sooth her, to let her know he was there for her in her moments of need and fear.

That was when he saw the wound.

It was huge, and it was steaming. The poor beast's innards were oozing over her chocolate pelt.

He reached out a hand, wanting to stem the bleeding, but couldn't. There was too much of it to stop.

The something that caught his eye moments earlier did so again, and he whipped his head around to catch it.

It shouldn't have existed, it was impossible, but there it was, notwithstanding.

It hovered about three feet from the ground; its curved body was pointing towards him, and the long, lethal sting that protruded from the end of its body glistened in the fading light. A drip of something hung from the point before falling onto the ground below. Where it landed, it hissed and the brush withered and died instantly.

The firefly hovered.

Philip couldn't move. He dared not even try.

The drone from the beast's wings filled the air. It sounded like someone sawing through wood, but at the most rapid pace he had ever heard in his life. The insect didn't move. Its dark, alien eyes stared at him. *Through me?* he thought.

He moved slowly and slightly to the left.

The thing moved with him.

Philip's eyes roamed around the clearing, hoping to find a way out of this situation.

Slowly, he drew his sword from the sheath that was hanging on the horse's saddle. The noise of the metal sliding from the leather was deafening to his ears, and he noticed the firefly heard it too.

It flexed its body. He watched as its bloated thorax began to glow in the failing light of the day.

The sword released from the sheath, and he stood slowly, facing down the hovering abomination. 'Come on then,' he whispered. 'Let's do this.'

As he held the sword, the firefly took that moment to attack.

The noise of its wings heightened, and the monstrosity flew at him at high speed.

Luckily, Philip was well trained in battle.

As the beast came at him, he dropped and angled his sword.

The steel was of the best quality and had only recently been sharpened. As it touched the thing's body, it sliced through its flesh like a warm knife passing through freshly churned butter.

The lethal sting missed him by inches as it fell from the bisected body, hitting the floor with a hiss. It screamed, and it was a worse sound than Bessie's scream, as the rapidly beating wings slowed and it fell from the air behind him.

It died in the grass, twitching and buzzing.

Tentatively, Philip leaned in and poked the remains with the tip of his sword. He had never seen anything like it before in his whole life.

He coughed.

As he did, fresh, dark blood spattered from his mouth.

It confused him as he looked down, tracing the path of the blood. His eyes fell on something protruding from his stomach. It shouldn't have been there. It was long and tapered into a point, and it was covered in blood.

His blood.

That was when he noticed the drone of beating wings coming from behind him. He turned his head. The small movement produced waves of intense agony that flowed through his body.

There was a second firefly.

The thing poking from his stomach was the firefly's sting.

As he dropped to his knees, the sting ripped from his body as the beast moved away.

His head swam and his vision doubled. Bizarrely, he felt hungry.

As his head hit the soft ground of the forest clearing, the air was filled with the buzzing of the firefly hovering over him.

His last thoughts were of his family.

'Alverna, Cassandra … I love you,' he whispered. A single tear welled in his eye as he thought about the unborn baby growing in

Alverna's belly. A son or a daughter he would never see, who would never know the feel of a father's loving arms around them.

As he struggled for breath, a face appeared in his blurring vision.

It was a human face.

It was a female face.

~~~~

Unbeknownst to King Philip of Azuria, everything that had happened had been witnessed.

An unseen purple wraith hovered in the shade of the forest.

She had attempted to move against the enormous firefly, but something had stopped her.

It was a second wraith, who had appeared next to her.

Zadamare.

'Halt, my child,' she whispered. 'We cannot interfere.'

'But he is a descendant of the Sisterhood,' the first ghost argued.

'Of that, I am aware,' Zadamare replied, her eyes watery as she halted the other ghost's interference. 'But so is she.'

She pointed to the woman who was leaning over the stricken body of King Philip. Her clothes were ragged, torn, and dirty. Her hair was long, unkempt, and tangled. The wraith could see that her face, beneath the dirt and the malice, was beautiful.

She was smiling as she watched the second firefly rise into the air, still with the king's blood, mixed with its own poison, dripping from its sting.

'Is that …?'

'Endellion?' Zadamare finished for her. 'Yes, it is.'

'She is such a lost soul,' the first wraith said.

'She has lost her innocence. The poor girl has been through much. We helped her years back. She was beaten, humiliated, raped. There is no doubt she would have died. As she is a direct descendant of a sister, we could not allow that to happen.'

'How have we not saved her from this existence?'

Zadamare shook her head. 'Sometimes she is difficult to see. Other times we cannot see her at all. Walls of red bind us.'

'Bind us?' the first ghost asked. 'As I am tethered to this forest?'
~~~~

'It is the power of the Glimm. It blinds us when she wants it to. There is nothing we can do about it.'

Both sisters watched the girl lean into the dying man. As his eyes rolled back into his head, she whispered something that sounded like names.

There was a broach on the cloak the man had been wearing. Endellion attempted to remove it. She took a diamond encrusted stiletto blade from the folds of her dress and cut it away from the fabric. She looked at it as if it was something she had never seen before.

It was the Crest of Azuria.

She smiled as if this was something she had planned, then hid the broach and the knife in the folds of her dress before disappearing into the undergrowth of the forest.

'Sister Zadamare, this is not good. She is a sister, and she has gone feral.'

'That is true, but there is something else about her. She is custodian of a Glimmer,' Zadamare said as the king died on the forest floor. 'This one, we need to watch,' she concluded.

And watch they did.

Part Four:

1.

THE SKY OVER Outpost Three was as dark as night, perhaps darker. The clouds that had amassed over the castle were thick, heavy, and dangerous. They were filled with menace and foreboding, and they were pregnant, stuffed, fit to burst with cargo.

Matthew, with Linda in his arms, was running across the courtyard, heading towards the safety of the kitchens. He thought about the tents, they were closer and would provide shelter from the madness that would inevitably ensue after the first drops fell, but they would be difficult to defend when the dancing began.

'Get to cover … immediately!' he bellowed across the courtyard. 'That is a direct order.'

The men scattered everywhere, darting between the tents and heading anywhere they could find cover. Some had seen these clouds before; they knew what would come next. Inside the tents, the men were lined up, swords drawn, anticipating the onslaught from their friends and brothers once the black rain began to fall.

Matthew made it to the safety of the kitchens, where he roughly shoved Linda through the door. She landed on her knees and looked at the man she had waved at only moments ago. His eyes were manic, his grimace stretched across a face that was shining with sweat. He looked at her, and his features softened, just for a moment.

'If I get any of that black rain on me,' he said, taking deep breaths in between the words, 'if you see *anyone* with the black rain on them, you get away, you do *not* open this door. Do you understand me?'

Linda blinked as the big man shouted the last four words.

She nodded, blinking again as she cowered into the corner of the room.

Without another word, Matthew left, slamming and locking the door behind him.

~~~~

As he sprinted back towards the courtyard, he ran into two soldiers who were standing and gawping up at the churning clouds. 'You two, did you not hear my orders? Get yourselves to shelter. Now! Do *not* allow any of that rain to touch any part of your body, do you understand me?'

'What's happening?' one of them asked.

Matthew recognised them both as Carnelian guards, both of whom had been present during the first black rain.

'I don't know, I think it might be the black rain. Remember when Carnelia fell so quickly?'

The soldier looked at him as if he were telling him a children's fable.

The other soldier understood instantly.

'There's a nurse in the kitchens. She's to be protected at all times and at all costs. She's the difference between life and death in this place. If I understand what's about to happen, she's about to be very busy indeed. Stand inside and protect the door. Protect it with your very lives.' With that, Matthew back across the courtyard. It was a treacherous run. The clouds had blotted out the light of the day, and a few times, he nearly fell over guidelines from tents that housed the sick and injured. He was making his way towards the barracks, where a group of men were staring up into the sky, talking amongst themselves.

'Inside, all of you. Right now!' he shouted, surprising them.

He could see others inside the doorway attempting to coerce these men inside to no avail. The men were ignoring them, continuing their investigations of the black sky.

More soldiers began to pour from the doorway, pushing past the men inside in their rush to get a look at the phenomenon. As they made it into the courtyard, they were greeted by a crash of thunder. The sky turned purple for a moment, illuminating the whole of the courtyard.

Matthew knew he wasn't going to make it inside before the rain began to fall, he also knew that he couldn't afford to get even one drop of the dammed stuff on his skin. He stopped running and spied a wagon that
~~~~

had been left to the side. The horse that had been pulling it had been removed, and the wagon was abandoned. One of the wheels was lying on its side, halfway through being changed. He dived beneath it, relishing the cover it would give him from what was about to happen.

From his vantage point, he watched first drops of rain fall.

He was helpless as he witnessed the oily liquid drop onto the men who had gathered outside the barracks.

Everything after that seemed to happen in slow motion.

2.

AMBRIC WAS DEEP within the castle walls of Azuria. It was a place he knew he was not welcome, or particularly safe. It was an unsettling feeling, but one that was necessary for what he was here to do.

He was in a vast room surrounded by towering shelves filled with books. In some places, the shelves were stacked fifteen high, and in every one of them, leather-bound tomes filled every space. He took a moment to appreciate the deep, musky smell of the old paper. It was a smell he enjoyed from his childhood, growing up in the confines of the Kingdom of Carnelia. He had always been bookish and had taken a fair bit of ribbing from the other boys because of it, but his knowledge of the ways of the library had helped him with his studies of war, conflicts, and defence techniques during his cadet years, and helped him rise to the ranks he had so quickly.

He understood the ways of books and was a better man for it.

A large tome was open before him as he stood at the central desk; behind him, a looming tower of books he had already consulted had grown. Carlos Gardine watched from the doorway, his thumbs tucked into the thick leather belt straining around his large belly. A grin covered his face as kept watch over his bookish counterpart. Hanging from his belt was a long sword. The hilt was unsheathed, and Ambric knew why. The big man was ready for anything he might throw at him.

He smiled as he continued reading.

Occasionally, Ambric saw the big man's eyes shift between him and the corridor outside. He knew Carlos would be in as much trouble as he if it was discovered he had given access to their centre of knowledge to an enemy combatant.

A number of young people had already been chased away. It was obvious they were not visiting the library at such an hour to study. The place was a notorious *meeting* place, an illicit rendezvous for lovers. Each time, after a sharp word from the soldier, they turned on their heels and hurried off in the opposite direction.

As Carlos regarded the books Ambric had already amassed, he shook his head. The sight of the smaller man darting off in numerous directions, up ladders, and sliding around the room towards destinations that only he knew amused him, and he openly laughed at the activity. As Ambric returned from one such mission, Carlos scoffed at the book he was holding.

'Ambric, you have gone soft,' he sneered. 'Why are you reading children's books? What possible help can you get from that?'

Ambric regarded the book he had selected. 'You would be surprised, Carlos. There are many truths written and passed off as children's fables.'

The big man laughed. 'I know that one,' he boomed. '*The Red and Blue*. A simple tale of opposite colours. Every child is told this story. Why would this help you now?'

'Look here,' Ambrose said as he opened the book, walking towards the big man.

Carlos laughed again. 'I remember the colours merge at the end of the story. They become purple, or something like that.'

Ambric pointed to the page that was open. 'The story tells of colours made by small orbs.' He pointed at a drawing of two hands holding coloured balls. Each glowing, one red and one blue.

'Were they called Glamorgons or something?' Carlos asked, looking amused.

Ambric looked at him, humour on his face. 'What a student you are, Carlos. I'm impressed.'

Carlos's face fell as he glowered. 'Remember where you are, Robert,' he warned.

'Well, you see, my learned friend,' Ambric continued, ignoring Carlos's threatening response, 'it appears these things are real.'

'You're not making sense. This children's book is real?'

'That's exactly what I'm saying. The books were written based on reality. If the information I have received is true, and I have every reason to believe it is, some of the things I've witnessed are testament to it. They are called Glimmers, and they do indeed hold the power of the red and the blue.'

Carlos shook his head. 'What power?'

Ambric flicked the pages and opened another story. He turned the book around so the soldier could see the pictures—he knew he would have issues with the text. 'This is a story about a little girl. Her mother and father are dead, and she is very sad.'

'Stop, Robert,' Carlos laughed. 'You'll have me in tears.'

Ambric shot him a look before continuing. 'She finds a blue ball, and it glows. She is then able to talk to her parents again. They tell her they are in a nice place, they are very happy, but they miss her. The little girl is happy again, knowing her parents are happy. We have the same story in Carnelia, but the ball the boy finds is red.'

Carlos shrugged.

Ambric rolled his eyes and turned the book towards him. 'There is another story about a girl in trouble with an evil king. She finds a red ball, and it helps her escape the king's clutches. Another one, a gang bullies a boy. The ball he finds teaches him how to defend himself. A small duck can't fly with his brothers and sisters, he finds a glowing bubble under the water, and he becomes the best flyer in his whole family. Do you see what I'm talking about now? The truth has been out there all this time.'

'Are you trying to tell me these balls have something to do with your attack on our queen and our retaliation?'

'Think how easy it was for your men to walk into Carnelia and take it over. You never lost one man. All our men were too busy fighting and killing each other. The kingdom was already in chaos. There were nearly one-hundred-thousand men within the walls of the kingdom that day. The Azure war machine took it within a few hours. You're a soldier. How could this have been possible? Without the power of magic?'

Carlos's face was vacant. His eyes were shifting left and right as if he were attempting to process the information. 'It was commented on. Our queen told us it was testament to our superior forces.'

Ambric's shoulders dropped, and he shook his head. 'Do you think that to be true, Carlos? You are a master in the art of war. In the real world, would that be possible?'

Carlos didn't answer but bit at his lower lip.

'What about those fireflies? Where do you think they came from? They don't look natural to me,' Ambric continued. 'I have seen Queen Cassandra.'

Carlos's eyes shone at the mention of Cassandra's name.

Ambric was still shaking his head. 'She is not the woman who sits on the throne of your City of the Fireflies. She is being held prisoner somewhere by the witch. She was running with the Rebels and the Ferals.'

'Why would the queen run with such filth?'

'She ran with us as she is as much an outcast as we are. A witch sits on your throne.'

'Is our queen dead?' Carlos seemed to be taking what Ambric was saying seriously.

'If it serves the witch's purpose, then she may well be.'

'So, the woman on our throne, the one who destroyed the kingdom of Carnelia, is a witch and has one of these … what are they called? Slimmers?'

'Glimmers,' Ambric corrected him.

'She has one of these Glimmers, and has changed her appearance to masquerade as our queen?'

Ambric nodded. 'That's exactly what I'm telling you.'

'Robert, if this was coming from anyone else, I would think it was folly and kill the liar; but as I know you are a man of honour …'

'It is truth. I would stake my sword on it.'

Carlos moved in closer. Ambric could smell sweat and the tobacco that had been smoked in the guardroom. It was a smell he was used to; it was universal to men of the guard.

'I'm going to need some proof of this, Robert. I can't raise an insurrection against a witch pretending to be our queen based on some children's tales in a dusty old book. I'd be hung, drawn, and quartered as a traitor and conspirator.'

Ambric hung his head and shook it. 'Proof, I have none,' he muttered.

'If you can get me proof of this treachery, and I know it is a great *if,* then you will have an army at your side. We have always been on opposite sides, Robert, but I respect you, and I think there maybe truth to what you say.'

Ambric reached out and gripped the bigger man's shoulder and smiled.

'Now, Carnelian scum, get out of my kingdom. If any of my men have taken offence with me talking to you and allowing you access to our facilities, there will be bloodshed, my friend. I would rather it be someone else's, other than mine. If your tale proves to be true, then I don't want it to be yours either. You would be killed on sight.'

Ambric nodded. 'Can I take these books with me?' he asked.

The big man shook his head. 'Are you joking?' he replied.

Ambric smiled. 'Yes, I was.'

3.

MATTHEW WAS CROUCHED beneath the broken waggon as the first drops of the viscus rain began to fall around him. He was holding his breath, hoping none of it would splash into his shelter and infect him. He could see the men, the ones he had been shouting at, still outside the barracks. They were holding their hands into the air, laughing at the strange phenomenon falling from the darkened sky. He now wanted exactly the opposite of what he had been shouting earlier. He needed the men to turn away from the barracks and not think about entering inside. He knew deadly havoc would ensue on their entry.

Even though he knew it would end badly, he was relieved when the three of them turned on each other.

The first man threw his sword onto the black, oily floor before plunging himself towards a second man. As he reached his victim, he sank his bared teeth into his neck. A thick arterial spray of blood arced into the air, splashing the third, mixing with the horrible black rain.

This incensed him.

He was bigger than the other two and used this to his advantage as he leaned into the melee. To Matthew, it looked like he was trying to split the fight up, but he knew better. He'd seen this before.

The bigger man grabbed the biting man on either side of his head. As he gripped his ears, he pulled. Matthew winced as both appendages tore from his head. To his horror, the big man stuffed them into his mouth and began to chew.

The first to be infected stopped biting his victim and staggered away from the fight, weakened from the loss of his ears. He turned to look at his attacker, bared his bloody teeth again, and launched himself at him.

The force, coupled with the surprise of the lunge, knocked the big man off balance, and he stumbled backwards, banging his head on a hook that was protruding from the wall. His eyes widened and his mouth opened. The half-eaten ears fell from the maw, followed by a blacked, pinkish drool. His body twitched as he died, hanging from the barracks doorway.

Matthew felt sick as he watched more of the men caught outside rushing towards the fight. Four of them had already drawn their swords, one of them crawling with what looked to be a bloodied stump trailing behind him. There was fresh meat still hanging from the bone, but it didn't stop him from getting involved in the carnage all around him. Fingers were inserted into eyes and mouths, necks were snapped, and swords were swung as men who had been friends and colleagues moments earlier battled each other to the death.

One of the new attackers screamed as he was grabbed from behind. The man holding him tugged on his slick hair, pulling his head back, further and further, to an almost impossible angle. It wasn't long before a seam ripped in the scant flesh of the poor man's neck and the head was torn from his body. As the corpse crumpled to the floor, the man holding the head swung it like a weapon, connecting it with another man's head. One soldier responded to the knock by thrusting his sword deep into his attacker's chest. He continued to thrust until his arm was deep inside the man and the sword protruded from the other side.

Fists, swords, limbs, were swung. Blood sprayed and flowed. Bodies dropped as more men, covered in the thick black slime, joined in the fun. Others, obviously trying to help their colleagues, came running out of the shelter of the barracks and were instantly covered in the falling madness. Without even a second thought to what they were doing, they joined in the carnage.

Matthew had to look away.

There were now maybe thirty, or even forty, men killing each other or already dead. There was open fighting in the courtyard. Old women were attacking soldiers, who had absolutely no problem dispatching them with their swords before continuing to hack away at the dead bodies. There was a couple, a man and a woman, who looked like they were dancing in the rain; however, on closer inspection, they had their hands gripped around each other's throats, stepping around each other in circles. It was almost beautiful, until a soldier came up behind the man and cut away the tendons at the back of his knees. He fell instantly, and his struggling body was attacked.

Linda, Matthew thought as he turned his attention towards the kitchen.

To his dismay, there were several black, glistening monsters heading that way. His breathing became rapid as he thought about the nurse holed up inside. *I hope the men I stationed in there are up to their jobs,* he thought. But underneath his thoughts, he knew there was another reason he wanted to keep her safe; this one was personal. He closed his eyes and prayed for the rain to stop, and soon. The ugly noises of battle raged around him, and there was nothing he could do about it.

He had never felt so useless as he did now.

~~~~

'What's happening out there?' Jarod asked as he tried to push Kevin, his companion, out of the way.

'By the looks of things, you don't want to be out there. Remember the sacking of Carnelia?' Kevin replied.

'I'll never forget it. I watched my old mother get ripped apart by one of the commanders of the watch that day.'

'It looks like the same thing is happening again. The lads are tearing into each other out there. I've just seen Caruthers rip one of the new guy's head clean off his shoulders.'

Jarod's eyes narrowed as he looked at Kevin. 'We're all on the same side now, aren't we?' he asked, trying to get a view out of the black-smeared window.

'Not when the black madness comes,' Kevin answered, moving out of the way to allow his friend a view of the goings on outside. 'If that stuff touches you, you're done for. You'll attack and kill anything and everything in your way. That's what happened to your mother.'

Jarod stepped down from the kitchen window and drew his sword. He looked back towards the nurse who was sat at the table, down a small stairway, in the centre of the room. She was biting her nails, and he thought she looked pale, too pale. *I hope she doesn't get sick,* he thought with a mirthless smile.

She turned and caught him looking at her. He tried to turn away, to make it look like he was looking at something else, but she had caught him, and he knew it.
~~~~

'What's happening out there?' she asked, looking up the staircase. 'I need to get out there and help. There are people who need me. I can hear them.'

'I'm sorry, ma'am, but you can't go out there, not now,' Kevin said, shaking his head, looking away from the window.

'I can go anywhere I damned-well please,' she shouted. 'I'm not bound by any military chain of command. I'm a civilian.'

'If you go out there, you won't be bound by anything ever again. It's the black rains, ma'am. They've come again.' Kevin was shaking as he spoke; Jarod saw this, so he interrupted the conversation.

'The black rains,' he reiterated. 'Me and Kevin, we've seen 'em before. It turns whoever it touches into maniacs. It makes them kill, and eat, friends and foe alike. If you were to go out there, with all those trained soldiers, you'd be mincemeat in no time.'

'But they'll need help,' she protested.

Jarod nodded. 'And they'll get it. But not until it's all over and the rains have passed.'

The end of his sentence was punctuated with the crashing of smashed glass. Both he and Linda turned to see what had happened just as Kevin dropped to the floor, covering his face. Without even thinking, Linda rushed to the stricken man. It was then she noticed the large, jagged rock that had been thrown through the window. It had hit the soldier square in the face. The blood flow was heavy, pumping from the wound on the man's temple.

'They're coming for us,' Jarod shouted as he looked through the broken window. A number of black-slime-covered men were looking into the kitchens; they had their weapons drawn, and their eyes were wide and wild. He took a step back and drew his sword from its sheath. 'We're going to need to get you and him'—he gestured to his fallen comrade on the floor—'to safety. We can't have them storming in here and killing you.'

'We can't move him, he's likely to bleed out from that wound,' Linda protested.

'He'll be likely to be torn apart by the baying mob if we leave him. You too,' Jarod whispered.

Linda looked through the window. She couldn't see anyone outside, but she could hear the screams and the violence of the vicious fighting.

She nodded.

'You keep his head supported while I drag his feet,' Jarod suggested. 'There'll be room for you both in that pantry over there. There'll also be provisions, in case this situation draws out.'

They dragged Kevin across the tiled floor, towards the large wooden door in the corner of the room.

'Won't they be able to follow the trail of blood?' Linda asked, looking at the red smear on the floor, from the stairs to the cupboard.

'I don't think they'll be in any state of mind to look for things like that. If I remember rightly, it's a pure bloodlust. There's precious little thinking involved,' he replied. As he opened the door and dragged his moaning colleague inside, he gestured for Linda to climb in too. 'Bar this door with anything you can. You stay inside until you hear a lucid voice telling you everything's OK. Do you hear me?'

She was about to protest when the heavy door slammed in her face.

Jarod looked around for something to put in front of it, something big enough to make it difficult for anyone to get inside. With some effort, he pulled over a large wooden table and parked it over the door's jamb. He then looked towards the window. *That's one route in,* he thought before shifting his gaze towards the main door of the kitchen. There were noises coming from behind it. *Shit, it'll be difficult defending two fronts,* he thought.

There was a small nook in a cupboard that would be hidden from the window. He decided it would be where he made his stand.

With one last look into the courtyard, he saw that most of the men who had been advancing upon his position had turned on each other. They were literally ripping each other to pieces. It was a sad sight to see, watching brother turn upon brother, but he was relieved the odds had suddenly narrowed in his favour. *Every cloud,* he thought with a cynical grin. He climbed into the nook, his sword drawn, ready to defend the nurse of Outpost Three with his life.

A loud crash heralded the arrival of the first crazed foes.

4.

ENDELLION WAS IN rapture. She was sitting on her Azurian throne, the docile Alexander on the floor next to her. She was holding both Glimmers in her hands and was half within the real world and half within the realm of the Glimm. Floating before her was a small portal that allowed her to watch as the black rain, *her* black rain, fell onto Outpost Three, causing everyone within to tear each other apart.

She was grinning uncontrollably.

With a wink, she flipped into the realm of the Glimm and regarded the sad, pathetic faces around the altar. 'Look,' she commanded. 'Look at what your beloved religion allows me to do.' She forced the men to watch the battle and the effects of the black rain. 'I now command the power of The Glimm, and, my friends, there is not a thing you can do about it.'

Each of the old men looked at the other. Not a single word passed among them, but the looks were not lost on Endellion. It made her laugh. 'I will be the one who brings about the destruction of the kingdom of Carnelia, and then, at my whim, I may or may not'—she shrugged to show her indifference—'destroy the Azurian Kingdom too. It bothers me not, either way.'

'Can we allow this?' one of the old men asked the others. 'Can we allow this debauchery?' he shouted.

'Brother, hush,' another chastised him. 'There is nothing we can do. She is custodian of both Glimmers. We are under her thrall. Alas, this is all our doing.' He dropped his head and reached out to the other men.

Some of them took up his offer and held onto him.

Endellion laughed again. It might have sounded exaggerated if the woman had not been so animated in her mirth. 'You,' she laughed, trying her best to keep her breath. 'You have failed me, Glimm.' She was pointing at the man who had asked the question. He looked back at her, fear etched on his spectral face, even through the thick, grey beard. 'Be gone,' she said and snapped her fingers.

The old man disappeared in a small cloud of smoke. The faintest of screams could be heard as he did.

The others looked at each other before huddling together at the throne.

Endellion blinked her eyes, and she was back in the real world. Alexander was still sitting, wide-eyed, staring at the remote portal floating above him.

They were alone in the throne room; she was alone in her moment of triumph. *Another battle won in a war I cannot lose,* she thought. She laughed again as the men in the outpost continued slaughtering each other.

5.

CASSANDRA SAT UPRIGHT in her cot. Her cell was darker now. Her eyes were closed, but there was rapid movement behind their lids.

She was focused on something important.

Tears were running down her cheeks.

Slowly, she opened her eyes and got off the bed. The pain in her legs shot arrows of fire in both directions, up and down, from her knees. She was dizzy, and she leaned on the wall to stop the room from spinning and herself from falling over. By the time she reached the window, she was tired and covered in cold sweat. Determined, she reached out and gripped the iron bars, pulling herself forward. The breeze from the small hole chilled her moist skin.

The sight she witnessed outside her prison filled her with joy.

Fluttering around in the breeze were the biggest butterflies that she had ever seen in her life. A smile broke on her face, bringing with it a small bloom of colour to her waxy complexion. She gripped the bars tighter and whispered one word.

'Go,' she said.

As one, the swarm of colossal butterflies lifted and took to the sky.

Their shadows passed over her, and the breeze from the beating of their wings blew through her hair. She closed her eyes again. Once more, her eyeballs moved rapidly beneath the lids, and she began to whisper another chant. The colour that had momentarily reappeared on her face drained in an instant, and she lost her grip on the bars of her cell.

She fell back hard on the cold stones of her cell. She turned her face to press it against the cobbles and whispered another word.

'Alexander!'

6.

JAROD WATCHED FROM his vantage point within the nook of the cupboard as three soldiers—men he had known for years, had joined the Carnelian Cadets with—crashed through the door and into the kitchen. Their wild eyes roamed the room; the malintent on their blackened faces petrified him.

He had never before seen men look so … vacant.

Each had his sword drawn, and he could hear them grunting and growling as they searched the kitchen for someone to fight, to maim, to kill.

He was expecting them to turn on each other, to fight each other, stab, maim, kill each other, but they didn't. He was hopeful the lack of the black rain falling inside the kitchen would turn them lucid. But they were slipping on the black slime they dragged in with them, the same tar-like substance that was dripping from their tangled, blood-stained tunics, and the madness in their eyes was still there.

He never once took his eyes from them as they made their way through the room. He was ready; he would wait for them to either turn on each other, as he had witnessed through the window, or for them to split up. He would then attack each man individually. He had no intention of killing them, they were friends after all, but he did need to incapacitate them if he and the nurse in the pantry were to survive this day.

He knew the men, and he knew how good they were with swords; luckily, he had confidence in his own abilities too. He knew in a one-on-one situation, he could take any one of these men; he thought that maybe given their aggression and rage, if he could keep his cunning together, then he might even be able to take on two. But there was no way he would survive an assault by all three at the same time.

He watched his savage friends as they approached his nook. His hands were wet as he gripped the hilt of his sword. Adrenaline was rising in his stomach and in his chest. He had to use every bit of his training to fight the urge to give in to it. When they passed, he considered an attack, but knew he would have to bide his time.

The men were grunting and kicking things, stabbing at places where a person could hide. He watched them head towards the pantry and the heavy table. He hoped they didn't have the dexterity to move the large table and search the pantry beyond.

They passed it without even a second look, and Jarod released the breath he had been keeping for too long. His head swam a little, but the relief of the men passing the cupboard was enough for him not to care.

A crash—it sounded like a smashing of glass—from inside the cupboard caused time to stand still. He was still only halfway through exhaling when he stopped.

The three soldiers ceased their searching and turned towards the table pushed up against the door. He realised then that the soldiers *did* have the intelligence to move the table. Two of them began to shift the heavy item while the third resumed his search for others. He walked back, passed Jarod's nook, stabbing at areas where bodies could have been hiding.

Jarod knew this was the moment he needed to shift the odds in his favour. Careful not to make a noise, he squeezed his body from the nook and crept behind the third soldier. He knew this one. It was Jeffory, a drinking buddy from the tavern he used to frequent. He didn't know his second name, but military types were never ones for over-familiarity. *First name, uniform the same,* was all a military man needed to become drinking friends.

No time for nostalgia now, he thought. *This is life and death!*

He placed his sword on the floor, with the hilt pointing towards him in case he needed it. He reached into his tunic and removed a small stiletto from a concealed pocket. He then lunged, grabbing the man from behind, wrapping his arm around his neck. There was a genuinely scary moment when the wriggling man almost slipped from his grip as the black slime, he was coated in allowed him to half turn. But Jarod was not playing a game. He knew it was either the soldier or him, and he had no other option but to kill the man. He slid the knife around the man's neck and applied the right amount of force. He felt the dagger bite into the man's skin before beginning to move more freely.

The blood began to flow, and the soldier's struggles weakened. He crumpled to the floor as Jarod lessened his grip on him.

He turned to see if either of the others had noticed one of their party had been removed but was relieved to see them still trying to negotiate the table.

Jarod looked down at his hands and his arms. There were smudges of the dark, greasy rain spread over where his skin was exposed. He watched as is sank into his pores. His head begin to spin. A nausea rose from his stomach, and a cramp almost crippled him in agony. His vision doubled, trebled. Then, the vilest homicidal thoughts flashed through his head. He could think of nothing else but ripping, stabbing, killing, eating. He looked at the body on the floor. He didn't see it as a fallen comrade but as an opportunity missed to hack and slice and cause pain.

The fuzz in his head doubled again, and he fell against the wall, holding out a hand to stop himself from falling as his eyesight failed him.

And then, as suddenly as it started, it passed.

He opened his eyes and saw he was wielding his sword, ready to … *to do what*?

The other two soldiers were still trying to remove the table, mumbling, and swiping at each other from end to end. They hadn't even noticed him. Taking a deep breath, readying himself, he adjusted his grip on the sword.

A muffled scream from inside the cupboard distracted him. It excited the two soldiers; they stopped squabbling and doubled their efforts removing the object in their way. He needed to get them away from the door, but he also needed to stay away from the black goo that covered the two remaining men. He now had a small understanding of their motives and knew he couldn't afford to have anything further to do with it.

He angled his sword and crept stealthily towards them, hoping not to make any sound.

The table had been successfully removed, and the two men were now fighting about how to open the door.

As they scrabbled, Jarod could hear Linda shouting from inside. The sound buoyed him to advance on the mindless soldiers, knowing they could attract more of the maniacs inside.

Without any further ado, he thrust his sword into the first man's back. He hadn't wanted to kill him, but there was no other recourse. He pushed the weapon deep, almost to the hilt, until he could feel the warmth of the soldier's blood pouring over his hands. His first instinct was to flinch in case it was infected like the rain. He didn't want that horrible feeling coursing through his body again. However, it was too late, the blood was on him. He held his breath, waiting, but none of the uneasiness came.

The soldier turned on him. His eyes were wide, and the rictus on his face told of pain and frustration.

Jarod recognised him as Marcus Fraiton. They had grown up together and had saved each other in the sacking of Carnelia the last time it rained black. Deep down, he was saddened by what he'd had to do, but there was no time for remorse now, he needed to protect the nurse in every way possible.

He was shocked when his old friend at the end of his sword began to push back. If he was as wounded as Jarod knew he was, he wasn't showing it. Under the force of the push, he slipped backwards, losing his footing and hitting the floor hard, releasing his grip on the weapon in the process.

Grinning, Marcus, his old friend, advanced upon him, the sword protruding from his chest. Black rain, dark blood, and the pink of his innards as his insides spilled from the wound clashed, but it didn't stop the soldier's advance.

Jarod reached up, careful to dodge the blade of his own sword, and thrust his hand deep into the bloody wound.

Marcus screamed.

As he did, it alerted the second soldier, who was still trying to open the door to the pantry. Sensing easier prey than what was on the other side of the door, he gave up and began to manoeuvre around the table to get at the two fighting men.

Jarod raised his other hand and thrust it into the widening gash in the man's stomach, then pulled with all his strength.

He tore his attacker apart with his bare hands.

He removed his hands from the warmth of the wound just in time to unceremoniously roll out of the way and onto the floor. He dodged the falling body with ease. The last thing he needed was to be stuck beneath his dead friend. Also, he didn't want any more black rain touching his skin.

He struggled to his feet and grasped the hilt of the sword lodged in Marcus's body. He tugged it, but it wouldn't move. He turned to see where the second soldier was and was dismayed to find he wasn't far away at all. He continued to tug at the sword in Marcus's chest, but it wouldn't budge.

The third soldier's shadow was behind him now, raising his weapon, ready to bring it down on him. He swivelled, avoiding the strike, but the movement caused him to slip on the blood still leaking from Marcus, and once again, he lost his footing.

If it hadn't had such dire consequences, it might have looked comical. He fell again, onto the body of Marcus, and the small stiletto, the only weapon he had at hand, clattered across the floor. The remaining soldier advanced upon him. His eyes whiter than they should have been due to the drying black on his face and the fact that they were open wide, staring unblinkingly at him.

All Jarod could do was raise his hands, close his eyes, and wait for the inevitable attack. *At least I kept the others safe,* he thought.

He waited for the agony of cold steel piercing his body.

It didn't come.

Eventually, he opened an eye, just in time to see his attacker and potential murderer drop his sword. The man's head turned slowly around to look behind him, then he crumpled on top of his fallen comrade.

Jarod grasped at the falling man's blade. He had been given a moment's reprieve and needed to be ready for whatever, whoever had killed his attacker.

A firm hand gripped his shoulder, and he turned, throwing a heavy punch. Whoever it was almost dodged it, but not quite. His fist connected squarely on the jaw of this next attacker, and he felt the satisfaction of him falling away. Jarod struggled to his feet and held his newly acquired sword out before him.

'By the Glimm …' the man uttered, his face turned away from him.

'Come on, you bastard. Let's do this,' Jarod spat as he waited for his attacker to stand back up.

'Jarod, it's me, Matthew. I don't have any rain on me.'

He hadn't heard any victims of the black rain talk, and he didn't expect them to be lucid, so he relaxed, just a little.

Matthew looked at him, still holding his jaw. 'I forgot how good a punch you have.' He grinned.

Jarod sighed. He lowered his defence as he regarded his superior officer. He wanted to hug him, but he knew if he did, he would never live it down in the barracks.

'Has the rain stopped?' was all he could think to ask.

'Something has happened. I'm not sure what,' Matthew replied, looking at the three dead bodies in the room. He pointed to the window as he busied himself moving the first body and removing his sword. 'Take a look for yourself.'

Jarod looked towards the darkened window. 'The nurse and Kevin are in the pantry,' he informed his superior. 'Kevin was hit with a rock, so I got him and the nurse in there,' he said as he reached the window. He looked out. He didn't want to over commit himself just in case there were men, still mad, waiting to jump on him.

Once he was satisfied no one was there, he looked up at the sky.

It was undulating.

At first, he thought it was clouds crashing into one another, creating the madness, the maelstrom that had caused the black rain chaos. But this was different. There was something up there, something other than clouds; but he couldn't make out what it was.

'What is it?' he asked.

Matthew shrugged as he opened the door to the pantry. 'I don't know, but whatever it is, it's stopped the rain from falling. At least for the time being.'

7.

THE DARK CLOUDS churned and crashed against each other in the portal that hovered before Endellion. Her wide eyes were switching rapidly from side to side, tracing the fall of the black rain and the chaos it was causing in its wake. Outpost Three was taking a beating. *Nothing more than they deserve,* she thought.

Purple lightning flashed and forked through the blackness as death and madness fell from the obsidian sky. The hapless victims below were like puppets delighting a child. She clapped and laughed as men and women died needlessly at the hands of family and friends. *I will allow the black rain to fall until there is no one left alive in that cursed place.* She chuckled at the delicious, deviant thought.

'What?' Alexander said as his vacant eyes looked at her from his position on the floor.

'What did you say, boy?' she asked. Her lips drew upwards as she spat the last word as if he were a dog she detested.

'You called my name,' the boy replied.

'I most certainly did not,' she answered, dismissing him with her hand. 'You just carry on doing whatever it is you're doing. Stop bothering me.' She no longer wished to uphold the pretence of the relationship of brother and sister, not now she was custodian of both Glimmers. Her focus returned to the remote portal and the death and destruction happening within.

She had counted maybe twenty men fighting. The ground around them was strewn with severed limbs, black rain, and blood. She settled into her throne, ready to watch the outcome for the foreseeable future.

Something obscured her view.

It was large and was moving with a deliberation that denoted intelligence.

'What is that?' she muttered, attempting to move the remote seeing portal's angle so she could see the cause of the obstruction. There was nothing obvious.

Closing her eyes, she was back in the throne room with the Glimm. 'What is the meaning of this? What are you doing to interfere with my plans, you insignificant ants?' she snapped. 'Remove that deterrent stopping my black rain. Do it now!'

The men looked at each other. Bushy eyebrows raised and shoulders shrugged. 'What deterrent do you speak of?' one of them asked.

'Don't play your little games with me,' she roared. 'It would do you well to remember what I did to your colleague. You know what deterrent I'm talking about. Remove it now!'

The men of the Glimm stared at her, their faces as vacant as Alexander's.

'Oh, never mind,' she tutted. 'I'll deal with it myself, then I'll be back to deal with you.' She blinked her eyes and was back in the throne room in Azuria.

'Sister, you called me again,' Alexander said as he pulled on the sleeve of her dress.

'Get off me. I haven't called you,' she said, shooing the boy. She got up from her throne and stormed towards the main door. She wanted peace and quiet to watch the events at Outpost Three. As she opened the door, there were several officials outside. When they saw her, they ceased their chatting and turned towards her.

'My Queen,' the first said as he bowed low. 'I'm in need of assistance. There are certain areas of the …' he cleared his throat, hesitating, 'City of the Fireflies that require your attention. We need a decision on—'

'Get out of my sight!' she screamed, alerting the guards who were stationed outside the door. 'All of you, leave me alone.' She lifted the red Glimmer. It began to glow as a mist surrounded the officials.

As she stormed off down the corridor, they all struggled to get away from the mist that was binding them, but their struggles were in vain.

'Glimm help anyone else who gets in my way today,' she spat as she headed towards the disused underground chambers.

~~~~
~~~~

A short while later, Alexander exited the throne room. He encountered the officials bound in the red mist. The guards were attempting to assist them, but their efforts were failing. 'Help us, my prince,' the first official pleaded to the boy.

'I'll be back, I promise. But first, can you please tell me which way my sister went?'

They all indicated the same direction, and their wide eyes watched as the boy ran, following the queen.

He needed to tell his sister something very important.

~~~~

Endellion was raging. She couldn't believe what she was seeing. She was in a dark room, the only light illuminating her face came from the remote portal hovering before her. The vision it displayed disturbed her on many different levels. She had been happy earlier, as she watched the black rain fall on the Rebels and Ferals, making them kill each other at her bidding, but that delight had now turned sour. The object that was distorting her view earlier was still there. It was large, and it was … blue.

Her eyes narrowed at the portal, and her mouth hung wide as she watched a swarm of butterflies hover over the compound. She gawped as the beasts circled the castle. They had descended beneath the maelstrom of the filthy clouds, their wings sheltering the compound from the black rain—her black rain.

She had seen these butterflies before, but they had been smaller, and they had been … everywhere.

'The Glimm,' she hissed as the butterflies began to settle over the castle.

'Damn you, Glimm!' she screamed. 'Damn you all to Kor'nor!'
~~~~

8.

MATTHEW, JAROD, LINDA, and Kevin ran from the kitchen and out into the courtyard. The area was a battle ground—or more specifically, the aftermath of a battleground. The dark rain that had puddled on the ground was evaporating, and the men and women who had previously been fighting were staggering around looking dazed and confused. Some were kneeling next to the corpses of friends, friends who they had themselves killed.

The people who were not moping around or dying were looking up towards the sky, or what should be the sky.

It was as dark as night up there, much darker than it had been during the black rain. As they looked, what they saw should have scared them, but Jarod couldn't help but laugh.

'What are they?' he asked, gawping at the huge insect bodies, each with their six legs dangling in the air.

'Are they blocking out the rain?' Linda asked, not taking her eyes from the sky.

'I think so,' Matthew replied. 'I was underneath that old wagon,' he said, pointing towards the wagon with the wheel missing. 'There was carnage all around me, and a puddle of the black stuff was inching its way towards me. I grabbed a shield that someone had dropped nearby and put it over my head. As I dived out of the wagon into the rain, I felt a beating in my chest. It was as if the air itself had come alive. I got to cover just in time to see those beasts settling over the castle.'

'Where are they from?' Jarod asked.

'I have no idea,' Matthew replied, shaking his head.

As the black rain evaporated from the ground, Linda strode forth, ready to tend to the wounded and the dying. 'You, Sir Matthew, can you check on the tents? I believe that whatever bad magic did this to these good men wouldn't have stopped them from killing the sick and wounded.'

Matthew accepted his mission. As he walked off, he couldn't tear his eyes away from the sky, filled with legs and wings.

9.

'FIREFLIES … FLY!' THE command roared from the underground chamber. 'Fly to Outpost Three and destroy those dammed butterflies.' Endellion was furious as she stomped along the corridor, heading towards the trapdoor that would lead her deeper into the deserted underground corridors of the castle.

'Kill them all and then finish off every living soul there. I want the place decimated. I want those Ferals and Rebels dead by nightfall.'

She closed her eyes, and the red Glimmer in her hand flashed once, then continued to pulse its dull red glow.

Feeling a little more relaxed, she inhaled a deep breath and composed herself. She bent and lifted the trapdoor before descending into the gloom below.

~~~~

A cloud of insects ascended from the bowels of the castle and into the air, creating what looked like a thick fog, a fog that hummed and throbbed with the beating of hundreds of gossamer wings. The wings were small for the size of the insects but stronger than they looked.

The people of Carnelia flocked to their windows to witness the insects. Grown men and women crossed themselves, as was the custom of the followers of the Glimm. Small children cried at the hideous site while mothers and fathers tried their best to cover their eyes.

An ill wind blew through the kingdom.
~~~~

10.

MATTHEW WAS HEADING towards the medical tents in the centre of the courtyard. Jarod and Linda were close behind him. Both men had their swords drawn, ready for any interference they might encounter. Even though the butterflies had dried up the black rain, Matthew wasn't taking any chances.

Making their way across the courtyard was a slow business. They were stopping from man to wounded man, checking for life and tending to wounds.

Linda was shouting orders at the soldiers who were about, looking lost and confused. Once an order was barked at them, however, it broke them from any malaise they had been wallowing in.

'What on earth could have caused this madness?' Linda hissed as she hunkered down next to a young man whose arm had almost, but not quite, been severed. The man was, thankfully, in a state of shock and couldn't acknowledge anyone attending him.

'I'm not certain it was anything of this earth,' was Jarod's reply as he helped with the stricken man. 'We've seen the same phenomenon before, in Carnelia, on the day of the sacking.'

'You mean this is what caused the downfall of a kingdom?' Linda asked, looking up at the soldier helping her.

'Yes. Although the Azurians, your people, would have you think they won the battle fair and square, it would have been impossible for an army, no matter how large and no matter how well trained, to take a kingdom that quick. Well, without the help of something like this.'

She looked at Jarod and shook her head. 'Don't call them *my people*,' she snapped. 'I have no allegiance to either side in this stupid conflict. I cannot and will not condone the actions of the so-called queen.

As a nurse, and a midwife, my priorities lie in preserving lives, bringing them into this world, not supporting mechanisms that take them.'

As Matthew watched this debate, he was suddenly distracted.

Linda stopped arguing and looked at him. 'Are you OK?' she asked. 'You've suddenly turned—'

'Bernard,' Matthew uttered before hurrying in the direction of the medical tents.

Linda watched him go. She finished her triage on the wounded man, ripping his tunic and using it to cover the stump of his arm. 'Get him to the infirmary as soon as you can,' she ordered Jarod, who nodded and shouted towards another soldier who was passing. Both men carried the patient away.

Linda followed Matthew towards the king's tent. She noticed the guards who had been protecting the boy were no longer present. Absently, she wondered if these men had made it through the black rain alive. She pushed the tent flap open and entered the warm, gloomy room.

Matthew was leaning over the bed, his back to her.

'Is he OK?' she whispered, not wanting to speak aloud. She looked around the room and was surprised, pleasantly, that it had not been ransacked. It seemed the marauding had thankfully not spread to the tents.

'He's alive. I suppose that's a blessing,' he replied, mimicking Linda's hushed tones. 'He's not conscious, though, but considering what just happened outside, that is probably a blessing.'

'It might have saved him. If he'd been making noise, it would have made him a target,' she continued, rummaging through the small bag she'd left at the foot of his bed. The bag was filled with medication. 'Is he hot?'

Matthew leaned over and put his palm over the youth's forehead. 'A little.'

'This should help,' she said, shaking a bottle filled with a clear fluid.

Matthew stepped back, allowing the nurse access to the boy. 'It's thought his father killed his mother before taking his own life,' he said, looking at the sleeping boy. 'During the first black rain.'

'That's awful. It must be a huge weight on his shoulders.' She looked saddened at the news.

Matthew didn't reply, he just shook his head, his eyes staring at something that wasn't there, was in another time, another place.

'I'm going to assume you were there, by the way you talk about it.' She finished spoon feeding the sleeping boy the fluid from the bottle and put it down on the bed. She then put her hand on Matthew's.

He looked up at the unexpected contact. His eyes were the window of the soul of a much older man, one who had seen far too much for one lifetime.

'Do you want to talk about it?' she asked, meeting his gaze and raising her eyebrows. 'I'm a very good listener!'

'I bet you are,' he replied with a smile that brought his eyes back into the room. 'But alas, there's no time for that now.'

As he squeezed her hand, it was Linda's turn to relish the unexpected embrace.

'There's too much to do here. We need to assess this situation with the black rain and try figure out where those butterflies have come from.'

'Well, when you are ready to talk, know that I'm here. OK?'

Matthew smiled. His gaze shifted from Linda's face to the patient. She was a little disappointed at the loss of his attention, but she knew her duty must be attended to.

'Will he live?'

She cleared her throat and adjusted her tunic before answering. 'I'll not lie to the man who has just saved my life.' She smiled but instantly felt the humour was out of place. To her, Matthew looked like a boy in need of good news, or at least the affirmation of good news. It hurt her heart to be the bringer of bad news he didn't need. 'I don't expect him to last the week.' She bowed her head as she continued. 'I'm so sorry, Matthew.'

He nodded. 'I'll need to make preparations,' he replied, his tone business-like. He then kicked out at the small medicinal bag on the floor. The force of the kick caused Linda to jump.

'Damn it. I wish Ambric were here,' he cursed.

Linda reached out again, taking his hand. 'Hey, you can wish all you want, but he isn't. *You* are. You've done a fantastic job in his absence, and you'll make a good job of this too.'

As he looked at her, the anger fell from his face, and she was relieved to watch a smile crack his features. 'Thank you,' he replied, bowing his head. 'I needed that affirmation.'

The tender moment was interrupted by a scream from outside the tent. It was loud and sounded inhuman.

'What now?' Matthew hissed before turning towards the flap in the tent.

Linda noticed him hesitate before stepping out, looking into the sky in case the black rain had gotten through the giant butterfly cover currently protecting them.

She followed his gaze upwards.

The canvas was still there.

Another scream echoed around the courtyard.

They both searched for the source. As they did, they witnessed one of the butterflies being ripped from the overhead blanket. The black rain began to pour in through the hole the insect left.

Linda watched as the rain coursed down onto the head of an unsuspecting soldier. In a matter of seconds from when the first splash hit him, he was screaming and shouting, thrashing and lunging at anyone and everyone within his reach.

Matthew was saddened to see it was Jarod who had gotten wet.

The hole in the roof was not there for long as either another butterfly appeared to cover it or the others shifted to cover it. Either way, the rain stopped again. Matthew watched as four men approached Jarod with caution, their swords drawn and ready for whatever their colleague could throw at them.

'Bring him alive, if possible,' he shouted towards the men.

They looked to see who had given them the order. Once they saw it was him, they dropped their swords and dived onto the madman.

With some effort, they subdued him before he could do himself or someone else any damage. They dragged him kicking and screaming towards the barracks.

However, the reprieve was only short lived, as more holes were ripped in the insectoid cover, allowing more black rain into the courtyard.

'Everyone, get to cover,' Matthew shouted.

Everyone began to scramble when they saw what was happening.

Matthew looked up through the holes that were appearing. What he saw in the thick, dark clouds above chilled him to the bone.

Hovering just above the cover was a swarm of the mutant fireflies that had attacked them in the tunnels. Their thoraxes were bulging and glowing; their wicked bodies were bent, undulating their lethal stings, ready for attack.

11.

'ATTACK, ATTACK … ATTACK!' Endellion screamed from the throne deep in the bowels of the Azurian castle. The one made of mud and stone. The one surrounded by primitive drawings and primitive seats. The throne that dated back thousands of years.

Her hands gripped the arms of the chair, and the tendons in her neck strained and bulged as she cursed the remote portal with wide, bloodshot eyes.

Unbeknown to her, she was not alone in the room.

Unseen and unheard, hovering in the corner of the room was a wraith clothed from head to toe in purple.

~~~~

The fireflies were hovering above the castle. Their bodies were bent, their stings primed, ready for attack. Venom dripped from the lethal tips. Below them, the giant butterflies jostled with each other, keeping the castle grounds free of the black rain that continued to pour from the ugly clouds above.

'Attack, attack … ATTACK!' came the order.

Each firefly did as it was bidden.

The first wave of beasts dived into the blanket of butterflies below them, their stings ready to pierce and kill each blue winged insect they encountered.

As the first wave hit, their stings did their work, piercing the butterflies' skin. The large blue insects screamed. One was torn from the protective blanket, exposing the compound below to the continuous rain. A kind of panic rippled through the gentle insects as more fireflies dove into them, stings piercing the blue fur covering their bodies.
~~~~

The black rain fell, coating butterflies and fireflies alike. However, the insects were impervious to the devastating effects it had on the humans below.

Another butterfly was ripped from the cavass.

More dark rain poured onto the castle.

The butterflies grew restless of the attack and began to shift formation; this shift allowed more of the rain to fall below. Another wave of fireflies swooped in on the butterfly formation. As one, they shifted again, and the fireflies missed their marks, crashing through the holes in the cover and becoming trapped between the floor of the courtyard and the butterfly blanket above.

A single butterfly fluttered down towards a disorientated firefly buzzing angrily in the courtyard. The gentle behemoth descended onto the angry beast and wrapped its wings slowly around its wicked counterpart and closed them.

The insect within the embrace of the blue wings struggled and thrashed before ultimately falling still. The butterfly opened its wings, releasing the dead body of the firefly, allowing it to fall on the floor of the castle grounds.

A cheer of triumph rose from the shelter of the large blue wings.

Each firefly that had broken through the cover was dispatched in the same manner, smothered by the massive wings of the butterflies.

The rest of the blue cover rose like a blanket towards the waiting swarm above.

The black rain was beginning to falter. The dark clouds that had brought the death were thinning, evaporating into wisps in the air.

Unheeded by this, the battle raged in the air above the outpost.

Fireflies stung the butterflies, who in turn smothered the fireflies. Each firefly that fell into the compound below was met with a cheer, as the humans, seeing the black rain had passed, stabbed and slashed at each beast that hit the ground, careful not to get too close to their stings.

The butterflies were winning. The bigger they were, the more enemies they could smother.

All the fireflies could do was sting, and sting, and sting.

For each butterfly lost, another took its place.

12.

ENDELLION JUMPED FROM the throne, picked up an old table that had sat in the same position for thousands of years, and threw it against the wall, where it splintered into hundreds of pieces. In her fury, she kicked and broke pots, tables, small chairs. She threw herself back on the throne, growling and gnashing her teeth. She jumped up and down on the ancient seat until it cracked beneath her violence.

Her rage hadn't even begun to subside when she realised what she had done. The moment her weight was off it, it crumbled into pieces.

Breathing heavily, she looked around her, witnessing the fruits of her anger. She had destroyed some of the paintings and etchings that adorned the walls, the ones that led to the Throne of Glimm.

She dropped onto the floor. As she lay amid her destruction, she screamed.

She yelled, shrieked, and cried until she was exhausted.

Eventually, red faced and out of breath, her anger subsided, only to be replaced with an experience she had not felt in years.

Tears spilled down her face.

They were tears of anger, sorrow, and sadness.

She cried because everything she had wanted had been so close. It had been in her grasp. *Why had that attack been stopped?* she sobbed.

Then the thought evolved. *How had it been stopped?* she asked.

'Endellion …'

She cocked her head to one side, unsure if her name had been whispered or not. She thought she had heard it but, for some reason, didn't want to acknowledge it.

'Endellion …' it whispered again.

'Who's there?' she asked, searching the room for whoever had had the audacity to spy on her. Suddenly, she felt spooked by the old place, even though she had been there many times. She could feel the presence of ghosts, ethereal presences, watching her, stalking her, judging her.

'Endellion ...' the voice whispered again. 'See me.'

On the far side of the room, the air began to shimmer. A form emerged. It was shrouded in a thin purple mist that swirled around the room, making her dizzy.

'Endellion, see me.' This time, it was not a request.

She reached into the secret pockets of her gown and produced both Glimmers. Holding them before her, her face lit purple from the glow of the orbs.

The wraith regarded her. The purple mist spun around Endellion as it reached ghostly arms towards the Glimmers. It wrapped around them like metal filings attracted to a magnet, encasing them in its mystery.

The ghost began to solidify, and Endellion was able to see it completely.

It was a woman. She was young and pretty. *Like I used to be,* she thought with bitterness. The apparition was wrapped in a purple shroud, and her long blonde hair, with a hint of purple running through it, blew back in a wind she couldn't feel.

'Endellion,' the ghost said. Her voice had all the hushed qualities of a whisper, but it filled the room. 'You have allowed your rage to defeat your purpose.'

Endellion looked around her, regarding the broken throne, the smashed pots and tables, and the destroyed artwork. Shame ran through her. She shrugged it off. She had promised herself long ago she would never again feel shame, especially now she was custodian of both Glimmers.

'I have destroyed the directions to the Throne of the Glimm, haven't I?' she asked.

The woman regarded the walls with emotionless, shimmering eyes. 'You have,' she replied, her voice flat.

'I care not of such things,' Endellion spat in defiance. 'I stand before the Great Lord Glimm as custodian of both Glimmers. I don't need a throne to make me great.'

'Maybe not, my lady. There is another way to the Throne of Glimm.'

'There is?'

'Yes, Lady Endellion, there is. The blood of the purple flows strong through your veins. Your mother was a true Sister, as was her mother before her, and the mother before her too. Your lineage can be traced back to the origins of our society. I am honour bound to help you, as you have been helped by the Sisterhood of the Purple before.'

Endellion was salivating. It had been a long time since she had been addressed as Lady Endellion, and she liked it. She licked her lips at what this ghost had told her. 'Tell me the other way, spirit,' she commanded. As she did, both Glimmers began to pulse, strong and fast.

The wraith closed her eyes. 'You need to follow the purple in your heart. It will guide you to where you have been before.'

Endellion could feel her temper rising as she became impatient with her ethereal visitor. 'I don't want to go somewhere I have been before. I want to go to the Throne of Glimm.'

'As I said,' the woman replied as she began to fade into the walls of the ancient room. 'Somewhere you have been before!'

~~~~

Cassandra was finding it difficult to breathe in the confines of her cell. She lay on her back on the uncomfortable bed, her body covered in a thick sheen of sweat. Even though the room was warm, the young queen shivered.

In the corner lay the meal that had been roughly shoved through the door last night. The potatoes, bread, and jug of water had been untouched since its delivery, but she thought she needed the water now, urgently.

Gingerly, she sat up, leaving a damp stain on the bed. Cramps, aches, and pains tore through her as she leaned forward, attempting to get to the water. Her clammy hands grasped the warm jug, and with shaking limbs, she lifted it to her mouth. She drank lightly, knowing too much might make her vomit and she would lose the precious liquids her body required to get her through this ordeal.

'When will this pass?' she croaked into the empty cell.

'Not long now,' came the whispered reply. 'Be patient, child. It's not long now!'
~~~~

13.

ALEXANDER FOLLOWED THE sinister voice down the ever-darkening corridors of the castle. He found himself in places he didn't like, places that scared him; the places he had thought of as his sacred, secret locations, where he would come when he felt like he needed to prove himself. It was here where he'd met the strange old woman from his dreams. He tried to remember what happened after their meeting, but everything was a blur. All he could remember was he saw Cass and everything became all right again.

Only, it hadn't.

Nothing was right.

There was a nagging ... *something.* It bothered him that he couldn't figure out what that something was.

Cassandra had spoken his name in the throne rom. Of that, he was certain. If he had only heard it once, he might have been able to shrug it off as his mind playing tricks on him, but it had been persistent. Each time he heard her voice whispering his name, she was sat on the throne, not talking, lost in some rapture or other.

Admittedly, there had been a fog around his thoughts and actions recently, but the calling of his name had cut through that. The lifting of the mist had left him realising something was amiss, something he should be concerned about. It was a feeling akin to having a word on the tip of his tongue and he just couldn't wrap his head around what it could be.

It was only when she'd run from the throne room, screaming at her subjects who were waiting outside, and headed off in this direction that the fog became a whisp. He'd known he was supposed to follow her.

He didn't have any choice in the matter.

He was her royal guard, after all.

He did his duty, and he followed. He needed, or wanted, to see where she was going and to make sure she was safe when she got there. He didn't want her knowing he was following her, though. Not that he was doing anything wrong, but in the mood she had been in lately, she might not take kindly to his interfering. So, he maintained a good distance between them, that way he could easily slip into any nook or cranny and avoid detection. If there hadn't been something dark gnawing at his soul, he might have thought this exciting, a kind of elaborate game, but the ugly feeling in the pit of his stomach told him otherwise.

All he could think about was the colour purple.

He watched from afar as she held aloft the metallic orb he had given her what felt like a lifetime ago. He was confused about the second one she held, the one glowing red. He had never seen her with two before. The one he had given her had been blue, he was sure of that. He had seen it turn red for a while, but now there were two.

He didn't know what was going on anymore.

She held them both aloft. It looked like she was conversing with someone, but if she was, it was with someone he couldn't see.

The red and the blue lights merged. The purple light made him shiver. He felt he'd seen it before, in a dream maybe. It unnerved him even more than he already was. He looked behind him, into the darkness that he had already travelled, and his fevered mind conjured all kinds of trickery to scare him.

Ghosts, vampires, werewolves …

He had been worried that Cassandra was losing her mind.

He was now petrified he was too.

This place was alien to him; he had been into the bowels of the castle before, but he had never braved this far. The corridors looked like they hadn't been used in hundreds, maybe even thousands of years. He closed his eyes, but all it did was conjure images of disgusting things reaching out from the murky walls, grabbing at him, biting him, pulling him in to live with them in their vile wall world forever.

He opened his eyes and chastised himself. He was scared, yes, but he had a mission, and he was determined to see it through.

In the purple illumination of her orbs, he watched Cass bend and open a trapdoor that was hidden in the floor. He waited a few moments in the pitch dark after she had climbed down, then lit a small candle he had brought with him and found the trapdoor for himself.

He took a deep breath.

The air was dank and musty, but he could smell Cassandra's perfume; it spurred him on.

With trepidation and more than a little mental effort, he convinced himself to open the door. Thrusting the candle before him into the almost impenetrable darkness, he drew on his deep sense of duty to his sister. He needed to continue this quest. *I need to keep my queen, my sister, safe,* he thought.

'Follow me, Alexander!'

He recognised the whisper as her voice. It was unmistakably her voice. She was speaking to him, directly into his head. He turned to see if anyone was behind him, but his candle had burned down to the bottom of the wick and was in the process of extinguishing. Hurriedly, he searched his pockets for another and lit it with his trusted flint. He needed to see who else was down here, who else was speaking to him in his sister's voice.

'Show me your courage, my brother. Follow me. I need you.'

The candle lit. The dim light it gave did not pierce deep enough into the darkness for him to see who, or what, had been whispering to him, but the voice gave him strength. He continued into the darkness in pursuit of Cassandra.

He crept down corridors that were danker, darker than the ones above. Before long, it felt like he was walking on soil or clay, as opposed to stone. The uneasy feeling he experienced above reared its ugly head again. His stomach was in knots, and even the sound of his shallow breathing scared him. He envisioned real ghosts down here. Wraiths of people killed in vile, inexplicable ways, stalking the unused corridors, looking for victims to vent their anger and vengeance upon.

The age of the castle was imposing, claustrophobic.

From the dim light of his flame, he could see twists and turns in the … he thought the word corridor didn't quite describe where he was now, it felt more like a tunnel. This thought didn't comfort him in any way.

Eventually, almost two candles later, a breeze blew on his face, and the sweet smell of fresh air, so different from the staleness of the tunnels, graced his nostrils. It gave him hope, and he began to walk faster. He needed the breeze. *If there's a breeze,* he thought, *there's a way out.*

He turned a corner and was surprised to find himself in a large room. It was shaped in a circle, and there were benches around the walls. In the centre of the room, sitting on the floor, surrounded by bits of what looked like an old wooden throne, was his sister.

She was shrouded by a wispy purple mist that was entwining itself around the orbs she was holding.

~~~~

'Follow me and the Sisterhood will show you the way,' the purple wraith, still hovering in the corner of the room, said.

'You'll show me the way to the Throne of Glimm?' she asked.

The wraith replied. It was only a one-word answer, but it was the word Endellion wanted to hear.

'Yes,' she said.

Endellion closed her eyes and breathed deep. When she opened them again, there was smile on her face. 'Are you my mother?' she asked. There was an innocence in her voice. It was a child talking to a kindly stranger.

The wraith said nothing for a few moments. She just looked at the woman on her knees in the dirt. 'I am *not* your mother,' she whispered eventually.

Endellion bowed her head.

'But,' the wraith continued, 'she is close. She will make herself known to you when the time is right.'

Endellion looked up. The smile on her face didn't belong to her. As she stood, dissipating the mist around her, she put the orbs back into her pockets. 'Well then, my lady wraith, lead on.'

'My name is Valaiden,' the wraith said.

Endellion smiled again. 'Well then, lead on, Lady Valaiden. I have important work to do.'

~~~~

As Endellion made her way out of the opposite side of the throne room, Alexander watched her and the thick purple mist that was still surrounding her leave. She had stood and turned as if in a daze or a trance. It scared him to see her like that.

He waited. He wanted to leave a distance between them before he would begin to follow her again. As he passed through the ancient throne room, he looked at the smashed items all around. He thought it wrong that such things of age and beauty had been destroyed, and his heart hurt as he saw the ruined drawings and sketches on the walls too.

'Alexander ...' the whisper in his head returned, sending goosebumps up and down his spine.

'Wh ...Who's there?' He shuddered in the near darkness.

'Alexander ...' the female voice whispered again.

'Who are you? What do you want?' he asked, trying to sound braver than he felt.

'Follow her, Alexander. You need to be there when the time comes.'

'Need to be where?' he asked, feeling silly talking to himself.

'You need to be there,' it repeated. 'You will know when you are there, when the time is right. The purple will guide you.'

A hissing sound heralded the sight of a glowing purple mist rising through the floor, giving the room an eerie glow. 'This will be the most courageous thing you have ever done, Alexander. You will be long remembered as the knight who saved two kingdoms.'

'I will?' he asked.

'You will, for a long, long time to come. Follow the mist to where it leads. It will lead you to where you need to be.'

The boy breathed deep of the musty air. He checked the hilt of the sword dangling at his side.

He hiked up his breeches.

Without a look back, he set off in the direction the purple mist led him, the same direction he had seen his sister take.

As he left the room, a single thought brought a shiver through him.

Ghosts!

14.

AMBRIC ARRIVED AT the gates of Outpost Three. He had given the correct signal on his approach and had given the correct password at the portcullis. Even though he was instantly recognisable, he had left word that no one was to cross into the outpost grounds without the correct security.

As he made his way through to meet with Matthew, who he had left in charge, he was surprised to see the remains of what looked like a battle, and a bloody one at that. He passed the tents of the sick and wounded before being directed towards the tent that Bernard occupied.

'Nurse, how is the king? Has he healed?' he asked.

His loud voice in the quiet tent made her jump, and she turned and scowled at him. Ambric looked at her and saw that she had not had much sleep. 'Are you the nurse or the doctor?' he asked.

'A little of both.' She smiled, wiping her hands on a towel at the side of the bed. 'I'm Linda, and you are Sir Robert Ambric, if I were to hazard a guess.'

'Maybe the sir part can be dropped, but yes, I am,' he replied. He looked at the boy in the bed and shook his head. 'I take it the prognosis is not good.'

Linda raised her eyebrows as she turned back towards the patient and released a sigh. 'It won't be long now,' she whispered her reply.

'How long?'

She shrugged. 'Days, if we're lucky. Maybe less if the same thing happens again.'

'The same thing?' Ambric asked. He looked back towards the ruins of the courtyard. 'What happened while I was away?'

'Black rain,' she said.

Ambric's eyes widened. 'Again? Did we lose many men?'

'Eighteen dead, another twenty-two maimed or wounded. It would have been worse if it wasn't for the insects!'

'Insects?' Ambric asked, trying to make sense of what he was being told. 'The fireflies?'

Linda nodded. 'Oh yes, there were fireflies,' she replied, her voice hushed. 'And butterflies too.'

'Butterflies?' He cocked his head. 'I haven't heard of butterflies in the mix. Were they friend or foe?'

Linda smiled again. 'I would err on the side of friend. They hovered over the courtyard, sheltering us from the rain. If they hadn't been there, I don't know what would have happened. There would have been a lot more dead, that's for sure. Then, the fireflies came and began to pick them off, one by one. We thought that would have been the end of it, but the butterflies fought back.'

'They attacked the fireflies?' Ambric asked, narrowing his eyebrows.

'Not only that. They beat them. They smothered them within their wings. Then they disappeared. Once the rains stopped falling and the fireflies were dead, the butterflies flittered off into the skies. No one has seen them since.'

'Pray, tell me, who oversees the outpost now?'

'Matthew. He's currently residing in the main offices.'

'Thank the Glimm for that.' Ambric sighed as he turned to walk out of the tent. 'Will you keep me apprised of Bernard's progress?'

'I will.'

As Ambric turned again, Linda grabbed him by the arm. 'Sir Ambric, Matthew deserves your praise. He handled the situation to the best of his abilities. He was honourable and brave. That deserves to be recognised.'

Ambric nodded to her. 'It will, believe me, it will.'

He then took his leave.

~~~~

'Robert!' Matthew shouted as Ambric entered the meeting room.

All the other men in attendance stood to greet their commanding officer.
~~~~

'Matthew, it's good to see you still alive, my old friend.' The older man grabbed the younger man's arm and squeezed.

'I'm thankful you're here. Have you been briefed on the events since you left?'

'Kind of. I bumped into the nurse on the way in here. Linda, I think her name was.' Ambric squinted for a moment when he noticed the slight change in his friend's face at the mention of the woman. The squint turned into a smile, albeit a small one. 'She informed me about the battle and regarding Bernard's condition.'

Matthew's head fell at the mention of Bernard. 'It's grave news, I'm afraid. It's a shame, as he has been a great source of motivation for our movement.'

'Aye, that he has,' Ambric agreed, along with the other men in the room. 'We must see to it that we make him proud with our actions. I have news that I want to share with you all. Please sit, and I'll tell you of my travels.'

Everyone in the room sat around the table. Everyone except Ambric. 'I've been to Azuria,' he announced.

There was murmured consternation around the room at this titbit of news.

Ambric raised his hand to silence the hubbub. 'There, I did some studying. I have learned of two talismans. They're known as Glimmers. They are the fabled orbs of the Glimm, an ancient folk who followed the teachings of the Great lord Glimm many thousands of years ago.'

'Aye, we know of the Glimm, Ambric,' one of the men in the room replied. 'But they're just stories told to naughty children to get them to sleep at night, to allow them to believe in fairy tales and magic.'

Ambric nodded at this interruption. 'That is exactly what I thought. But now I know otherwise. I'm about to tell you something, it may take a little jump of faith on your side, but I swear on my kith and kin, on my very sword, it is truth.'

He looked around the room; all the faces looking at him were serious. He nodded his approval and continued.

'Everything Cassandra told us is true. The witch, Endellion, I have had dealing with her in the past, dealing that does not awash me in glory but was at the command of my king. This woman is in possession of one of these Glimmers. She may have both by now. The legends tell of any person who holds both Glimmers also holds unlimited power. Somehow, she must be stopped.'

'Who is she?' another of the men in the room asked.

'She is the one who brought about the sacking of Carnelia.'

The men in the room mumbled again.

'She is masquerading as the Queen of Azuria. Queen Casandra.'

'If this is true—' Matthew began.

'It is true, believe me,' Ambric interrupted.

'In that case, what can we do to stop her?' Matthew continued. 'If she can organise the destruction of an entire kingdom in one day, and if she is in control of the black rain and the fireflies, then I repeat my question. What can we do to stop her?'

'That is what we are here to talk about, my friends,' Ambric replied, offering a cold smile to the room.

'We also need to agree about what must be done in the event of Bernard's demise,' Matthew said.

Ambric shook his head. 'Believe me, this is of a higher importance than that. Bernard would not want us discussing what we do when he dies, not when there is other, more important work to be done.'

Matthew stood. 'I agree,' he proclaimed, nodding to the group.

'Me too,' another man added. 'But the question still remains. What are we, a rag tag unit at best, going to do to overthrow a witch with unlimited magic and the might of two kingdoms, not to mention those fearsome fireflies, at her disposal?'

Ambric smiled. The nature of the grin made some of the men shift in their seats. 'I have allies in the Azurian army. They have informed me of a new, important prisoner at the castle. I have managed, partially, to convince them that if I can prove their queen is indeed a witch in disguise, they will join our cause.'

'How do we do that? How do we prove this is true?' Matthew worried.

Ambric smiled again. 'I propose an old-fashioned prison break. A skilled team of four to infiltrate Azuria and break her free. If my theory is correct, then I believe she is the source of our mysterious butterflies. It will need to be done soon, within the next day, two at the most.' Ambric folded his arms as the room exploded into questions.

15.

LINDA WAS IN Bernard's tent. She had been tending to the sick, aided by several others, civilians and soldiers who had been drafted to help with the burden of her rounds. But she had insisted she be the one to look after Bernard.

He had been in decline since the black rain, and she was concerned he wouldn't last the week.

A noise from his bed surprised her, as he had been silent for the past few days. He was awake and looked almost lucid.

'Nurse, are you there?' His voice was little more than a rasp, and it looked like it pained him to speak.

'I'm here,' she whispered her reply; it felt fitting to the situation.

He held out a hand for her, and she took the offering, giving his sallow skin a slight squeeze to let him know she was there.

'Could I beg your council, only for a moment?' he asked, struggling to sit up.

Linda watched as the makeshift bandages over his wound strained. The discolouration of his skin around the wound was what told her he didn't have long left in this world. It was testament to his tenacity that he had lasted this long.

'How can I be of service, my prince?' This was the first time she had called him that, as he, technically, wasn't her prince. But it seemed fitting now.

He smiled. The effort of just that small movement caused him to grimace. 'Have I asked you to not call me that?' He laughed a little. 'I have nowhere to rule and no one to rule over; therefore, I cannot be a prince, or a king.'

'Well, it's good to see you haven't lost your faculties,' she laughed, squeezing his hand again. 'What can I do for you, Bernard?'

'I'm dying!'

Linda gripped his hand and began to utter a counter exclamation, but he shushed her protestations.

'I know I am. You don't need to pretend around me. Trust me, I can feel death creeping. I hear him while I sleep as he gets ever so closer. So close, I sometimes feel his bony fingers gripping my shoulder.'

Linda shuddered at this image.

'I want from you a simple promise. Can you offer me that much?'

The intense scrutiny with which he looked at her was so compelling, she had no other option than to agree. 'I can offer you one promise,' she conceded.

'Promise me that when Cassandra gets here, you will tell her my final thoughts were of her. Would you do this for me?'

She removed her hand from his, pulling herself away from his light squeeze. 'Bernard, this is not a promise I can say I can keep. We do not know if Cassandra is even still alive.'

Bernard closed his eyes; his chest began to rise as small, painful coughs racked him. The intense fit passed. 'She is. I feel her. I don't know how, but I do.'

'Ambric, Matthew, and the others, they are devising a plan for a rescue mission. Matthew told me this himself last night. But there's no guarantee how successful it will be. If it is a success, and she does indeed live, then you'll be able to tell her yourself when she gets here.'

Bernard shook his head; a small smile appeared, only briefly, on his lips. 'I fear not, my lady. My time in this world is drawing to a close. I will not see Cassandra again this side of life.'

Linda stood. 'Stuff and nonsense,' she scolded. 'You're young and strong. You will make it to see your queen.'

Bernard physically grew weaker before her eyes as he relaxed back into his pillow. He closed his eyes; however, the ghost of the smile survived on his lips. 'I fear not, Lady Linda. But you have at least given me hope. I know you will keep your promise.' His smile grew as he relaxed further into the bed. 'You … will make a great Queen, Linda,' he whispered as he drifted into a troubled sleep.

Linda watched as he twitched. Sadness and confusion etched her features.

16.

FOUR SOLDIERS WERE selected for the infiltration and extraction mission, hand-picked by Ambric and the council for their skills in battle, their cunning, courage, and stealth.

Ambric addressed the men. 'This is to be a covert mission, that much is obvious. You will be required to infiltrate the Azurian stronghold, locate the prisoner, extract her, and bring her back here.'

'That all sounds a little too easy,' Bryan, one of the soldiers, said with a laugh as he listened to the orders. He was a slight man with a good-humoured face. His wiriness belied his training. He was one of The Ferals' top men. Having been one of Bernard's original hunting party, he was at first considered unruly and erratic, but Ambric had seen much potential in him and had nursed it, coerced it, and he had now sculpted him into a fine soldier.

'It will not be easy, Bryan. It is a tempered mission. I've had to pull almost every string and every favour I have left within the Azurian guard to get passage into that stronghold.'

The smile on Bryan's face fell on hearing Ambric's chiding. 'You've secured us access into the castle?' he asked.

'Yes. You'll meet with minimum resistance. I can't guarantee you'll meet *no* resistance. If you do, you're not to engage the enemy, do you hear me?'

The men present looked at him as if he were somebody wearing an Ambric mask. 'What?' Bryan asked.

'If there is bloodshed, my fragile alliance will be invalid. You'll then be on your own behind enemy lines. The agreement I have with the guard will be gone, and we'll have failed our mission. Do you understand me?'

The four men hesitated before nodding.

'So, there's no pressure then?' Bryan asked, the smile returning to his face.

Ambric looked at him and couldn't help but smile himself. 'No, Bryan, there's no pressure at all.'

'What do we do if we do run into resistance?' one of the other men asked. He was another small, wiry man with shifty eyes. Ambric knew this man would see every detail of the mission down to the minutest point. He was also deft with a sword and lethal in hand-to-hand combat.

'Estefan, if you do run into resistance, you improvise. Choke holds only, I do not want any unnecessary killing. Death only as a very last resort.'

Estefan, Bryan, and the other two men shook their heads. Ambric knew they were not the type to go against orders, it was why he picked them in the first place. 'Matthew and I will be with you, but we will remain outside the city walls. Our faces are a little too well known in Azuria for us to chance this mission. We'll be the extraction team and facilitate the meeting with our contacts within the Azurian guard. Does anyone have any questions?'

'Just one from me.' Bryan had his hand in the air like a school child. Ambric kept forgetting that these men were not long out of the Academy. 'When we extract the queen, what do we do with her?'

'We return to base,' Matthew answered. 'She has a bigger role to play in this battle than any of us can imagine.'

'Understood,' Bryan replied, nodding his head. He was mimicked by the others.

'Excellent,' Matthew said. 'Make your plans, we leave at sundown. We will be travelling light.'

With that, the meeting was disbanded, and the council members wished them the very best of luck.

As they left the meeting room, Matthew nodded to Ambric. 'That seemed to go well,' he commented.

'I knew there would be little resistance. These are good men we are surrounded with,' the older man replied.

Matthew put his hand on his superior officer's shoulder. 'It is a good plan you have put together, Robert. If there's one thing we can rely on, it's your ability to pull it out of the bag when the heat is on.'

Ambric smiled and patted his friend's hand. 'Your face tells me you have somewhere to be before we commence our mission, my friend.'

Matthew smiled and shook his head. 'Nothing gets past the wily old Robert Ambric, does it?'

Ambric shook his head.

'I have a feeling things are coming to a head here and that something … I don't know, maybe momentous, is happening.'

'I have the same feeling. Now, you go and see to whatever, or whoever, it is you need to see before the mission begins. I will keep our king vigil.'

Matthew smiled. 'I'll meet you there shortly.'

As Ambric watched his friend walk off towards the officer's quarters, there was something about him he hadn't seen before, something he couldn't quite put his finger on, and it troubled the wily old soldier, in a good way. He bit the inside of his cheek as he regarded his friend. *There is something ... regal about him,* he thought, then dismissed it and walked off in the direction of the courtyard.

17.

ENDELLION HAD BEEN trudging through the forest for more than two days. She was tired, and she was hungry. Her temper and patience with the purple wraith she was following were reaching breaking point. The wraith had advised her that on this mission, she was not to use her Glimmers to expedite the journey. This was a pilgrimage that must be completed on foot. Although, the wraith did allow her to use the Glimmers to attract animals for her to kill, cook, and eat. It was also good for divining fresh water for her to drink.

'Wraith,' she snapped as they made camp on the second night, 'I fear we have been to this location before. Either that or I am going mad. I recognise this place. Are you affording me a wild goose chase?'

'I am taking precautions we are not being followed. The Throne of Glimm is a sacred place, a hidden location. It would not be prudent to allow anyone who might be following us to enter its hallowed grounds. It is not for everyone. Just for the custodian of the Glimmers.'

'So, you *are* taking me on a goose chase, but one that is for my own wellbeing?' she snapped again.

The wraith bowed. 'You are correct, mistress. Now, please eat, and do not fret. We will be at the Throne soon enough. You need to keep your strength. When you present both Glimmers at the Altar, you will need to be at your very best. There is another long day of travelling ahead of us, and you need to rest.'

As the wraith disappeared, Endellion removed both Glimmers and held them before her. She closed her eyes and was instantly transported into the dark altar room of the Glimm. There, the old men were ready for whatever they were instructed to do, no matter how unsavoury it would be.

'What can we do for you, Mistress of the Glimmers?' one of the men asked, bowing low. His long face was not smiling, his eyes telling tales of woe and suffering.

Beaten, Endellion thought with a grin. *Beaten, and they know it!*

She smiled. 'I want nothing of you. I just want you to look upon my face time and again. I want you to know I am the one who tips the balance. I am custodian of both Glimmers, and when I present them at the Altar of Glimm, I will destroy you all forever.'

'To what end is this, ma'am?' another asked.

Endellion's eyes glowed in the darkness of the altar room. 'To my ends. Mine and mine alone,' she snapped.

Before she opened her eyes into the real world, she took the time to appreciate the despair she felt in the room as the men vanished before her.

She took the cooked rabbit off the spit over the small fire and began to eat.

The purple wraith hovered nearby, watching her every move.

~~~~

In the woods, not too far away from Endellion's camp, Alexander had caught his own rabbit. He had killed it and lay it down on the grass.

He stared at it.

He didn't have a clue what to do with it now. He thought about making a fire and putting the poor thing on a stick to roast it, but he didn't know how to remove the fur, or even how to make a fire.

He carried the poor thing out of his little camp and dug it a small grave. He then foraged for nuts and berries. He knew where to find them and how to eat them.

With his belly semi-full and enough water to wash his meal down, he settled onto a bed of dried moss to sleep.

His dreams were filled with visions. Old men with long beards and women dressed from head to toe in purple veils. On more than one occasion through the night, he woke startled as his dream body fell down a hole or from a cliff. Whatever it was, it was always close to a deep purple mist, and even more strangely than that, he was sporting a long white beard and a purple veil.
~~~~

18.

'I HAVE TO go. I don't know when or if I'll be back. I'm fully aware of how this might sound to you, but from the first moment I laid eyes on you, I had a notion we were supposed to be together.'

Matthew and Linda were in a room that was being used as an office in the area that was now a makeshift hospital wing. They were holding hands, and Matthew was fumbling, looking away towards the small window as he spoke. 'I don't know why, but I needed to tell you that before I left.'

Linda was trying to look into his eyes; there was a smile on her face. 'I've felt this compulsion too,' she confessed. 'It felt like something clicked into place when you entered my life.' She let go of his hands and moved away from the desk where they were sat. 'Would it be strange if I was to tell you I'm in love with you?' She said this looking out of the same window he found so interesting.

Matthew stood from his seat but stayed where he was.

'If I've spoken out of reason …' she started.

Before she could finish, his rough soldier's hands were wrapped around hers and he was behind her. 'No,' he said softly.

She turned to look at him. She felt silly, but there was a something within her forcing her to tell him how her heart felt.

He swallowed before he spoke. 'I was going to say the same thing to you,' he gushed. 'It's the strangest sensation I've ever had. It's like, and this is going to sound like madness,' he paused to take a breath, 'there's something pushing us together. I feel like I've known you all my life.'

'I feel the same.' She shook her head and looked away. 'We must put these feeling aside while you're away on this mission. I have important work to do here. Can we resume this on your return?'

Matthew nodded, shuffling his feet. He sucked in a deep breath. 'You're right, of course. We can make plans for our future on my return. Until then, I'll take my leave, but know this: you will be forever close in my heart.'

'And you in mine,' she replied.

A moment passed between them where they both leant in to steal a kiss from their newfound love … and very nearly banged heads. They laughed before Matthew took the initiative and took the trembling woman in his arms. He held her for a few moments, savouring the smell of her hair and the feel of her warmth next to him. As he moved away, she surprised *him* with the missed kiss.

'Good luck, and come home safe to me,' she whispered as he walked out of the room.

19.

THE PARTY MARCHED for two days. The journey was uneventful, mundane, and completed in silence. They knew the mission before them was of the utmost importance, and that fact weighed heavy on all of them.

'My contact will be meeting us in a few hours,' Ambric announced as they made camp in a clearing in the forest. 'If you gather around, I'll outline the plan.'

They built their small camp, gathered wood, and set about boiling their water.

When the chores were completed, Ambric assembled them around the fire. The five members of the team hung on his every word as the night drew dark around them. 'You four,' he pointed to the men, excluding Matthew. 'You will enter the castle via the underground tunnels. Carlos will show you the entrance and will act as your unofficial guide to Carnelia.'

'Who is this Carlos you speak of?' Bryan asked.

'He's a soldier, like me. We've been on the opposite sides for far too long not to know each other,' Ambric replied.

'Do you trust him?' Estefan asked.

Ambric stared at him. 'More than I do you,' he replied eventually.

Estefan took the meaning and quietened down.

'He will guide you beneath the castle to this point.' He drew a sketchy drawing in the dust with a stick. 'The main dungeons are here. If my contact is trustworthy …' he looked up at Estefan, who nodded and smiled a little, 'then this is where they are keeping the prisoner.

'We think this area is guarded more intensely than the rest of the castle,' Matthew continued. 'Carlos tells us that he cannot guarantee the allegiance of the gaolers. They are new men appointed by the witch herself. *This* is the area where you may meet the bulk of the resistance.'

'How are we to avoid killing anyone if we meet resistance?' Bryan asked.

Ambric took over this question. 'Carlos's men will be your guides. They'll talk the guards down; they know them and trust them. If this doesn't work, use them as a distraction and take them all out. Remember, nonlethal force. If there's any killing to be done, leave it to Carlos and his men. He'll authorise it. Is everyone OK with this?'

The group nodded their approval.

'When will Carlos be here?' Simon, one of the other men, asked.

'After full sundown,' Ambric answered, sliding himself into a comfortable position. 'Until then, we need to get much-needed rest. It's going to be an eventful night.'

'Ambric, a word if I may,' Matthew whispered to the older man.

Ambric rolled his eyes. With a sigh, he forced himself up from his comfortable position and got to his feet. The two men walked to a shaded area, away from the ears of the other men.

'I understand what we're trying to do here. But what are we going to do with the queen once we've liberated her? It's not as if she can just blend in. We need an extraction plan.'

'When Carlos's men see her sitting on the throne and in the jail, then they'll know who she is and who, or what, is running their kingdom.' Ambric smiled. 'Don't worry, Matthew. Everything will run smoothly.'

'I hope that's true,' Matthew worried.

Ambric winked. 'If not, and everything I've heard about these Glimmers is true, then I'll ask Cassandra to perform a few parlour tricks. That should convince them.'

'And then what? We march on Azuria?'

Ambric leaned against the trunk of the tree they were standing beneath. 'If we have enough backing, then why not? We need to move against this tyranny as quickly as we can. Bernard will not last the week. Once he dies, the men will no longer have anything to tie them to their Carnelian heritage. I fear the Rebels and the Ferals may flitter away into nothing. Then, the witch has won. We need a moral victory and someone for everyone to rally around. I've seen Cassandra, worked with her. She is every inch the queen and figurehead we need right now.'

Matthew was nodding. 'I understand all of this,' he replied. 'But do you think we could rally enough Azurian folk to mount a serious offensive?'

'Carlos is influential. He is also very loyal. I'm not naive in believing it'll be a push-over to convince him and for him to convince others. But we cannot hide anymore. How long will it be before the black rains come again? They could wipe us out like it did our kingdom. How long can we last against an army of overgrown, vicious insects?'

Matthew shrugged. 'I don't know, the butterflies seemed to do a good job of dispensing them for us last time.'

'But we don't know where they came from. We don't control them; we cannot rely on them. We need to take this chance. We need someone to lead us for when the inevitable happens and Bernard passes on.'

Ambric stopped talking for a moment as Matthew dropped his head.

'I don't know how powerful this witch is, or the Glimmer that she is in possession of, never mind the power combined *if* she has both. I know there's a red one and a blue one; I believe, or hope, that the real Queen of Azuria will have at least some knowledge, maybe even an understanding of the blue one.'

'I hope you're right, Robert. I really do. For our sakes and the sakes of future generations,' Matthew said, squeezing Ambric's shoulder. Both men returned to the camp and settled down to get some rest.

20.

'WE HAVE ARRIVED, mistress,' Valaiden said. She was hovering above Endellion as she struggled her way through the long grass, brambles, and thick trees of the forest.

'We're here?' she asked, her weary Cassandra face instantly lifting at the good news. 'I was beginning to think this throne was a myth.'

'It is no myth, mistress,' the spirit of Valaiden said. 'It is just over that ridge. You have been here before.'

'You keep telling me that,' Endellion replied as she struggled through the overgrown weeds. 'But I assure you, I have not. I think I would have remembered having been to a sacred throne room before.'

The wraith above her smiled. 'It was a long time ago. I personally led you here.'

'Well, I'll take your word for it then,' she snapped. She stopped for a moment to catch her breath and familiarise herself in her surroundings. She kept forgetting that even though she looked young and had the body of Queen Cassandra, in reality, she was the aging Endellion. She stood panting, with her hands on her hips, and looked about her, searching for landmarks she might recognise or remember. There was a huge oak tree that seemed kind of familiar. She might have remembered climbing it once or twice, or she might have been tricking herself into remembering places because she had been told she had been here before. 'When was I here?' she asked the wraith between gasps for air.

Valaiden just looked at her.

'Did you not hear me, ghost? I asked, when was I here?'

Valaiden still ignored the question.

With anger building in her stomach, she reached into her gown and produced both Glimmers. They were pulsing with their strange light. 'You will tell me when I was last here, woman, or so help me, I'll—'

'Stop this nonsense,' Valaiden said, her voice calm as if the Glimmers were of no threat to her. 'Come and see for yourself. When you see it, you will not need me to remind you of your time here.'

Endellion glared at the floating woman and made her way up the last section of the ridge to the area that would give her a full panoramic view of the countryside.

'Behold, The Throne of Glimm!' Valaiden said, gesturing ahead of her.

Endellion's eyes opened wide as the afternoon breeze blew through her hair. 'I *have* been here before,' she whispered. As she fell to her knees, tears were filling Cassandra's eyes.

Part Five

1.

THE SISTERHOOD WATCHED the young girl with interest. She was pretty, she was wild, but most of all, she was sad. Despite her only being twenty-one years, she was making a real attempt at living in the forest.

They were content with her progress.

She had built a small holding, away from civilisation and hidden from the more independent, wilder tribes that still dwelled in the darkness of the trees. She lived off the land and seemed rather content.

The Sisterhood had kept her under surveillance. Since she was a custodian of a Glimmer, they needed to know that it was in her control. Until now, they'd had nothing to worry about. She had led a quiet, unassuming existence.

The thing that worried them most was her insistence on sleeping with the Glimmer held in her hands. Each night, it would glow, a fierce red pulse. Sometimes her sleep was peaceful. When it was, the Glimmer would throb in a slow, constant rhythm. Other nights she would toss and turn, and the Glimmer's light would glare and flash in conjunction with whatever nightmares haunted her sleep.

The Sisterhood was mindful of this.

Some of them had advised preventative action against her. They wanted to remove the Glimmer from her possession. 'For the sake of us all,' they argued.

'She is a sister,' Zadamare countered during these heated debates. 'Yes, a terrible injustice was done to her by King Leopold, and yes, he deserved everything that came to him. We had to intervene. I just hope she does not want to bite back at the abuse, the injustice, she was subject to. If we remove the Glimmer, we remove that temptation, but we will also be removing any chance she has at thriving in her current environment. She would be living in the woods, wild as a bear, with no protection. Do any of you want that on your conscience?' Zadamare looked at the faces of the other wraiths in attendance. 'She is a sister, after all.'

It was agreed that the Sister of the Woods, Valaiden, should take care of her and lead her to safety.

'Where would I take her?' she asked the council of spirits. 'I cannot lead her to Azuria; they would imprison her instantly as a spy, they would have her head. And, equally, I cannot take her Carnelia. She committed regicide; she would hang for treason. The other regions are too far for her, unless she used the Glimmer, and I fear she doesn't know the ways of the orb yet. She is, right now, an easy target for any marauding hordes.'

'Then she needs to learn the ways of the Glimmer,' another spirit said. 'Why not lead her to the Altar? There, she would be safe, dry, warm. The Glimm that reside there could teach her everything she needs to know regarding the mystic powers she holds. Then she can make her way through the world with purpose.'

'That is a very good idea, Sister,' Zadamare praised. 'Valaiden, you will lead her to the Altar. She will seek refuge at the Throne of Glimm. We can watch over her as the years go by.'

Valaiden looked to the sister who had offered the quest and nodded.

The sister, a warm smile on her face, nodded back. 'Guide and advise her well,' she whispered.

~~~~

Valaiden appeared to her in the small, ramshackle hut she called home. The poor girl was lying in the corner of the dirty room; a rough blanket fashioned from the pelts of small animals she had trapped and cooked was warming her.

'Endellion, see me,' she whispered into the ear of the sleeping girl. She didn't want to frighten her. The appearance of a glowing purple wraith in one's home sometimes had that effect on unsuspecting victims.

'Endellion, wake now, child. Wake and see me.'

Slowly, Endellion's eyes flickered beneath their lids, then opened.
~~~~

She thought she was having another of her wild dreams. It had been a long time since she had heard the voice of another person, a person that was not in her imagination, talking to her. She smiled to herself, playing along with the dream.

'Who are you? What do you want?' she whispered into the cold morning air, her words forming plumes of mist from her mouth.

'Be calm, Endellion. I am here for good, not ill.'

At the sound of the voice answering her, her eyes shot open. She darted out of the bed and cowered into the corner of the room. Her arms and hands covered her nakedness in fear there was someone there, someone who wanted to harm her, or worse.

'State your purpose,' she commanded.

'I am here for good,' Valaiden repeated.

'Show yourself then. People who are here for good don't usually sneak up and hide in shadows.'

'Look, child. Look with your heart and you will see me.'

Endellion didn't know what she was talking about. She didn't know how to look with her heart. 'I am no child,' she stated as she retrieved her makeshift gown, made from the same materials as the bed covers. When she stood again, she saw the purple woman floating in the opposite corner of the room. Endellion gasped and grabbed at a small cup that was languishing on a table fashioned from collected wood. She threw it at the vision. The cup sailed through the glowing spectre.

Endellion's eyes widened again. She picked up the entire table this time and readied herself to throw that.

Valaiden held up her hand. 'Child, stop,' she commanded. 'I am here to guide you to a better place. It is a place for you to thrive and learn the ways of the Glimmer. You can stay until it is safe for you to return to where you came from.'

'I'll never be safe anywhere,' she said, still holding the table.

'Maybe this is true. Your future is clouded. However, if you follow me, I can introduce you to men who will teach you how to understand the Glimmer you possess.'

'Glimmer?' she asked.

'Your orb. It has magic beyond anything you can comprehend. At present, anyway. The Glimm will show you how to harness that power.'

'Who are these Glimm?'

Valaiden smiled and held her hand out to the scared woman before her. 'They are an ancient race, long dead now.'

'If they're dead, then how will I learn anything from them?' Endellion asked, lessening her grip on the table.

'They hold court at the Altar. They have done for thousands of years. They, like me, hold the powers of limited life after death. They will teach you the skills you require.'

'Skills?' Endellion's face changed. She put the table down on the floor and looked at the glowing woman. 'What skills?'

'The power to control nature and the elements. Power to see into the future, power to harness your very own spirit guide. All these are attainable from the Glimm.'

'Is this altar far?'

'A few days' journey,' Valaiden answered.

'When can we leave?'

The glowing spirit smiled. 'You must rest now, child. You are going to need your strength. We will leave in the midday.'

~~~~

It was an arduous trip. They made a rough camp, and she slept beneath the stars. She used her limited knowledge of the orb to attract wildlife, and she ate well.

The next day was more of the same.

She was exhausted and almost ready to give up this fool's errand when Valaiden proudly announced, 'Behold, the altar!'

Endellion looked to where the spirit gestured. There was a high tower protruding from the ground … and very little else.

'I'm to live here?' she asked. 'It doesn't look like much of an altar,' she mused.

'The sum of the swan is not all you see above the water, child,' Valaiden answered. 'You will be happy and, most of all, safe here. Now, I must take my leave. The Sisterhood will check in on you from time to time.'

Before Endellion could ask who the Sisterhood was, the glowing woman was gone. She looked towards the tower and smiled, put her hands in the pocket of her gown, and wrapped her fingers around the orb
~~~~

hidden inside. With the smile still on her face, she strode towards the tower, and her destiny.

~~~~

The years passed in the tower. The Glimm were her constant, if not entirely earthly, companions. They taught her the ways of the Glimmer, how to use it to bend the laws of nature and control the elements to her favour. They were always polite, informative, and, at times, funny. They taught her the difference between dark and light magic, and the responsibilities of traversing different realms.

She was a bright student, and she was interested in absorbing as much knowledge about the strange ball in her possession as she could. The old men of the Glimm grew to love her, and they treated her as one of their own. She was the first to come to them for knowledge in over a thousand years, since the old tribes had begun to delve into the magics and to develop what would become the great kingdoms of Carnelia and Azuria. To them, she was the embodiment of their ways continuing into the future, and in a funny way, they saw her as the saviour of the Glimm.

However, unbeknownst to them, Endellion was learning faster than they gave her credit for.

She learned how to block their thoughts from entering certain chambers of her mind. She was learning how to command the Glimm without their knowledge. She had discovered that they must obey the custodian of the Glimmers unconditionally. She found she could manipulate them into imparting knowledge of the darkness of their magic. She mastered the art of remote seeing. She could create vortexes and portals into anywhere, giving her knowledge of what people were doing without them knowing they were being observed.

As her powers grew, she was able to take control of a small insect that had been buzzing about her all day. She was about to kill it, but something about it spoke to her on a different level. Somehow, she knew this small, innocent firefly would play a large part in her life.

She performed experiments on the poor beast and the rest of its nest. She had blocked this part of her burgeoning skills from the Glimm. She didn't want them prying and giving her boring lectures on the responsibilities of what she was doing.

It was fun, and her powers were growing.
~~~~

It wasn't long before she mastered the art of enthrallment. She could command animals to do her bidding. She also mastered the magic of disguise. She could now take on the appearance of anything or anyone she wanted. She could change into one of her precious fireflies. She could take on all its characteristics, including flying, and producing their deadly venom.

Something else she kept from her teachers was the darkness she held in her heart, including the devastating plans she had for the kingdom that had done her so much wrong. She used every ounce of her newfound magic and laid out a plan to capture and kill her first victim.

This would be the catalyst for her long-term schemes against everyone who had wronged her.

She tracked the King of Azuria as he was on a hunting trip in the forest. She disguised herself as a firefly and killed him.

As a trophy, she took his broach. The seal of Azuria.

She watched remotely, and with a growing lack of empathy, as his wife continued as queen with no king, and as his daughter and son grew up fatherless.

Over the months, and the years, she lost her respect for the Glimm but gained herself a masterplan in return.

~~~~

Now, all these years later, she returned to the place where it had all begun. Where her dark journey started.

She stared at the tower rising majestically out of the ground. Her shoulders sagged as she took in its height. *I was living in the Throne of Glimm all that time,* she thought with wonder. *No wonder my skills with the Glimmer grew so quickly.*

She then thought about the time Cassandra had been imprisoned here too, locked in her tower.

She had wanted to kill the girl but didn't know if she could keep up her appearance as the Queen if the youth was dead. It was a part of the Glimmer's power that she couldn't see and couldn't risk. So, she'd kept her here, until she had escaped.

She pondered if Cassandra had been custodian of the blue Glimmer all that time and her powers increased exponentially too. *Maybe the*
~~~~

Glimm should have taught her better and me not so well. She laughed aloud at this amusing thought.

As she regarded the tower, the one she had called home for so long, she thought about what Valaiden had told her. *The sum of the swan is not all you can see above the water.* She looked at the glowing wraith above her. 'Am I to believe there is more to this tower than I ever saw for all the years I lived here?' she asked.

'The tower is merely the tip of the greater whole. If you had opened your heart while you were here, you would have heard it calling to you.'

Endellion stared at the top of the tower, where she had imprisoned Cassandra. 'Down below?' she whispered. 'That's where the throne is, isn't it?'

Valaiden nodded. 'Yes.'

'All those years I was sat on top of what I needed, what I wanted, for so long.'

'That is the nature of things, Endellion. You were there, yet you couldn't see it. You didn't care for it. You were wrapped in your own hatred and lust for vengeance; it clouded you. You refused to see it.'

Endellion turned to address the ghost directly. 'Refused?'

Valaiden nodded again. 'Yes, mistress. You *would* not see it.'

'Well, I see it now. It's better late than never,' she laughed. 'Lead on, Valaiden. I'm eager to enter, to fulfil my destiny. To take my rightful place at the Throne of Glimm!'

Valaiden didn't move. 'Alas, mistress, I cannot lead you inside. We are assigned areas in this afterlife. Mine does not include the Throne itself. You must enter alone.'

Endellion scoffed. 'I have no issue with that. I have no need for you anymore. You're free to leave.' She walked off towards the tower, not once looking back to see where the wraith who had guided her here had gone.

'Do I not receive thanks for my services?' Valaiden asked as her ward began the incline towards the tower.

'Not from me.' Endellion laughed. 'This is now about me and what is mine. Be gone, wraith. I *will* see you again. By that time, I will be endowed with the powers of Glimm and will be all powerful. You and all your Sisters will bow to me.'

Valaiden sighed as Endellion walked out of her sight.

2.

THE BAND OF six had set up their camp for the night. They were sat around the fire they had built, eating from their metal pans. Morale was high, and light-hearted banter was being passed around. Robert Ambric was sitting with them but was refraining from joining in with the joviality. He had heard footsteps around the camp earlier and knew they were currently surrounded.

He just hoped he could trust Carlos to keep his word.

Matthew had heard the sounds too. Ambric had grown rather fond of this soldier, as he had personally watched his growth from a recruit in the Carnelian army to a leader of men with a strong instinct to do the right thing.

There was something else about him too. He had become … *regal is the only word that comes to mind,* he thought again as he put his dish down and rested his hand on the hilt of his sword.

Matthew did the same, and it alerted the other men in the camp. The banter died, and the men began to stand.

'How many do you think there are?' Bryan whispered.

'I hear three,' Simon whispered.

There are a lot more than three, Ambric thought as he looked to the bushes around the clearing.

'Not three,' came a gruff voice from what seemed like everywhere.

Ambric smiled; it was a trick they had been taught to put fear into the enemy.

All the men drew their weapons and took defensive stances. Ambric was proud of their readiness.

'Try sixteen,' the voice continued.

Sixteen heavily armoured men strode out of the trees, surrounding the makeshift camp. Each of the newcomers had their weapons drawn and their face covered with mud so just their eyes were visible.

'You are surrounded, and you are outnumbered. Place your weapons on the ground and position yourselves to become prisoners of the Azurian guard and the annexed City of the Fireflies,' the large barrel-chested man, the leader, growled.

No one flinched.

The man looked around the camp at the five men. He was grinning like the cat who had gotten the early morning cream. Suddenly, as he looked from man to man, his face fell. 'Where is …'

'Ambric?' Ambric whispered as he stepped out of the bushes behind the big man, his stiletto drawn and resting in the fold of fat at the back of the big man's neck.

'Tell your men to drop their weapons, Carlos. Do it right now, or we will be finding our own way around your castle tonight.' Ambric's wild eyes looked around at all the newcomers. He could see their eyes passing from one man to the next, wondering what they should do.

Then Carlos laughed and nodded to his men.

They all relaxed their weapons.

The five Rebels quickly did the rounds and took the swords from the newcomers.

'Tut tut, Carlos. You're getting sloppy. Sixteen of Azuria's finest bested by six dirty Rebels.' Ambric removed the knife from the big man's neck. 'Did you not think we would be ready for your attempt?'

Carlos laughed as he turned on Ambric. He shrugged his wide shoulders. 'I had to try, did I not?'

Ambric sheathed his knife and laughed. 'Yes, I suppose you did. It's what I would have done, after all.'

The two men then embraced like old friends who hadn't seen each other for years.

'Men, this vagabond is Lord Carlos Gardine of Carnelia. He is Man at Arms to the queen herself,' Ambric announced as he pushed the big man away from him to arm's length. The group relaxed as they regarded the weapons they had gained from the Azurians.

'I think my men will be needing them back now,' Carlos said, pointing at the cache.

Matthew looked to Ambric, who blinked and nodded. The word was given, and the weapons were returned.

'Maybe that title of Man at Arms to the Queen might not be the full truth, eh? If all this is to be believed,' Carlos announced, sitting down by the fire and picking up one of the tins the Rebels had been eating from. He sniffed it, then put it back down, holding his nose. 'What rubbish are you feeding your men, Ambric?'

Ambric smiled. 'One of my own recipes, passed down through the generations,' he laughed. 'Enough play now.' Ambric's face was suddenly all business. 'We need to talk.' From the folds of his tunic, he produced a detailed layout of the underground dungeons and spread it over the ground.

As the men huddled around to look at it, Carlos raised an eyebrow. 'And just where did you get this?' he asked.

Ambric didn't even look at him as he weighted the corners down with stones. 'Never let the enemy into your library, Carlos. And if you do, never leave them alone while you go to the privy!'

Carlos shook his head. 'You really are a wily old goat,' he said with a smile.

'Come and share with us, Carlos. We need to get this done as soon as we can.'

Carlos looked at the large drawing and pointed to an area. 'So, you will hit no real resistance until you hit this section, here.' He pointed to a bottleneck corridor on the layout. It looked like the only real way in or out of the prisons. 'It's here that you'll hit the most loyal force to the queen. I've tried to lay hints and winks towards their leniency, but I've had no success. They're either far too loyal and blinkered, or, if what you say is true, they may be under her thrall.'

'Will they be hostile?' Estefan asked, looking at the map.

Carlos looked at him. 'Very,' he said.

'Do we have your permission?' Ambric asked, still not looking up from the map.

Carlos sat back and picked up the discarded dish he had sniffed earlier. He dipped his finger into it and licked it. 'Yes,' he said eventually.

'Right then,' Ambric said, rolling up the layout. 'I'd say we're ready to go. How many of your men are going to go in with them?'

'I'll send two men with your party of four. A party of six will be harder to locate than a party of twenty. I'll stay here with you two, and I'll disband the other thirteen back into the castle to mingle and infiltrate. Looks like this is something we're going to be able to sing songs about in years to come, eh, Robert? Tales of brave deeds and stupidity!' He laughed as he slapped Ambric on the back, causing him to spill most of what he was currently drinking. 'We can fill your underling here with a brief history of us.'

'That sounds like a plan,' Matthew said, smiling. 'This one is a closed book. There must have been some times he has let his hair down.'

'We'll do no such thing,' Ambric said, wiping his tunic of the spilled drink. 'I wouldn't want to subject the boy to talk of our foolhardiness.'

Carlos bellowed a laugh and stood up. 'Darrid, Golthwait, you two will be joining the Rebels on the mission. The rest of you, get back to the castle and await further orders. Now go …'

The two men who had been singled out checked their weapons and readied themselves for the mission ahead.

'Bryan.' Ambric signalled for the larger of the four Rebels to come forwards. 'You are to be in charge in there. There's to be no killing unless it's a last resort. Have you got that?'

'Yes, sir, no lethal force.'

'Unless we come across those filthy pigs in the prison,' Darrid offered.

Bryan, Estefan, Simon, and Garry all nodded at the two new members of the team.

'Look at them.' Carols bellowed with laughter. 'Best friends already.'

'Let's hope so,' Ambric replied.

'Glimm speed to you all,' Matthew offered and shook hand with all six men.

With that, they were off. It was a good hour's journey to the concealed entrance the two Azurian guards would lead them to. This would then lead to the tunnels that eventually fed into Castle Azuria itself.

3.

THE GUARDS STATIONED outside Cassandra's cell were checking in on her as they had been ordered to do every hour or so, as the queen had wanted a report that was human, not just from the fireflies who had been looking after her.

She was on her makeshift bed with a threadbare blanket draped over her. Her form was shaking uncontrollably, and she was muttering to herself, something that neither of the guards could understand, as her head tossed and turned.

'I think she's dying, you know,' the first guard stated as he watched her writhing. 'She hasn't eaten a bite in the last two days.'

'If this witch dies, then the queen's not gonna be happy with us,' the second guard grunted as he watched the girl shivering and shaking on the bed.

'Well then, maybe she should come down here and see to her herself then, instead of galivanting off with that jumped up brat of a brother of hers, eh?'

The other guard's head snapped around to face his colleague. 'Shh,' he warned with a whisper. His eyes roamed around the corridor. 'You do know she has ears everywhere inside the castle?'

'Don't you know that she hasn't even been in the castle for Glimm-only-knows how long?'

'That's as may be, but she's put us in charge of her most important prisoner—'

'Important? Seriously? She's a little girl. What is she going to do to two blokes like us, eh?'

Both men turned to look back into the cell. The bed was still shaking.

'Well, do you want to report that she died under our watch? I know I don't,' the first guard pointed out.

'Maybe we should get someone in to take a look at her. She doesn't look too good at all.'

'The queen said absolutely no visitors. None whatsoever. Only the fireflies and us. Not even anyone from the kitchens is allowed to bring her food and water.'

'Do you think she could have foreseen anything like this, though?'

Both men looked back through the cell door towards the bed. Cassandra was still mumbling to herself, but it had gotten faster and louder; her thrashings were becoming violent.

'Should we go in? You know, just to check she's all right and everything?'

The guard blew air out of his mouth, then grimaced. 'Yeah, maybe we should. Just to check that she's all right.'

The other guard shrugged and inserted the key into the old, rusted lock on her cell. It turned and the lock clicked, and both men jumped back away from the door as Cassandra sprung from the bed in a flash.

'Close the door! Lock it …' the second guard shouted as the young girl, who had an uncanny resemblance to their queen, was heading for them. Her eyes were open wide, but there was a vacantness about them that unnerved the two men. The guard struggling with the key thought she wasn't looking at them but rather past them. He exhaled as the lock clicked back into place before the wild girl could get out of the cell.

'I need to get to the throne room,' she said. Once again, the guard didn't think she was talking to him. She gripped the bars of the cell and brought her head closer. Her hair was wet, wild, and dirty, her lips dry and chapped, but it was her eyes that scared them the most.

'I need to get the throne room,' she repeated.

'Y-you're not going anywhere, missy,' the guard with the key stuttered as he backed away from the door.

'The queen will have our heads if we let you out,' the second guard said. He didn't know why he was telling her this, but he felt like he couldn't lie to this girl. 'Besides, you'd never get past the royal guards. The queen told us of your trickery. She said you can change your appearance to look like who you want … so, no, you're not going anywhere.' His speech got braver the more he spoke.

'I need to get the throne room,' she repeated.

'There's nothing for you in the throne room, little girl.'

Cassandra whipped her head around, and her gaze landed on the guard. He instantly regretted calling her *little girl*. He cowered, stepping backwards, making sure she couldn't reach out for him if that was her intent.

'It's not *that* throne room I need to get to,' she whispered. Her voice was dry and croaked. 'I *will* be out of here and on my way to the throne room within the hour,' she continued.

'OK, love,' the second guard said, nodding and giving a sideways smirk towards his partner now that the door between them was locked and they were out of her reach. 'Whatever you say.'

As the two men walked away, back to the safety of their station room, the guard with the key was laughing. 'Mad as a box of frogs, that one.'

The other guard turned, only to see the girl still looking at him through the bars. 'Yeah, crazy,' he said as a shiver passed through him.

4.

LINDA HAD BEEN busy in the hospital tents, not only from the battle with the black rain and insects but from the ones who had turned up with Ambric too. She was currently doing the more pleasing job of discharging two soldiers who no longer required her attention. 'You're going to need to keep that leg elevated when you're inactive for more than an hour, but after a few days of exercise, you should be back to normal duties.'

The man thanked her and limped out on makeshift crutches.

She turned to the second man. 'And you, that scar should heal eventually. You can help to speed up the process by rubbing this lotion on it twice a day. It'll itch like hell, but that is just the skin healing.'

'Thank you, ma'am,' he said, bowing low. 'And thank you for all you've done for the plight of Carnelia.'

As she watched him leave, she shook her head. *Why is everyone talking odd to me recently?* she thought.

'Nurse Linda.' The fresh but pink face of a new nurse thrust her head through the canvass door of the tent. She took in a few deep breaths as she attempted to calm herself. 'Nurse Linda, come quickly,' she wheezed.

Her stomach dropped into what felt like her boots. *What now?* she thought. 'What is it, child?' she asked, following the frantic girl out of the tent. Outside, a group of women and a few men who had been helping her with the medical requirements of the compound were standing around, looking lost. Her eyes flicked between their faces. *Someone's dying,* she thought. *That's the look people have when someone is ready to pass!* 'Who is it?' she asked.

No one answered, but their eyes fell towards one of the tents. She knew exactly whose tent it was. With a curt nod to the congregation, she made her way inside, where one of the other nurses, one of the few who had any real training, was tending to the patient on the bed.

She looked up on hearing the canvas flap. She turned and bowed her head.

'What is it, Nurse?' she asked, not really needing an answer.

'Oh, thank the Glimm you're here,' the older woman whispered. 'It's Bernard. His fever has shot up, and his breathing has slowed. It's become shallow. Too shallow, if you ask me.'

The woman moved aside, allowing Linda access.

'He was convulsing a moment ago. I put a wooden bit between his teeth so he wouldn't bite his tongue and held him. It passed on its own, but he's far too hot.'

Linda put her hand on Bernard's forehead and grimaced as she felt the heat of his skin. *A sickly fever,* she thought.

Suddenly, the boy opened his eyes. Linda watched as his eyeballs rolled wildly, trying to find focus. He grasped her arm, his fingers making white welts on the pink of her flesh.

'Queen Linda, is that you?' he asked, his pupils narrowing on her face. 'Thank the Glimm. I need you to—' He began to cough. As he did, his grasp on her arm tightened. He was hurting her now. 'I need you to tell Cass … Cass, tell her …'

'I'm no queen, Bernard. I'm just your nurse. What would you have me tell her?'

'I need you to tell her—' He coughed again, and Linda watched as pink spittle flew from his mouth. '… tell her I love her. I—I don't think I'll get the chance!'

Something happened to her then, something she hadn't done for a patient in many a year. She felt the stinging of tears welling in her eyes. 'That's all stuff and nonsense, of course—'

Bernard cut her off by squeezing her arm even tighter. She knew how much energy it was taking for him to exert such force, so she stopped the pretence of him getting better; he was worth more than that.

He pulled her closer, and she went willingly. 'Linda,' he rasped. 'You … you are not queen yet. But you … you will be … believe me!'

She thought he must already be delusional from his fever and the pain suppressant medicine that had been administered.

'Listen to a dying man, please.' He began to cough again, turning his head away so as not to spray her with the dark blood spraying from his mouth with each heave. 'I need someone … I can trust. Please, tell Cass I love her, and that my dying thoughts … were of her.'

Linda squeezed his hand as her tears flowed for a doomed young man in love.

'Tell her … tell her the butterflies worked … her butterflies worked!'

His grip loosened as his arm flopped back onto the bed. He was now in a deep sleep. A sleep Linda thought he may never wake up from.

Joilet, the other nurse, was behind her. Her head was bent low. She passed a basin of water from the side of the bed, and Linda accepted it. She took the flannel that was inside and wrung it out. The hackles on the back of her neck were standing on end, and she turned to the other nurse. 'Joilet, are you staring at me?' she asked in hushed tones.

The nurse shook her head. 'I—I don't know. What was he saying about you being the que—'

'Stuff and nonsense,' she tutted. 'The ramblings of a dying man, that is all.'

She was still shaking her head. 'I don't know about that, ma'am; there's something different about you.'

'Different? You're talking riddles, woman.'

'I have other patients I need to see,' Joilet said, her head still bowed low. 'May I take my leave, ma'am?' she asked.

'Of course. Why do you even ask?' Linda said.

'I don't know; it just feels right, that's all.' And with that, she left, leaving the canvass door flapping behind her.

Linda was left alone with the sleeping Bernard. She wrung out the towel and began to wash the boy's arms and head. 'I'll tell her,' she vowed in a whisper. 'I'll tell Cassandra you love her.'

5.

THE SIX SOLDIERS sliced their way through the winding labyrinth of the underground tunnels into Castle Azuria. They used their swords to cut back the thick undergrowth that had built up over the years—in some places, maybe even hundreds of years. One of the Azurian guards had taken point, as he knew the layout of the tunnels better than anyone else. He held a torch that had been dipped in pitch and set alight. He illuminated the treacherous pitfalls and obstructions that were in their way.

Bryan, not completely trusting of the two Azurians, volunteered to take the rear. He kept a watchful eye on the way they had come, making sure they were not ambushed from behind while also keeping his eye on Darrid and his colleagues. The journey had been long. They had been wandering around in the stinking sewers for over an hour, and Bryan was beginning to get restless. 'How much further?' he whispered.

Darrid replied with a fist in the air, instructing him to stop and be quiet.

Bryan, ever the soldier, did as was instructed. He watched as the guard at the front listened to the tunnels. After a short while, he must have been confident that whatever he had heard had passed, and he signalled for the group to huddle together in the light. Darrid produced a smaller map than the one Ambric had. It looked to be exclusive to the sewers.

'OK,' Darrid began. 'We're now starting our ascent into the castle. If we go this way, there'll be less resistance. Gardine has put word around to others who are sympathetic to this cause, soldiers who are not happy about what happened to Carnelia. His word is as good as his name around the castle.'

The four Rebels nodded at his appraisal of the situation.

'We may only meet cursory resistance. If we do, we'll take the lead and let you know who is on our side and who is dispensable. Is everyone OK with that?'

Again, the Rebels nodded their approval.

'If anyone uses lethal force in a non-hostile situation, then our treaty is over. Is that understood?'

'I'll vouch for my men,' Bryan said, looking around at the other three.

'Good. Stay close and watch me for direction. None of us have any love for the royal guardsmen who watch the prisoner. So, if any of those bastards start, they're free game.' He smiled.

Bryan shared the smile and chinked his muddy sword with Darrid's. 'That's good to know,' he said.

'OK then, if everyone is ready, let's go.' He turned and opened a small door that Bryan and the rest of the party hadn't noticed. He doused his lamp in the filthy water, and all six of them entered the castle.

'I didn't see this on the maps,' Bryan whispered as they exited into an unused corridor. 'Where are we, exactly?'

'Were coming up onto the kitchens. We'll enter a large chamber. It will be busy with cooks, waiters, and the like. They'll only notice us if we have our swords drawn. So, all of you, put your swords away and don't act suspiciously.'

Bryan gave the signal, and the others sheathed their weapons.

'Good,' Darrid said. 'Are we all set?'

'Yeah,' Bryan answered. 'Let's go and rescue ourselves a queen.'

Darrid smiled and opened the door.

Inside, ten Azurian guards greeted them, all heavily armoured with swords drawn. Darrid turned towards the four Rebels. 'Ah,' he said with a fake grimace. 'I forgot to mention this, but we won't be rescuing any queens, not today anyway.'

'What is the meaning of this?' Bryan snapped.

'Tell your men to surrender to the Azurian guard, Bryan. We don't need there to be any bloodshed. Please, forgive me, my friend,' he said, giving the instruction to the newcomers to strip the men of their weapons. 'I'm only following my orders!'

Bryan and the others gave their weapons up grudgingly.

'Bastard!' he spat as he was dragged out of the tunnels.

6.

THE DOOR WAS well hidden, but Endellion knew exactly where it was. This had, after all, been her home for the better part of twenty years. She attempted to open it, knowing it would be tough, there had always been an issue with the rusted hinges and the swelling of the heavy wood. She stood back and blew her hair out of her eyes. She removed both Glimmers from her pocket and held them up.

The door burst open before her. With a smile, she returned the orbs into her dress and entered. The gloom of the night cast scant illumination through the doorway, so she removed the Glimmers again. The red and blue lights illuminated her way, and instantly she recognised her old home. She took the seat where she had sat for many a long, cold night, staring out of the window. She made herself comfortable and closed her eyes again. 'Glimm, come to me,' she commanded.

The spectral figures of the old men in the white cloth and the white beards appeared around her. Their faces were long and worried. Gone was the jovial appearance they once had when she first met them.

'Well, gentlemen. It would seem I have won. I've reached the Throne of Glimm with the help of my purple sisters, and with absolutely no help from you.'

None of them answered. They looked around at each other, careful not to make eye-contact with the witch.

'What is your bidding, mistress?' one of them asked finally, his head bowed low.

Endellion laughed. 'Did I surprise you with the mention of the Sisterhood of the Purple? Did you not know I am a direct blood descendant of them and, as so, entitled to their protection and guidance?'

'I … I mean, we—' another Glimm began, but Endellion cut him short.

'What are you saying, old man? You didn't know? You mean, after all this time, there's actually something that you *didn't* know? I'm about to end you, to blow your existence away for good, and all you can do is stand there stuttering.' She threw her head back and bellowed a laugh. 'Here I am, challenging the Great Lord Glimm himself. You, the Sisterhood, the whole of humanity, Koll'nor and Koll'su themselves will bend to my will.' Eventually, she stopped laughing and stared at the Glimm, who looked at a loss as what to say. 'Do you know what the best thing about all of this is?'

The old men stared at her, twitching and shuffling as they waiting for her to finish her tirade.

Her grin spread slowly across her face. 'The best part of it is that *you* are going to help me do it. You are about to bring about the end of you all. The irony of it is it will be the second time you have done it!'

'No, mistress. We implore you not to do this,' the stuttering Glimm sobbed. 'You can't. We're—we're the balance. We're all that stands between the power and the rest of humanity.'

Endellion raised both Glimmers and closed her eyes. 'Be gone, filth,' she whispered.

The Glimm raised both of his hands to his face. He looked like he was attempting to protect himself from something coming at him from afar. Then, in a cloud of purple smoke, he disappeared.

The rest of the Glimm watched silently as their colleague vanished.

'If anyone else would like to protest me and my powers, then be my guest,' she mocked, holding the Glimmers before her. After a moment, a long moment, of silence, she smiled. 'I thought not. Now, I want to be taken directly to the Throne. I will not delay my crowning glory any longer.'

'This way, mistress.' Another of the Glimm stepped forward.

The rest looked at him, a few reached out, attempting to stop him from moving forward. 'Don't,' they whispered. 'If she ordains herself at the Throne, it is the end of everything!'

The Glimm turned to look at his brother. 'It is the end of everything anyway. That is inevitable now. She *has* the power. There is nothing to be gained in delaying it. This way, at least, we will all be together when it happens.'

The Glimm brother let him go.

With his head bowed low, he stepped forward. With a wave of his hand, a previously unseen door creaked opened. A plume of dust and the stink of a thousand years issued from beyond. The Glimm spared a look at his brothers, then at Endellion. His head fell again as he walked through.

Endellion grinned as she followed him into the dark room, lifting the Glimmers and closing her eyes. The brother who had tried to stop the opening of the door vanished like the other, in a cloud of purple mist.

As she passed into the time-sealed corridor, the door slammed shut behind her.

'This way, mistress,' the remaining brother sighed.

A natural luminescence shone from the Glimm; it lit the way along the drab corridor.

'How far is the altar?' she asked, looking past him into the darkness of the corridor beyond.

'It's not much further now, mistress,' he said. His flat, monotonous voice echoed around the empty room as he trudged onwards and downwards, deep into the bowels of the castle. He turned and looked at Endellion. A sickening smile was plastered across her face, or Cassandra's face, as she held the two orbs before her in the darkness.

7.

THE FOUR REBELS were frog-marched through the castle at sword point. Their weapons had been seized and their hands bound by tight rope. Darrid seemed to be enjoying the humiliation the Azurian guard were putting them through. He jabbed Bryan with his own sword at every opportunity. 'Get a move on, you dirty Carnelian scum,' he hissed as they passed by castle dwellers and soldiers alike. As they exited a door into a busy courtyard, their appearance caused much consternation with the people who were busy going about their daily lives. 'We caught this filth trying to infiltrate the castle,' Darrid would tell anyone willing to listen.

There were many boos and even some throwing of rotten fruit at the caravan, all of it aimed at the prisoners.

As they crossed the courtyard, they were met by a large man wearing the uniform of the Azurian Royal Guard. This man was a monster. Bryan looked him up and down. He towered over Darrid and the others, and they were not small men. The big man sneered at the Rebels. He pulled a face like he had stepped in something unsavoury that a stray dog might have left on the street before turning his attentions back to Darrid.

'Are these the infiltrators we have been warned about?' he growled.

'They are. We led them a merry dance, lulling them into a false sense of security. We then secured their arrest with minimal effort. They'll be no trouble to you,' Darrid replied as he grabbed Bryan by the collar and pushed him towards the big man. 'This one seems to be their leader. He's the one we need to make an example of.'

'Understood,' the big man rumbled. 'What about the others, the ones outside the castle?'

'They're being rounded up as we speak. They'll be paraded through the castle like these pieces of filth are.'

'Good. Follow me then. They'll soon be getting to where they want to be, just under different circumstances.' The big man laughed at his joke as he gestured towards a group of men dressed similar to him.

'You're a traitorous bastard, Darrid. You know Ambric is better than twenty of your men. Your company will never catch him,' Bryan hissed as he was thrust forward, forced to follow the big man.

'Well,' Darrid laughed, 'it's a good job I sent twenty-one men out there then, isn't it? Now, shut up, Carnelia, or I'll cut the tongue from your filthy mouth.'

'What's happening?' Garry asked as he pushed up front.

Bryan shook his head. There was fire in his eyes, and his mouth was merely a thin white slash. 'We were set up. It was that treacherous bastard, Carlos Gardine. I just hope Ambric has the fore sense to kill the scum for this deception. I fear they'll kill Ambric on first sight. He's already proved himself too dangerous. That will be a huge blow to the Rebels, and to the Ferals. To lose Ambric and King Bernard.' He put his shoulders back and walked through the door with the sign DUNGEONS on it.

If he was to go to his death, he would do it with his head held high.

As the four men, accompanied by the twenty or so guards, entered the room, Bryan heard the heavy door slam behind him, trapping them in the gloom of the prisons.

8.

BERNARD'S TENT WAS quiet, serene. Linda had lit candles; they added to the calming ambiance of the scene. She was alone with the patient, although she was aware of the gathering crowd in the courtyard. She kept vigil as the boy slept, monitoring the slowing rise and fall of his chest. *It's so sad,* she thought. *A prince destined to never take his rightful place at the throne of his kingdom.*

The night was drawing on. She had delegated her nightly rounds to the other nurses so she could stay at the boy's side. It wasn't fitting for him to die alone, in a cold tent, in a lawless castle, in no-man's territory. A basin filled with cooling water was at her side, and she had been dipping a towel in and dabbing his forehead periodically. She wanted to keep him cool and wanted him to know he was not alone.

Many of the well-wishers outside had lit candles. The light issuing from them cast a lustre of daylight through the fabric of the tent. There was barely a noise coming from them, such was their respect for their fallen comrade.

His breathing had begun to labour, and what little breath he had was rattling with every exhale. She took another towel and dipped the corner into the basin, allowing the water to drip into the boy's mouth. It was received with a sluggish lick of his lips as he enjoyed the moist sensation.

She looked out of the tent, towards the people lining the courtyard. She sighed as she worried about breaking the news when the inevitable happened, then shook her head and returned her attentions to her ward. *I'll cross that bridge when I come to it,* she thought.

Something was different about this death.

Tears welled in her eyes as she dabbed the boy's brow once again. Instinctively, as her training instructed her, she put two fingers onto the boy's neck.

What she was searching for was not there.

The skin was cooler than it had been.

Cool, and still!

She had witnessed many people releasing their mortal coil; it never got any easier to watch, but she had built an immunity to the deeper emotions of the event. This instance, however, took her back to her first.

The boy was so young and so loved. He was seemingly so much *in* love too, and his whole life was mapped out before him. He was strong and he was worthy. This should not be, and yet, here she was witnessing it.

Her hand passed further down to feel for any pumping of his heart. Alas, his chest was as still as his neck.

The king, Bernard, was dead!

Through a sheen of tears, she looked at his young face. It was so peaceful. He had passed in his sleep, and it looked like he was still in that state. That had been a blessing to her, and to him. She had not wanted to be the one who closed his eyes forever.

Her training took over as she wiped the salt water from her eyes. She tucked his blanket at his sides after straightening his arms. She then took the thin sheet from underneath the heavy, coarse blanket that had been keeping him warm and pulled it over his face. She gave one more check, just to see if the sheet rose from any breath that might still be in his body.

There was none.

She straightened her tunic, closed her eyes for a moment, and took in three deep breaths. She raised her head and spoke a few words in blessing to the Great Lord Glimm.

Taking the candle that was at the side of his bed, she exited the tent.

Hundreds of pairs of eyes fell upon her.

She could feel their scrutiny instantly.

With a stuttered breath, she licked her fingers extinguishing the candle.

A whispered gasp rippled through the crowd before they began to extinguish their own candles in reverence to the passing monarch.

The message was clear.

A whispered chant filtered through the crowd. 'The king is dead,' it sang in hushed tones. 'The king is dead, the king is dead, the king is dead!'

9.

CASSANDRA LAY ON her back in her cell. The fever pulsing through her body continued to grow. Despite the cool air of the night blowing through the bars, a thick sheen of sweat covered her body, causing her tunic to cling to her emaciated body.

She was shivering violently as her eyes rolled freely in her head.

However, she was sleeping.

In her dream, she was riding another huge butterfly. She'd had this dream before, only this time, it did not start as enjoyable as the first. The warm wind was whipping through her hair, but the sky around her was anything but blue. It was a dull, uninspiring grey. The clouds that had once been white and fluffy were now black and heavy, ready to spill their load onto the ground beneath her.

Only, their load didn't look like water. There was a black, oily thickness to it.

She watched helpless as the viscus liquid spilled from its pregnant prison. Looking down, she was horrified to see the outpost where the Rebels and Ferals had made their base was directly below the rainfall.

The butterfly obeyed her order to fly closer to the rain, even though she knew it didn't want to. *Black rain,* she thought as she got closer. *I need my butterflies, now.*

With the thought still in her head, the beating of huge wings filled the air around her. The sky became thick with flying insects, and for the first time in what felt like a long, long time, a smile cracked her face.

The great blue wings flew close; so close she could feel them tickling her face.

She laughed out loud.

'Fly, my beauties. Fly to the outpost and block the black rain.'

Without a moment's hesitation, the kaleidoscope of butterflies shifted direction, heading now towards the courtyard of the compound. Her own mount began to buck beneath her, causing her to grip the sides of the animal to stop from falling. A thick fork of purple lighting streaked through the sky before crashing into one of the ugly black clouds. The explosion within briefly illuminated it, and what Cassandra saw inside scared her badly.

A huge insect resided in the confines of the cloud.

As she noticed it, it noticed her.

Her stomach dropped, and she gripped tighter onto the beast she was controlling. With her eyes closed, she ordered her mount to retreat from whatever it was, to avoid it seeing her.

But it was too late.

The massive silhouette turned within the cloud and headed towards her. Whatever it was, it was fast, and it scared her butterfly. She sent the order to retreat again, but again, it was too late.

At first, she thought it was a firefly, but it was bigger than any of the other beasts, it was also faster. *And it's not glowing,* she thought as it closed in on her. Her butterfly swerved to avoid it, but as if sensing its thoughts, the hideous silhouette swerved in the same direction. Her butterfly tried the same manoeuvre another two times, but the great black insect was coming for them, no matter what direction they flew.

Why does it not glow?

As the beast closed down on them, she was surprised to see that it was another butterfly. But this was nothing like the ones she commanded. This insect was obsidian, lightless, with the exception of its eyes. They shone like two suns in its massive head.

One glowed red, the other blue.

There was someone riding on its back.

As she strained to see who the skilled rider was, she missed the battle raging beneath her. The clash of swords, the cries of pain and anguish as people died, were muted by the screaming of her butterflies as they were picked off, one by one, by the ugly newcomer. Then the counter screams made by the fireflies as the butterflies, the ones defending the outpost, smothered them in their wings were also ignored by her.

Her only thought was who it could be riding the hellish butterfly.

She thought it might have been Endellion, but she would be riding a firefly.

She could think of no one else.

Eventually, the figure revealed itself.

A flash of purple lightning illuminated the rider atop the vile courser. Bernard's smiling face flashed briefly as more purple lightning smashed into another cloud.

His smile was not long lived.

His face began to change. It became a map of bruises as dark rings formed around his eyes. His skin turned pale, and his beaming grin faded.

The version of Bernard riding the fast insect looked like he was about to drift off to sleep. As his head rolled, there was a glowing from his chest. It pulsed the same colour as the fireflies.

One word came to her. It felt like it filtered into her ears, into her very being, from everywhere all at once.

'Dead!'

'Bernard is dead,' she screamed.

She let go of her mount and allowed herself to fall. As she did, Bernard opened his eyes and looked at her.

Their eyes locked as she continued her descent.

When she woke on her bed in the cell, she was sopping wet, her clothes and bedding were soaked, and agony wracked her entire body. Every bone, every fibre of her being burned. Her body was a dead weight made of stinging fireflies.

A noise came from somewhere outside her cell. She welcomed the distraction from her horrible realisation.

10.

THE TIP OF Bryan's own sword was poking him in his back as he was shoved roughly through the door into the cell block. 'Get in there, you Rebel filth,' Darrid snarled as he followed closely behind.

The cell block was old, one of the oldest still-used parts of the castle. It was dark. Very little natural light made it into the room, or maybe it just didn't want to come into such a dismal place; either way, darkness prevailed, broken only by the few flaming lamps mounted on the dripping walls and from the tiny, barred windows of the cells.

Bryan glared at Darrid as he was pushed inside the stinking jail. He tripped over the mantle and almost fell into the lap of the surprised guards.

One of the scruffy men stood at the surprise delivery. His face wrinkled as he regarded the unexpected newcomers. Cups of dark liquid and playing cards were scattered on the table beneath limp candles. The other six men remained seated but glowered at the melee shattering their normally quiet existence.

All seven guards were armed with long, sharp broadswords. Bryan thought they were better suited for the battlefield than the close quarters of the cell block and wondered how he could take advantage of this if the opportunity arose.

'What is the meaning of this?' the standing guard snarled. He was trying to keep eye contact with Darrid while simultaneously eyeing his broadsword. 'Why are you bringing prisoners in here?' The wrinkled-faced man looked at the four prisoners and snarled again. 'Who even are they?'

'Have you not heard about the Carnelian infiltration into the castle?' Darrid was looking at the faces of the other guards, who were only just beginning to stand.

Bryan could smell alcohol in the room, and his own searching of the guards' faces told him they were more than half inebriated. While their attentions were on Darrid and his men, he was going to try something. Anything. It was his Carnelian duty to escape capture, even if he died doing so.

'These are them,' Darrid continued. 'We caught them red-handed as they entered the main thoroughfare of the castle. We've been ordered to house them here until we can make an example of this one,' he said, kicking Bryan in the rear end, edging him closer to the other guards' discarded broadswords.

The wrinkled man shook his head. A dangle of turkey skin flapped beneath his chin. 'Not in here, you don't. This block is for political prisoners only. Just the one prisoner here. On the queen's own seal.'

Darrid stared the man down. 'When did you last see the queen?' he asked.

'No one has seen her in days. She left with that brat of a brother of hers,' one of the other guards chirped in.

The guard looked at his colleagues. 'What's that got to do with—'

He didn't finish his question as Darrid thrust Bryan's sword into the man's scrawny neck. His little speech culminated in a deep gag before blood that was almost black poured from his mouth.

Bryan, who was halfway towards grabbing a sword, looked to see what was happening, and before he knew it, his tight bonds had been cut free, as had his companions', and a sword, his own sword, was at his feet. Without invitation, he picked it up and swung it at one of the surprised guards. The poor man didn't have a clue what was happening as the blade sliced through his head. The sharp, well-maintained metal made easy work of the man's skull, and he crumpled, his head split neatly in two. He was dead well before he hit the dirty floor.

Darrid disabled another guard by swinging his weapon into an arch and cutting deep into the man's neck. The drunkard fell back onto the card table, clutching his wound, ruining the game that had been set out.

Estefan was on the floor, struggling for his sword, when a guard bore down on him. Garry blocked the potentially fatal blow easily, but the weight of the weapon knocked him to the floor. The guard raised his arms, both hands gripping his heavy sword, ready to take a swipe at both men. A blade burst from his chest, causing him to stop what he was doing and die in a twitching heap next to the two Rebels.

Estefan got up from the floor just in time to see Simon receive a blow from one of the remaining guards. The swipe gutted the Rebel, and both Estefan and Garry watched helplessly as his steaming innards sluiced from the wound.

Before he died, Simon turned his blade around and swiped his weapon at the man who had dealt him the blow. The attack was true, and his severed head toppled to the floor.

Before long, all seven guards were dead, as was Simon, and another of Darrid's men mortally wounded. He was trying his best not to cry out in agony as blood from the wound in his stomach pooled around him.

Darrid looked at him and nodded slowly.

The man nodded back, understanding what needed to be done.

Darrid then plunged his sword into the dying man's chest, killing him instantly, quick and painless.

The fight was over in less than five minutes, and the cell was a blood bath. The prison guards, one Azurian guard, and Simon lay dead on the floor.

With a growl, Bryan swung his sword in an arch, aiming it towards Darrid. The Azurian was ready for the attack and easily blocked it.

'What is the meaning of this?' Bryan roared. He could taste his own blood, such was the ferocity of his shout.

'It was Ambric's idea,' Darrid countered, pushing Bryan away from him. 'Him and Gardine knew we would never get you through the castle if you didn't think that *you* were real prisoners. You would have been too eager. So, they devised this plan and made us swear we wouldn't tell you about it. We had to march you through the population in plain sight; it was the only way.'

Bryan exhaled as Estefan and Garry relaxed their battle stances. The other Azurian guards did the same.

'And what of Ambric, Matthew, and Gardine?'

Darrid smiled and stepped off a small manhole cover where the blood from the battle was seeping. He stomped on the metal lid four times and looked back at Bryan. A smug smile was growing on his face.

A rusty scrape came from the lid as it began to turn in its hole.

Eventually, Ambric's blood-covered head popped out and regarded the carnage before him. 'Have we missed anything?' he asked.

11.

IMAGINE BEING STUCK in here, all on your own, Alexander thought as he peered into the entryway to the tower. The thought brought a shiver down his spine, and he felt his skin cover in goosebumps. As he stared into the velvety darkness, he was convinced he could see things inside, things that were staring back out at him, things that were waiting for a young boy to enter their lair so they could eat him alive.

He had watched Cassandra enter after talking to herself at the top of the hill. The knowledge she was in there, someone he knew and loved, gave him the courage he needed to step in and brave the darkness.

He was scared of monsters and wild animals, he was also very scared of the thought of ghosts, but most of all, these days, he was scared of … *Cassandra,* he thought, hating the feeling as it bounced through his brain. *I'm scared of her. She isn't the same loving sister she used to be.* He laughed at his own absurdity; he also chuckled that he had thought himself the bravest knight in Azuria. How could he fear his own sister? He scoffed as he stepped into the blackness on the other side of the door. 'Scared of my own shadow,' he whispered as the inky fingers of darkness embraced and then enveloped him.

'Alexander …'

The whisper came from the darkness. It raised the flesh up and down his arms, making him shiver uncontrollably. *Ghosts, after all,* he thought.

The door behind him slammed. He jumped, and the darkness became complete. There were no windows, and even if there had been, it was night outside, and the heavy cloud cover was suppressing any light the moon was attempting to issue.

'Don't be afraid, Alexander,' the voice whispered again. 'It's me, Cassandra, your sister. I need my brave knight now more than ever. I need you to enter the Throne of Glimm. There, you will find me. You have a legacy and a prophecy to fulfil.'

'A prophecy?' he asked, swallowing a chunk of his fear. 'What prophecy?' He spoke the question aloud, feeling more than a little foolish talking to the wind.

'Find me,' the voice whispered again.

'Where is the Throne of Glimm?' he asked. He could feel thick tears welling in his eyes, ready to fall down his cheeks. 'How am I supposed to find you if I don't know where I am?' he shouted.

'The Throne is here, Alexander. Follow your instincts and you will find it.' The last voice didn't sound too much like his sister, but he recognised it from somewhere; he just didn't know where.

His fingers grasped for the hilt of his sword and relaxed a little at its reassuring cold. He dusted down his tunic in the darkness, wiped the tears from his eyes, and began to walk. He didn't know where he was going, but he trusted the voice when it told him to use his instincts.

12.

'AMBRIC, WHAT THE Kor'nor is happening here? First these guys are our allies, then they turn on us, then they are allies again. I'm getting confused,' Bryan shouted when the three men who had stayed behind during the infiltration climbed out of the manhole.

Ambric was wiping the other men's blood from his face. 'We needed you to let us in,' he explained. 'Besides, these tunnels are too fragile for a team to pass through, and we knew there was no way an armed force was going to be able to make it through the castle unmolested. So, Sir Gardine came up with the ruse. If you had known about it, it wouldn't have looked so real. Darrid and his men needed to march into the dungeons with you as prisoners, with a legitimate reason to be there.'

'Simon was killed for your ruse,' Bryan spat. 'He died saving Garry and Estefan's lives.'

Ambric's face was stern as he eyed the younger man. 'He knew the risks when he volunteered for this mission. He will be remembered as the hero he is,' he whispered. 'He will be mourned when we have freed the queen and Carnelia is free from the tyranny of Endellion and her fireflies.'

'So, how do we go about freeing the queen? What's the next stage of your plan? That is, if you want us to be privy to the information,' Bryan asked, not making eye-contact with Ambric.

'I have a feeling, and that's all it is, a feeling, that we will be getting some unexpected help in this escape. If I'm wrong, then I do have a plan *B,* but that one is a lot bloodier and a lot more dangerous. Anyway, there should be keys somewhere in all this mess,' he said, shifting body parts with his feet.

'I have them,' one of the Azurian guards shouted, dangling a large ring of keys, dripping blood, in the air.

'Pass them over,' Carlos grunted.

They were thrown, and he caught them, just about. The blood made them slip in his grip for a moment, and they almost fell into the innards that had escaped Simon's wound. The correct key was located, allowing them access to the cell block and the single cell that was populated beyond.

As Ambric made it to the door, he slid open the small viewing hatch and looked inside. Cassandra was there, lying on the floor. He could see she was still alive, as her body shook, but he could also tell she was in poor condition. He turned the key and entered. 'She's alive,' he half shouted down the corridor to the others guarding the door. 'She's going to need help, and fast.'

'Will she make it back through the tunnels?' someone shouted. Ambric didn't know who, nor did he care.

'I'm hoping she won't have to,' he replied.

A scratching noise from outside the barred window distracted him, and he looked to see what it was. The sky was growing brighter as morning was creeping upon them. However, it wasn't this that caused him to grin.

It was the swarm of blue butterflies fluttering on the morning breeze outside the bars that lifted his spirits.

He looked down at Cassandra and was relieved to see her eyes open. She still looked sick, but there was a small, mischievous glint in her eyes.

'You sent them, didn't you?' he whispered. He didn't think she had the strength to speak, but he smiled when she gave a small nod.

Some of the smaller insects fluttered into the cell. Ambric stood back and regarded them. *They're not going to be able to get us back to the compound,* he thought, but he was enjoying the way they frolicked in the light of the new day. He appreciated the effort Cassandra was putting into producing them. *Plan B it is then,* he thought. *Today just might be a good day to die.*

Four of the small insects fluttered around Cassandra's body, fussing around her like moths around a handheld lamp. He watched as they fluttered themselves into a fluster. Their beating wings, coupled with the speed of their flight, began to whip up a small wind within the confines of the cell. He scrambled out of the way, ducking to avoid the crazed creatures.

As he got to the corridor, the men at the guard station looked at him, concern and amusement merging within their features.

'What's going on in there?' Matthew shouted.

Ambric looked at him and grinned. 'If I'm right, then it's something amazing.'

He was right!

13.

ENDELLION WAS FOLLOWING the glowing Glimm deeper into the underground castle. The cold was biting into her skin, and she pulled the Glimmers from her pockets to create a purple mist around her. There was warmth within it, and she smiled, content in her powers.

'We're not far now, mistress,' the Glimm said without looking at her.

They entered onto a large spiral staircase, and without stopping for a rest, her guide continued downwards.

'You best not be trying to trick me, old man,' she warned. 'You witnessed what happened to your friends back there, didn't you?'

'I saw, mistress,' he replied. There was no emotion in his voice, just acceptance at what was happening. 'I have no desire to end up like my brothers.'

Keep that attitude, old man, she thought. *You'll end up like them anyway.* She smiled amid the purple mist. As she stepped onto the staircase, there was a different feel to her footsteps. They sounded like they were echoing in the darkness.

'Hello,' she shouted. 'O … O … O,' came her reply. The echo came from all around her, as if the walls her words were bouncing off of were far apart. 'Glimm, look at me,' she ordered.

With a heavy sigh, the old man turned. 'What is your bidding, mistress?' he asked with no enthusiasm in his voice whatsoever.

'Did you hear me shout just then?' she asked.

'I did.'

'So, you heard the echo too?'

'I heard it.'

'Are we here? Have we reached the Throne of Glimm?' There was excitement in her voice, like a child expecting gifts to celebrate their birthday.

'Not quite,' he replied. The dullness of the Glimm's voice did not undermine her excitement. 'We need to pass through the Altar of the Glimm first. It is a place you should be familiar with.'

As he reached the bottom of the stairs, he raised his hand in the air, and the room lit up like a stage.

Endellion's breath was taken from her as she gazed around. She had been here, many times. *Every time I close my eyes with the Glimmer, this is where I go.*

The room was huge and sparsely decorated. The walls had carvings on them, depicting formulas and magic symbols, and there were benches dotted along them. In the centre of the room stood an old altar. The only ornaments adorning the table were the skeletons of two men. Men who were long dead.

Endellion reached the bottom of the staircase, still gazing all around. Her mouth was pinched into a pout, and she raised her arms, spinning in three-hundred-and-sixty-degree turns, taking in the whole of the room. It was old, musty, and dirty with over a thousand years of dust and grime; other than that, it was exactly how she had seen it in the Glimmer.

Among the drawings and symbols were portraits of old men dressed in the garb of the Glimm. Old men with long white hair and white beards, dressed in simple robes. All of them looked the same but had different names beneath their portraits.

Endellion didn't care for any of them.

She only had eyes for the altar.

She ran towards it like a child in gay abandon. 'I'm here,' she whispered. 'I'm actually here.' She put her hands on the stone, then rested her face upon it. The cold bit at her skin, but she didn't mind. After a moment, she raised her head and swept her hands across the top of the table. Her intention was to push the bones off. But they wouldn't budge.

She tried again, but they still wouldn't move.

'They are fused to the stone,' the Glimm said.

Endellion had honestly forgotten he was still there.

'They cannot be moved from the Altar. They have been in situ for millennia; they are, as now, one with the altar itself.'

Endellion turned to look at him. Her eyes were wild, and the grin on her face caused the Glimm to grimace. 'Is that so?' she asked. 'Well, I'll have to see about that, won't I.' It was not a question.

She took the Glimmers from her pocket and raised them into the air, closing her eyes. Two bolts of light issued from each ball and hit the altar. As they crashed into the cold stone, it exploded. Shards flew into every corner of the room.

When the dust settled, the Glimm cast his eyes over what had just happened. His mouth hung open as he regarded the damage.

Endellion raised her eyebrows and laughed. 'Now they are no longer as one with the altar; now they are as one million.' She looked at the distress on the face of the Glimm, and it made her laugh louder.

After a while, the Glimm looked to be back in control of his faculties. He breathed deep and bowed his head as if in prayer. 'Come now, mistress,' he said eventually. 'The Throne of Glimm is this way.'

To Endellion's ears, he sounded like a broken man. This was fine with her. She wanted him broken before she cast him into oblivion. *There will be no room for the old ways in my new regime,* she thought as she followed the glowing man.

14.

THE BUTTERFLIES WERE growing.

Ambric watched as the four insects flying around Cassandra doubled in size before doubling again, and then again. They were flying in such a way that they were careful not to touch the body of their mistress. When they were big enough, they hovered over her, two of them sliding their wings beneath her. Working together, they elevated her from the cold floor.

Two more expanding insects appeared at the bars in the window and positioned themselves between them. The two others already in the room hovered over the sleeping body of Cassandra.

The butterflies in the window were getting so big that the iron bars and the stone surroundings of the small window were unable to accommodate them. Ambric watched dust from between bricks begin to explode as cracks formed in the masonry.

Matthew appeared at his side. His eyes were wide, as if witnessing something that shouldn't be happening, which was exactly what he *was* witnessing. 'They're the same butterflies that saved us from the black rain. The same ones that battled the fireflies … and won,' he uttered.

Ambric didn't know if his second in command was talking to him or himself, but it didn't matter. 'I believe they were sent,' he whispered to his colleague.

'From where, and from whom?' Matthew asked, not taking his eyes from the beasts destroying the prison cell.

'From her,' he said, pointing to the still sleeping form lying on the wings of the butterflies. 'I think she controls them, much like Endellion controls the fireflies. It was my gamble they would appear to help us get her out of here.'

Matthew turned towards his superior officer. '*Did* you have a plan B?' he asked.

The wink that Ambric replied with was all he needed to know. A man like Ambric didn't go the toilet without a plan B.

'What in the name of Glimm is going on in there?' Carlos asked as he turned up to see what all the noise was about. 'All that noise would wake the de—' He didn't finish his sentence. His features widened as he looked on, agog at what he was witnessing.

More of the growing beasts had positioned themselves in the window. The rate they were expanding was too much for the ancient wall to take. Bricks and mortar were cracking under the pressure, and the hole where the window used to be, was now big enough for a man to climb through.

'I believe we are watching a prison break,' Ambric replied to Carlos's unfinished question.

The huge Azurian shook his head as he watched the wall collapse. 'If I wasn't seeing this for myself, I'd never believe it could be happening,' he said.

Again, Ambric didn't know if the big man was talking to him or to himself.

'Ambric,' Bryan shouted as he made his way halfway down the corridor. 'There are noises behind the door. I think we may have attracted a bit of unwanted attention.'

A loud bang shaking the locked dungeon door emphasised his point. Carlos made his way back up towards the guard station.

'What's happening in there?' demanded a muffled voice from the other side.

'To whom am I speaking?' counter-demanded Carlos. 'Who is demanding a report? Identify yourself.'

'It is I, Captain Mylos of the guard. To whom am I addressing?'

'Lord Carlos Gardine.'

The voice on the other side hesitated for a moment. 'Lord Gardine, we're here to investigate the commotion happening in there and the reports of fighting in this cell block.'

As the Captain spoke, a chunk of masonry broke away from the cell wall. The crash as it shattered onto the stone floor was impossible to disguise.

'Lord Gardine, I must insist you open this door.'

'I can't right now, Mylos, it's not safe in here. There has been … an explosion. The fighting you heard were the prisoners caught in the castle earlier today. You may have seen them. We're attempting to get information from them.'

'Gardine,' the voice had lost all the respect it had at the start of the conversation, 'open this door, in the name of Azuria and Queen Cassandra!'

Carlos looked down the corridor at the disintegrating room and grinned.

The butterflies continued to grow, and where the window had been was now a large hole. The ones protecting Cassandra were moving away towards the opening. Smaller ones were fluttering in from the outside, where they instantly began to grow as they hovered over Ambric and Matthew.

The young girl was sleeping as she lay on the great wings, but Ambric could see her muttering, her body twitching and flicking.

'Sir Ambric,' a voice spoke to him. He couldn't tell where it was coming from, but he seemed to be the only one who had heard it. It was a sweet voice, it was a young voice, and it was also a voice he recognised.

It was Cassandra.

'Sir Ambric,' it continued. 'Order the men to climb aboard the butterflies. We need to leave now. We need to fly to the Throne of Glimm as soon as we can.'

'The what?' Ambric asked.

Matthew looked at him, his sword was drawn and ready to fight. 'Who are you talking to?' he asked.

Then the voice spoke to Matthew. 'Matthew, you need to be present at the Throne of Glimm. Destiny awaits you there.'

'Did you just hear that?' Matthew asked Ambric as he looked at the growing butterflies. 'Are these insects *talking* now?' he asked.

'I heard it. We need to climb aboard the winged beasts and fly to somewhere called the Throne of Glimm. Call Bryan, Estefan, and Garry back here now,' he ordered.

Matthew did as he was bid.

'Carlos, we need to go. Get you and your men aboard these butterflies. We need to leave this place.'

'Where are we going?' Carlos asked, his mouth pulled back in a rictus as he looked at the door. 'I was rather hoping for a fight.'

'I believe there is much for you and your men to witness. We'll need allies on both sides of the kingdoms if a truce is to be forged today.'

Ambric tagged a hovering beast, and it lowered enough for him to jump on its back.

'Do you even know how to fly one of these things?' Matthew asked.

'Of course, I do. Butterfly handling is a required course at the academy.' Ambric smiled—a rare moment of levity from him. 'Alas, no,' he continued in his usual dour tone. 'I'm rather hoping they know where to go,' he said as his mount began to rise and follow the other butterflies out of the hole in the wall.

The other insects were now of a size where they could easily accommodate a fully-grown man wielding a weapon.

Carlos shook his head. 'What have you got me doing here, Robert?' he muttered, then ordered his men onto the beasts. He waited until they were all safely mounted before he flicked the lock on the door to the dungeons.

'Hurry, Carlos,' Ambric ordered.

Carlos smiled. 'I want Mylos to see what has happened right under his nose. I never did like the snivelling little dog.' He turned his attention to the door. 'Mylos,' he shouted. 'The door is open. You may enter, you sightless fool!' As the door opened, he backed down the corridor towards his awaiting butterfly.

~~~~

Mylos, a big man, almost as big as Carlos, burst through the door. The first thing he saw was the blood from the dead men spattered around the floor and the walls. He then heard Carlos laughing. He turned to see the soldier leaping onto what looked like a large winged creature. Something the likes of which he had never seen before.

'He's getting away,' he shouted to the men behind him. 'I want that traitor alive.'

He and his men ran down the corridor, towards the cell where Cassandra had been held captive. When they arrived, they stopped, gawping at what they saw.

The wall to the cell had been destroyed, and there were several men flying away into the dark morning sky, riding what looked like blue butterflies.
~~~~

'Alert the archers on the wall,' Mylos shouted. 'I want them shot out of the sky.' He then walked up to the broken wall and rubbed his hands on the burst brickwork. *That wall is one meter thick!* he thought in wonder.

~~~~

By the time the archers were mobilised, armed, and ready to shoot, the butterflies and their cargo were out of range.

The captain of the archers watched as they fluttered away. 'Where are those damned fireflies when you need them?' he muttered.
~~~~

15.

HIS CANDLES HAD all run out, and Alexander cursed his stupidity at not bringing more illumination devices, like a lamp, *or even a firefly,* he thought. *Yeah, a firefly would be brilliant right about now.* He closed his eyes and wished for one to appear, but something inside told him this was not going to happen. He was on his own now, alone with his scary sister.

He'd heard ghostly whispers in his ears, felt the touch of cold fingers in the dark, caressing him, prodding him, whipping past him, brushing his hair. He had tried to take his mind off what was happening with thoughts of fireflies and the like, but it was a fool's errand. He could feel the darkness, real darkness, seeping into his soul.

His feet, however, had other ideas to the fear the rest of him felt. They seemed to know exactly where to go as he strode forth, step after step.

It had been cold when he entered the tower, but now there was a strange, comfortable warmth in the darkness, as if he was walking with an invisible blanket wrapped around him.

~~~~

What Alexander was not aware of, as he trudged through the darkness, were the Sisters of the Purple walking with him. There were several of them guiding him in the right direction, ensuring he didn't head off on a tangent and fall down steps or break his neck on obstacles in the darkness. They knew where he needed to be, and they were going to make sure he got there.

From time to time, they physically touched him, steering him away from pitfalls and boobytraps and preventing him from taking the wrong
~~~~

corridors at junctions. 'You must make it to the Throne of Glimm, Alexander,' they whispered. 'There, you will stand next to Endellion.'

~~~~

A name he had never heard before popped into his head.

Endellion!

Who is Endellion? he thought. 'Endellion, who are you?' he shouted. It was a little bit for fun and a bit to oust the eerie feelings he had running through him.

He was surprised at the extent of the echo his voice caused. He smiled in the darkness, but his heart knew it was a forced smile. He wanted to feel happy about the echo, but deep down, it made him feel worse. He had no idea he was passing through the room where the recently destroyed Altar of the Glimm had stood for a millennium before being smashed into pieces by a vengeful witch.

He had ideas about something called the Throne of Glimm. He also had an idea that wherever this was, it was his ultimate destination. 'The Throne of Glimm? Is that where Cassandra is?' he asked aloud to the whispers that may or may not have been in his head.

No one answered.

He felt something change, like he had entered another room. The air around him felt closer, like this room was considerably smaller than the one he had just left.

Guided by the Sisterhood, he continued his journey towards whatever fate had put before him.
~~~~

16.

AMBRIC CLUNG TO the butterfly's neck for dear life. He had only once ridden anything that was bigger than a horse, and that was a firefly. He had no intentions of reliving that ride. He was hating this one. Normally, he found the wind whipping through his hair as his horse galloped through a forest or a glen thrilling, exhilarating even, but this was a different level. He looked down and saw the ground hundreds of feet below, zooming past at a break-neck speed. He swallowed hard, his mouth moist in what he knew was a precursor to vomiting. His head was spinning, and his sweat-lined hands kept losing their grip on the beast beneath him.

He turned to see Matthew not so far away. He was dismayed that the younger man seemed to be enjoying his ride. His smile was as wild as his hair flowing behind him.

Everyone else was enjoying it too.

Just me then? he thought as his stomach lurched.

His mount stayed behind the four beasts who were carrying the sleeping queen. She was on her back, and the two beasts carrying her had wrapped their legs around her, securing her, while the other two flapped their great wings, propelling them forward. He could see she was still twitching as the wild ride continued.

'Bernard is dead …'

The voice came from nowhere and everywhere at the same time. He looked around to see if anyone had gotten close to him, but there was no one within hearing distance that wouldn't have warranted a shout or a scream.

'Bernard would never be king,' the voice continued. 'That was his destiny all along. That was why he was never comfortable with the mantle. Why he would never allow anyone to call him it.'

If it is only *I who can hear you, I will assume you can hear my thoughts*, he shouted within the confines of his own head.

'You are correct.'

Who are you? How do you talk to me?

'I am a Sister of the Purple.'

'That name means nothing to me,' he yelled from his mount.

'To you? Maybe not. To others, it might. They would know us through fairy tales, fables, songs. None of that is important now. What is important is that Bernard is dead. This fact will have an impact on the forthcoming events.'

'Events? What events?' he screamed again.

This time, the voice didn't answer.

Matthew's mount flew closer to his. 'Ambric?' he shouted. 'Are you OK?'

Ambric looked at him and shook his head. 'Have you ever heard of the Sisters of the Purple?' he shouted.

Matthew shook his head. He turned towards Carlos's mount, who was flying close by. 'Carlos, have you ever heard of the Sisters of the Purple?'

Carlos shook his head as he looked over at Ambric. 'No,' he shouted. 'Unless they were in those children's books Ambric likes so much. Do either of you have any idea where we're going?'

'The Throne of Glimm,' Ambric shouted in reply.

'Where?' Matthew asked.

Ambric shrugged his shoulders before he realised where he was and gripped onto his butterfly tighter. 'I don't know, but apparently, it's paramount that we get there, or at the very least, Cassandra does.'

'Well, if we have no choice but to go there, we might as well enjoy the ride,' Carlos shouted as his butterfly dove low beneath Ambric.

This turned Ambric's stomach again, and he leaned forward, gripping his butterfly tighter.

17.

ENDELLION HAD DAYDREAMED. Ever since she had heard of the Throne of Glimm, she had thought of it as a lavish room filled with bright jewellery, paintings of ancient kings and queens adorning the walls, and two large golden thrones in the centre of a huge staging area.

As the Glimm lifted his hand, illuminating the room, she was not disappointed.

The beauty of the chamber momentarily took her breath away.

It was magnificent.

The light danced everywhere, swirling from the gold and silver trinkets embellishing the cabinets, flirting with the splendour of the huge dangling chandeliers, and twinkling from the lavish ceiling adorned in what looked to Endellion like the finest gemstones she had ever seen. The walls were polished stone and decorated with paintings that looked thousands of years old.

She studied them, thinking she recognised some of the faces. They were of old men with white beards and long hair. *They all look alike anyway,* she thought. She amused herself with the thought of ripping them down and smashing them to pieces; it was, after all, her right as the custodian of both Glimmers to do such a thing.

However, something caught her eye. Something she was deliberately ignoring but at the same time desperate to see.

It was the throne itself.

She turned, allowing her eyes to bathe in its full glory.

It was a thing of devastating beauty.

It looked to be made of glass. The way the light shone through it, Endellion thought it might even be something better than glass. The refracted light sparkled in a rainbow of beauty, denoting that it was either pure crystal or maybe even diamond.

Behind the throne was a golden fireplace, and before the throne were rows upon rows of long tables with benches running alongside them. Each table could have held at least fifty men and women, and there were maybe twenty of them.

She raised her arms and danced before the throne. She was in rapture. She couldn't believe this was hers; no one, alive or dead, could take this away from her. *Not even the Great Lord Glimm himself,* she thought with a grin.

'My destiny has been fulfilled,' she whispered into the empty room.

However, the room was not *quite* empty.

She stopped spinning and looked at her spectral Glimm guide.

'What happens now?' she snapped.

The Glimm looked back at her. his stoic face difficult to read.

'I want my bidding to be done right here, right now. I have the Glimmers, both red and blue. Bring forth the Great Lord Glimm to ordain me. Do it now. I am in no mood for dalliances.

'I cannot do it right now, mistress. There are certain—'

A flash from the red Glimmer hit him squarely in the chest. There was a flicker of surprise on his face as his form began to dematerialise before her. He disappeared into a cloud of purple mist.

'Glimm,' she screamed, her voice bouncing off the walls of the great room. 'Show yourselves!'

Instantly, several more of the old men with long white beards and hair began to appear within the room. They stood around the chamber, none of them looking like they wanted to be there.

'I want what is mine,' she commanded. Her eyes passed over each and every one in attendance, challenging them to defy her.

To her pleasure, none of the old men met her gaze.

'Very well, mistress,' one of them replied, stepping forwards.

~~~~

There was a light ahead. It was still a way off, but any break in the darkness around him brought relief, even if it was relatively short lived. A sharp shout cut through the silence, making him jump. It was extra loud to Alexander, as his hearing had become accustomed to the almost complete silence around him.

It was a female shout, and it sounded angry.
~~~~

It scared him more than he already was, but he was determined not to allow it to interrupt the mission he was currently on—whatever that maybe.

Something inside told him that wherever he was going, he was supposed to be there, *had* to be there. It was his destiny, and nothing he could do could change it.

The shout turned into a maniacal laugh, sending shivers down his spine, and although he was rather warm in the darkness, it raised the flesh along his arms. *I hope that wasn't Endellion,* he thought, not completely understanding who this woman was. *I don't want to have to stand next to someone who sounds like that!*

His feet were working of their own volition. They seemed to know where he was going, even if his head didn't, as they took him forward, at some pace, towards the far-off light that was getting closer.

The laughter came again. It was followed by more shouting. It confused him how someone, assuming it was the same person, could be so angry and so happy at the same time. He wasn't close enough to hear what was being shouted, but it sounded intense.

The sensation of being pushed, coerced, guided, came over him again, stronger than before, and he had no choice but to head towards the light.

~~~~

Endellion was suddenly aware of someone outside the throne room, advancing on her location. She turned towards the Glimm, her eyes blazing and her mouth pinched into a white hole. 'Who is loitering outside on my big occasion?' she spat.

One of the Glimm closed his eyes and then opened them again a moment later. 'We cannot see, mistress. Our magic lessens when we enter the Throne Room. I think the destruction of the Altar has weakened us.'

Endellion tutted. 'Well, it has enhanced me.' She raised both Glimmers and closed her own eyes. She was granted the use of remote seeing.

A portal appeared before her, but all it showed was darkness. There was a little movement within the black emptiness, but not much. 'Light my view,' she snapped, and the scene became enhanced.
~~~~

It was a boy. A young boy of maybe fourteen.

Behind him, guiding him, was a group of purple wraiths.

'Alexander,' she spat aloud. 'Why is he here? Why are the Sisters of the Purple leading him? They told me they could not enter the castle.'

'Some can,' the same Glimm who addressed her earlier replied. 'They are assigned locations and can roam only within those regions. Others have free roam; they can go where they please, or where they are needed.'

Endellion's face softened, and a smile spread across it. 'Something about this feels … right,' she purred. 'Make sure he makes it to the Throne Room. I want him here to bear witness to the crowning glory of his sister before I break his little heart and inform him of her death.'

'Actually, it is fortuitous he is here, mistress,' the Glimm said. 'You need a witness for the ceremony to take place.'

'What?' she asked.

'In order for the transference of power to be complete, you will need a sacrifice. It must be from someone who loves you.'

'Someone who loves me? There's not anyone in this land who loves me,' she spat.

'That's not entirely true, mistress,' the Glimm said. He held up his hand, and a reflective surface was produced.

'What are you doing?' she snapped.

'I am showing you what you look like, *who* you look like.'

Endellion looked into the surface and saw a young, beautiful face staring back at her. 'So,' she shrugged. 'I look like Cassandra. I have looked like her for a while.'

'Mistress, who does Alexander love more than anyone else in this world?' the Glimm asked.

Endellion smiled as her eyes widened. 'Me,' she laughed. 'So, I needed that brat after all. I knew there was a reason not to kill him.'

'That is correct. Should I instruct the Sisters to hurry their efforts getting him here?'

Endellion continued to stare into the remote portal. The boy was unaware of the wraiths behind him, guiding him to his doom. He was also unaware of her watching his progress. 'Yes. I want him here as soon as possible.'

'Yes, mistress,' the Glimm whispered as he moved away. The other Glimm watched his movements. None of them spoke, but their faces told of disappointment in one of their own.

'Oh, Glimm,' Endellion said before he walked off.

'Yes, mistress?' he asked, wincing at the sound of her voice.

'Is there anything else I should know before this transference of power begins?'

The old man thought about it for a moment. 'No, mistress. If you have both Glimmers and the sacrifice, you are ready. Oh, except for at least one Glimm present to facilitate it.'

Endellion thought the Glimm had offered her a sly grin. *I'm beginning to like this one,* she thought.

'You are poised to overtake the Great Lord Glimm himself and become a deity,' he continued.

'Get him in here. I'll be the loving sister to the little brat. I'll trick him into this sacrifice to me and to Azuria. It will be simple.'

As the Glimm disappeared, Endellion took her seat on the glass throne. She was pleasantly surprised to find two indents, one on either arm rest, where the glimmers would fit perfectly. She rested her back into the cool glass slab and relaxed. She smiled. Everything was in place.

'My destiny,' she whispered.

18.

'WHAT'S THAT AHEAD?' Bryan shouted over the rushing wind as the butterflies continued their race through the morning light.

'Is it a tower of some kind?' Matthew asked as his eyes roamed the valley opening up before them. 'I've never been out this far before. I don't know the landscape.'

In the centre of the valley, a structure poked up, scratching at the sky above it. It was tall and thin, and there looked to be a room of some kind at the top.

'It's a tower,' Ambric confirmed. 'But it isn't one I'm familiar with. Carlos, do you know what it is?'

Carlos was still enjoying his wild ride and hadn't been listening to the conversation. 'What?' he shouted as he brought his mount closer to the group.

'The tower, do you recognise it?' Matthew shouted.

'I have no idea where we are,' he replied.

Ambric looked over towards the butterflies that were carrying Cassandra. *It's where they're heading,* he thought.

'Wherever it is, it seems like it's our destination,' Matthew shouted.

The caravan of butterflies and their riders swooped through the sky, heading towards the strange tower. *There's something about this place I recognise,* Ambric thought. *Have I been here before?* He manoeuvred his mount toward Cassandra's. He strained to look at the young girl. He was surprised, and more than a little happy, to see she was now awake and the shivering she had been plagued by had passed.

19.

ENDELLION WAS SITTING on the glass throne. Her Cassandra face was almost split in two, as the smile spread across it was as wide as it could be. Her teeth were dazzling in the light reflecting from the gold and silver and from the precious stones in the chandelier and ceiling.

Alexander walked through the door and gazed all around him with the look of a child who found himself stuck in a sweet shop overnight.

I recognise that look, Endellion thought, casting her mind back to when she and Thaddius used to *play* in the jewel room beneath castle Carnelia. The memory was pleasing, but she pushed it away, casting it aside. *For the good of my destiny,* she thought.

'Alexander,' she gushed. 'What are you doing here? You're so far away from home.' The moment she spoke to him in the faux kind tones, he smiled and the anxiety she could see in the stiff gait of his walk seemed to melt away.

'Cass,' he shouted. 'I thought I'd lost you.' He beamed as he ran towards her. Then he stopped and forced himself to act more professionally in front of his queen.

He is my bravest knight of Azuria, she thought with a silent scoff. She stood and motioned him forwards. He came willingly, and they embraced like brother and sister.

The wraith that had ushered him through the castle floated unseen in the corner of the room. She gazed down at the Glimm in the other corner; an anxious look passed between them.

When they moved away from each other, Endellion reached down and removed the red Glimmer from the folds of her dress. She placed it onto the arm rest in the throne. As it settled into place, a shudder tore through the room. It wasn't hard enough to break anything or make the pictures fall from the walls, but the chandeliers swung back and forth and dust fell from the ceiling.

'Alexander,' Endellion whispered.

'Yes, Cass?' he replied, whispering too.

There is more than thrall in that look, she thought. *He loves me unreservedly. This is going to be easy.* 'I have a job for you. It will not be easy, but I know that my most loved and brave knight will be more than capable of doing it, for his kingdom, his queen, and, most important of all … his sister.'

The light of pleasure fell from his face and was replaced with the dull glow of duty. 'Yes, my queen. I am the most loyal knight in Azuria. And I am your only brother.'

'You are true, most noble knight. It is true that you are the loyalist of the loyal. You will be long remembered after this deed. They will sing songs about you around campfires the whole land through.'

Alexander was beaming again. 'They will?' he asked.

'Yes, Sir Alexander, they will.'

He threw himself at her. She was surprised at the veracity of the hug, and instinctively, she hugged him back. Everything she needed to know was in that embrace. There was no doubt whatsoever that this little brat loved his sister with the fullness of his heart.

But still, something niggled at her.

She closed her eyes and thought a question to the Glimm surrounding the Throne. 'Do I need this boy to love me as Endellion or as Cassandra?'

The Glimm who had been serving her stood forward from the rest of the group watching the pantomime on the throne. 'It matters not who the boy thinks you are. If his feelings are cast in your direction and he gives himself freely, then the transference of power will be complete.'

On hearing this news, she hugged the youth tighter.

'So, what is this mission, sister?' he asked when the hug finished.

'You will see in a short while, my brave brother. Everything is in place. I believe we can now commence the ceremony.'

Gently, she pushed the boy away from her and removed the blue Glimmer from the folds of her dress. She placed it in the groove on the opposite arm from the red ball.

Once again, the room shook.

'Alexander, you are to stand next to me before the Throne of Glimm, of your own volition. This is our destiny, brother.' She turned and offered her hand to him. 'Will you stand next to your sister?'

The boy reached out his hand.

She watched as his finger stretched, reaching for her. Both their destinies coming to fruition. One legendary, one tragic.

The touch was just millimetres apart.

Alexander stopped. He pulled his hand back and looked up at her. Her face changed from a happy, blazing smile to a look of shock and surprise.

'Apparently, I'm supposed to stand before the Throne with someone called Endellion,' he said.

You fool, she thought. She wanted to reach out to him, take him by the neck, and strangle him. She wanted to watch as the light of his being dripped from his eyes as he died by her hands. Yet she knew this couldn't happen. She needed his cooperation.

'You will, my brave knight,' was all she could bring herself to say. 'You will!'

20.

OUTPOST THREE WAS waking to the reality of the death of Bernard.

The King of Carnelia was dead.

Linda had stayed awake the whole night for two reasons. The first had been to keep vigil on the body of Bernard. Her tradition was such that a body should have company as its soul passed from this world to Koll'su.

The second reason was that she was worried about Matthew and the mission he was undertaking. Breaking into the Azurian stronghold did not seem like a sensible thing to do.

When her time was done, she leaned over to embrace the washed body of the king before standing up. She stretched, listening to the bones in her knees, back, and neck, all pop at the same time. She winced as she rubbed at them. Sitting in the same position for hours had not been good for her joints. She surveyed the tent, making sure everything was as it should be. Once she was happy, she lifted the flap and exited.

There were a number of people walking around the courtyard, all of them going about their daily business as if nothing out of the ordinary had happened. *Life goes on,* she mused.

However, there was one difference she noted.

The folk of the outpost were behaving differently towards her. She received more than her fair share of tips of the hat, accompanied by 'Good morning, ma'am'. She was not used the people talking to her this way. She had always thought of herself as a woman of the people. An everyday kind of person.

'Would you like me to carry that for you, my lady?' a soldier offered as she strolled towards the barracks.

She had wanted to do a round of the sick who had been discharged from the tents before going to bed. 'Erm, OK then,' she stuttered, narrowing her eyes at the big man taking hold of her bag and walking beside her. 'Since when have I been addressed as *my lady?*' she asked.

He offered her a look that made her think the world had gone crazy. It was the kind of look people reserved for royalty.

'Will someone please tell me what's happening here?' she asked. 'I'm not your lady; I'm a nurse and a midwife. I'd appreciate being treated like one.'

'Are you not our queen now that the king is dead?' the soldier asked. 'The Queen of Carnelia?'

'I am most definitely not,' she snapped. 'Who has spoken these lies?'

'They haven't been spoken, my lady,' he continued. 'It has just been assumed. King Bernard is dead; he had no heirs. Lord Ambric has been gone for a while and would not accept the role anyway. It just seems fitting that it has fallen onto your shoulders.'

'Is that how things are decided these days?' she demanded again.

'That would be entirely up to you,' the soldier replied reaching the barracks. As they entered the room, all the soldiers who could stand did, each of them saluting.

21.

'HERE GOES NOTHING …' Matthew shouted as his butterfly dipped and swooped towards the tall tower looming before them.

Ambric was screaming.

Matthew turned to see his friend and mentor gripping onto his beast with all his strength. He offered the older man a thumbs up, as it looked like he was enjoying his ride almost as much as he was.

The flying beasts skimmed the floor of the valley as they flew in formation towards a small, almost concealed entrance at the foot of the tower.

The four butterflies carrying Cassandra kept the pace, and Ambric watched on in horror, as they showed no signs of slowing on their approach. He'd hoped the beasts would stop and let them off so they could make their way into the tower on foot.

That did not seem to be the plan.

The four beasts, along with their precious cargo, disappeared into the entrance that, at first glance, looked far too small for them to fit.

Matthew's beast was next. Ambric heard his friend hollering as he neared it, only for his voice to be cut off as they passed through.

Then it was his turn.

He closed his eyes tight. This approach was something he had no desire to watch first-hand. The roar of air rushing against his skin and through his hair cut off instantly, and he felt a sharp pain in his ears as the noises of the flight died.

Eventually, he opened his eyes. At first, he couldn't tell if they were open or not. It was as black as night all around him. Only the movement of the butterfly's wings, illuminated by the small hole of light behind him, told him they were indeed open.

'What is happening?' he shouted into the blackness. 'I can't see a thing.'

'Don't worry, Robert.' The voice reassured him he wasn't dead. 'The butterflies seem to know where they are going.' It was Carlos. He would recognise his voice anywhere.

'*The butterflies will take you to the Throne of Glimm!*'

Ambric was sure it had been a girl's voice he heard in his head, but he knew Cassandra hadn't been shouting; she didn't look to have the breath for it. 'Cassandra, is that you?' he asked anyway.

'*Yes, Sir Ambric. It is me.*'

'You're awake then?'

'*I am.*'

'Then, maybe you can tell me where we're going here,' he snapped.

'*I have already told you. The butterflies will take us to the Throne of Glimm.*'

'I have read about this place, but only in children's stories. Tales handed down over generations.'

'*There's a lot to be learned from children's stories.*'

'Cassandra?' Ambric said after a few moments of silence between them.

'*Yes?*'

'Are you dying?'

As an answer, she laughed. It was a light chuckle. '*No, Sir Ambric, I don't believe I am. I have a secret, one I needed to keep from the witch for as long as I can.*'

'Is Bernard dead?' he asked. He had wondered how to broach this subject to her and decided the direct method was probably best.

'*He is.*' Her voice sounded sad, distant somehow.

'He left no heir,' Ambric said, mainly just to break the silence.

'*That's not an issue right now,*' Cassandra said. Ambric could tell she was trying to conceal her grief with her words. '*There is no Carnelia to rule over. That does not mean it cannot or will not rise from its ashes like a great, fiery bird. This does not concern us right now, Sir Ambric. We're here now to bear witness. That is all. You and your men cannot stop what you will see today, Robert. Please do not try. It will not end well for you if you do, and may well inadvertently alter the course of what should be!*'

'Then, why bring us here?' Ambric asked.

'Men from both sides need to see what has, is, and will occur. Whoever survives will live to document this day. The documents will be testament for millennia. Today is a transference from the old to the new, however things transpire.'

'How do we document?'

'The act of seeing. Both parties will have the power of projection. What's left of Carnelia, which is crudely known as The City of the Fireflies, and Azuria need to see what Carlos sees.'

'How do you know this?'

'There are forces at work that you will not understand. I struggle to understand what the Glimmers can do myself. But I, it seems, am destined to be a conduit. That is the way of it.'

Ambric had no idea what she was talking about and realised that asking more questions was not going to remedy that situation.

'We will be at the Throne of Glimm shortly. Inform your men what I have told you. Save their lives, Robert; it is, after all, what you excel at.'

Cassandra's voice disappeared, and Ambric picked up on half of a conversation between Bryan, who was behind him, and one of the Azurian guards.

'Men,' he hissed. 'Hush, all of you, and listen to me.'

The men did his bidding.

'We are about to enter into the Throne of Glimm. We are to witness, for ill or for good, I do not know, the events that will transpire. We have no other part to play but to watch. What we see, our families in Carnelia and in Azuria will see also.'

'How?' Carlos asked.

'Projection or something,' Ambric answered.

'What's that?' Darrid asked as he flew his mount closer.

Ambric shrugged. He then realised no one would be able to see him in the darkness. 'I know not. It is just what I have been told.'

'What is this Throne you speak of?' Matthew asked.

'Once again, I don't know. But I think we're about to find out.'

Up ahead, a small light was growing brighter.

~~~~

As the Throne room got closer, Cassandra woke up. The first thing she saw was the light getting nearer. She sat up and yawned, stretching
~~~~

her limbs as she did. The pain in her body, although still there, was bearable. *At last,* she thought, elated for two reasons: the lessening of the agony and the Throne Room within her reach. *This has been a long time coming!*

~~~~

The wafting of the butterfly wings filtered into the Throne Room. It was Alexander, standing before the glass throne, who heard them first.

'Sister, do you hear that?' he asked. 'It sounds like the beating of wings. Have you ordered the fireflies?'

Endellion heard it. She cocked her head to listen. 'No, I haven't. Did anyone follow you here?' she growled at the youth before her.

'No, Cass. I was alone. Believe me,' he protested, moving a little away from her.

You were not alone, you fool. You brought a host of Sisters of the Purple with you, she thought. She sat on the Throne, grasped both Glimmers, and closed her eyes.

She saw nothing.

As she opened them again, they blazed as if an inferno was raging within them. 'What is the meaning of this?' she shouted.

Alexander looked around to see who she could be talking to.

The Glimm were standing around the Throne Room, their faces emotionless. The one who had been helping her was standing before his peers.

'What do you mean that you can't see them?' she spat. 'I don't believe your powers are limited in this room!' A flash issued from the Glimmers, and two of the Glimm who were in the background disappeared into a purple mist. The rest watched as their brothers evaporated out of existence.

Alexander couldn't see any of this. He was looking at his sister. 'Cass, you're scaring me. Who are you talking to?'

Her eyes flicked to look at him.

He cowered back from her intense stare.

'Don't you worry yourself about who I am talking to, brother.' She spat the final word. 'You wouldn't understand. Whoever or whatever is causing that pulse will be inconsequential very shortly.'
~~~~

Alexander was in the staging area before the throne; he looked younger than his fourteen years due to the fact he was cowering and crying. 'I wish the fireflies were here,' he sobbed. 'Cass bring the fireflies. I'm scared!'

'Most of them are dead,' she replied. 'I am preparing new ones as we speak.'

'I wish they were here now.'

'Stop your whimpering,' she ordered. 'You sound pathetic. Are you my brave knight, or a snivelling child?'

Alexander looked at her. His eyes were red and wet. 'I-I'm a knight,' he stuttered.

'Then behave like one. Defend your sister from whatever comes through that door.'

He drew his sword and stood upright, then wiped his eyes and nose and took a defensive position. 'You know I would die for you, sister,' he said.

'That is good to know, brother,' she replied, softening her voice. 'Very good to know.'

From the darkness outside the door flew four of the largest, bluest butterflies she had ever seen in her life. They swooped and fluttered around the room, causing a melee of confusion.

Alexander ducked as the first two skimmed over his head, narrowly missing him. He raised his sword to defend himself from the third, but the fourth flew past him and knocked the weapon from his hands.

Endellion was on her feet, furious. *Who is this, ruining my moment?* She closed her eyes and looked at the Glimm. They offered her nothing more than blank stares and scared eyes. She huffed, opening her eyes again. In the short time she had been with the Glimm, more beasts had invaded the Throne Room. There were men astride the great winged monsters, men she didn't recognise.

The butterflies landed on the opposite side of the room. As the last one folded its wings, her eyes widened so far, they looked in danger of falling out of her head. 'You!' she spat. 'How are you here?'

Cassandra dismounted her ride effortlessly, although Endellion was happy and interested to see that she was moving with care and delicacy. *She is weak,* Endellion thought with a smile.

As Ambric slid off his mount, Endellion turned to look to him. 'Sir Ambric,' she said. There was silk to her voice, the dangerous kind. 'Why, you are like a bad penny, you just keep turning up!'

'Sister,' Alexander shouted as he scrambled to retrieve his sword from the floor.

Both Cassandra and Endellion, who was still wearing Cassandra's face, turned to look at him.

'Brother,' Cassandra shouted, visibly pained by the effort.

The young boy looked up. He grabbed his sword and stepped back. His eyes narrowed as he looked at the newcomers. His defensive position dropped, just for a moment, as he regarded the woman who had dismounted the butterfly. Then he turned and looked at the woman who was standing before the throne behind him. 'Cass,' he said, backing up towards Endellion. 'Who is that? And why does she look like you?'

'She is a witch, Alexander. She's the reason we are here today. All the bad things you have witnessed over the last year are because of her and those men. She was responsible for your mother's and your father's deaths.'

Alexander turned towards Endellion. 'You mean *our* mother and father's deaths?'

'Yes, of course that's what I meant. She must be destroyed, otherwise she will bring destruction upon our great nation.'

'Alexander,' Casandra stepped forward.

The boy shifted his sword.

Ambric grabbed her by the arm. 'Be careful, Cassandra. The boy is confused and most probably in her thrall. He may strike you.'

'Alexander, please,' she pleaded before a coughing fit took her and she fell to her knees.

The boy looked at her as if he were looking at filth on the street. He gripped the hilt of his sword tighter and spat in her direction. 'You will die, witch,' he whispered. 'I loved my mother dearly, and you took her from me.'

'No, Alex. I didn't. She did.' Another coughing fit wracked her body. Ambric stepped forward to assist. She pushed the soldier away and looked at Alexander again. 'Glimm,' she whispered. 'Projection, please!'

Endellion closed her eyes and watched as one of the old men nodded towards Cassandra. Then, without warning, he was shrouded in a purple mist and disappeared.

'What just happened?' Ambric asked as a flicker flashed through the room.

Everyone looked for the source of the flicker, everyone with the exception of Endellion in her Cassandra guise and Cassandra herself. They didn't need to look as they were the only ones who could see the old men of the Glimm.

They began to appear in the real world, shimmying into existence like heat flies rising from the floor. They were simply not there one moment, then there the next.

As the men appeared, so did the women.

The wraiths that had coerced Alexander into the throne room shimmied in the same manner as the old men.

The soldiers and Alexander had drawn their swords and were standing ready to battle the entities suddenly surrounding them.

'Stand down, Ambric,' Cassandra croaked. 'They are the Glimm and the Sisterhood of the Purple. They are a part of what is happening here.'

'And just exactly what *is* happening here?' Ambric asked as he ignored Cassandra's request for him to stand down.

'What you are about to witness, Sir Ambric,' Endellion stood to address the room, 'is the final twist in my tale. I am about to bring about the transference of power from a long-lost deity to me. I will then be the ultimate power in this world. Invincible, indestructible, and eternal!' She paused in her speech to laugh theatrically. 'Your feeble armies will be defenceless against me.' She grasped both Glimmers in her hands, and her laugh turned into a roar.

Alexander had made his way over to where Cassandra knelt. The sword in his hand was close to his real sister's face. She was in no state to defend herself from her brother.

Ambric was still standing ready to defend his friend. Her hand reached out for the older man's sword. 'No,' she whispered. 'You are here to observe only.'

'Should I kill her, sister?' the boy hissed.

The malice and hate that was in the boy's voice shocked even Endellion, and she laughed again. 'I don't see why not, brother. She is of no more use to us. I am custodian of her Glimmer. She is worthless and useless.' She lifted the blue orb as if to emphasise her dominion over the real queen.

Alexander looked at the blue ball.

His face changed.

'Glimm, Sisters,' Endellion shouted, 'you may start the ceremony. I have more than enough witnesses present.'

The men of the Glimm and the women of the Sisterhood swapped worried glances. There was reluctance in their movements, but, as if they had little choice but to obey, they began to form two lines. The Glimm took up position on one side of the Throne Room, the Sisterhood of the Purple on the other. Without prompt, both sides began to chant. Their words were indecipherable, but it didn't matter.

It was happening.

Endellion sat back on the Throne. The smooth coolness of the glass eased through her clothing, causing a small but thrilling chill to run through her body. A purple light began to shine around her, emanating from inside the glass. It carved through the room like a mist, encircling the groups on either side.

Ambric and his men watched from the relative safety of the back of the room.

The Glimm and the purple wraiths began to levitate, while Endellion sat grinning on the Throne, a Glimmer grasped firmly in each hand.

22.

OUTPOST THREE WAS coming to terms with the death of Bernard. His body was lying in state in a tent that had been set up on the opposite side of the courtyard from the injury tents. Queues were forming to pay tribute to the boy king. As they stood, patiently waiting to light candles, an odd wind blew through the yard, ruffling people's hair and blowing out some of the lighted tapers they were carrying. Their eyes lifted to see where the wind could be coming from, many readying themselves to run, fearing a return of the black rain, and they witnessed a strange phenomenon.

Floating above the courtyard, where everyone could see, was an odd portal. A strange scene could be seen within the portal. It looked like a woman with an uncanny resemblance to Cassandra, the Queen of Azuria, sat on a glass throne, with a young boy at her side and a number of old men with long white hair and beards.

~~~~

In Castle Azuria, the same phenomenon occurred. The courtesans stopped their normal activities, and all eyes were set upon the strange, floating portal. The castle was silent as the people within the scene created two distinct lines. One consisted of old men in white, and the other of women dressed head to toe in purple.

Both lines were chanting. A red flame and a blue flame glowed from the throne where their queen sat in the background. It caused several confused and concerned looks to pass between the citizens of Azuria.
~~~~

23.

ENDELLION WAS ENJOYING herself. The two lines were chanting, the ritual was beginning, and she was in full control of the situation. Her Glimmers were glowing, emitting blue and red flames that were becoming more intense the longer the chanting continued. Her dark eyes stared hungrily at them, lost within their deep, mysterious beauty. *They won't be mysterious for long,* she thought. *Soon, I will understand every mystery in the universe.*

A Glimm, the one she had come to think of as her only ally in all of this, motioned to her. 'Mistress,' he whispered. 'You must stand and hold both Glimmers. The force of the Glimm must surge through your body. The boy must be near too; it's near his time for sacrifice.'

Cassandra heard what the Glimm said and looked at the boy. He was watching the chanting and the glowing of the orbs with obvious delight. The purple light merged from both Glimmers reflected on his face.

'Alex,' she whispered over the chanting, just loud enough to be heard by the enraptured boy. His head turned to regard his real sister. 'Stay away from that witch,' she warned. 'She is dangerous. You need to pay attention to what's happening here. This may not end well for you.'

The youth grimaced. He looked at her as if she were nothing more than something nasty on the bottom of his boot and turned back towards Endellion.

'Alexander, no … Do not go to her,' Cassandra shouted at the top of her voice. She staggered as the force of her activity weakened her. Ambric reached out to stop her from stumbling and falling.

The boy walked towards Endellion. She looked at him, her face glowing half blue and half red. Her eyes were dark, but her smile was genuine. He took hold of her dress wrapping his hand within the silk, and turned back towards the strange people chanting. As the incantations continued, the purple mist wound its way through the witnesses. Small forks of brilliant lightning streaked through it as it grew, stretched, and reached.

The Glimmers were pulsing. They looked hot, as if they were about to explode, but Endellion, still in her Cassandra form, clutched them tight in her hands.

The men of the Glimm had their eyes closed, as did the Sisterhood. A heavy humming thrummed in the air, signalling something important, monumental, magical, was occurring.

Everyone could feel it.

'Alex …' Cassandra hissed. 'Alexander, do as you must,' she spat. The physical act of talking was causing the breath to stutter from her body. She was struggling to form her words.

Alexander looked at her again before dismissing her and giving his attention back to Endellion.

'Alex,' Cassandra shouted again. 'Do as you must, but remember what our mother used to say …'

This caught the boy's attention. 'What do you know of our mother, witch?' he asked. 'Watch your mouth, or maybe I'll tear you a new one!'

The words caused Cassandra to recoil. Tears were falling down her cheeks. 'Remember, what she used to say, Alexander. Good things come to those …'

~~~~

The purple mist issuing from the Glimm and the Sisterhood reached the Throne. There, it entwined around the feet of Alexander and stretched towards Endellion next to him, holding the Glimmers in the air.

It began winding itself around Alexander's feet, climbing his legs.

Endellion tore her gaze away from the orbs and watched as the boy was slowly swallowed by the haze. A grin broke on her face. Soon he would be dead, the willing sacrifice of someone who loved her; she would soon be all powerful.

She would be the Great Lady Glimm!

~~~~

'... who are made to wait!' Alexander finished.

He watched as the witch who looked like his sister flopped to the floor. She was in obvious pain. The soldier next to her knelt and tended to her. Something was happening in his head, and he wasn't sure what it was. It felt like a fog was lifting, or something that had been flapping about in the wind was finally clicking into place.

He remembered his mother.

'Good things come to those who are made to wait,' he whispered. He let go of Endellion's gown and looked up at who he had followed as his sister for all this time.

Her appearance had changed; her veil had fallen and she was no longer Cassandra.

She was no longer young and beautiful.

Instead, she was an old woman. A crone.

The same crone who has been following me around the castle and the compounds, the horrors of my dreams, he thought. He looked around the room. He saw the old men and the purple ghosts, he saw the soldiers, *of both armies,* he thought. *How is that possible?* He then looked at the young woman on the floor. She looked tired, hurt, in agony, but determined. Most of all, more important than all of that, she looked familiar.

Cass? he thought.

He began to panic.

He looked down at his feet and was alarmed to see the mist with flashes of purple lightning coursing through it entwining around his legs. It was creeping up, grasping at him. It was thick, cold, and it was binding him. He thrashed at it, attempting to free himself from its icy embrace. His eyes were wide as he fought for breath. *My mission,* he thought. *It is my sacrifice for ...* he looked again at the crone holding the orbs, the one he had given his sister plus another one, the red one.

Her image flickered in his head. One moment it was that of an old woman, the next what he had thought of as his sister. He looked at the other young woman, the one lying on the floor with the soldier. Her eyes were open and locked with his. Something passed between them.

A secret maybe?

He couldn't be sure.

She nodded to him. '*Alex, I am your sister. You are my sweet brother!*'

The voice was in his head. He knew the voice was that of the one person in this world who he loved more than anything or anyone else.

'*Cassandra,*' he replied in his head, sure she would hear him.

She did.

She offered a smile; it was weak, but it was there.

He nodded a reply.

As the mist tightened around his legs. He heard Cassandra, the real Cassandra, speak in his head again. '*I love you, Alex. I am truly sorry for leaving you!*'

The boy smiled. It was a sad smile. He knew what he had to do. It was time for the brave knight he had pretended to be for so very long to come forth. He had a destiny to fulfil. He pulled a jewelled stiletto from inside his tunic. Gripping the small but heavy blade in his sweat-lined palm made the hilt slippery, but he had enough grip to do what was required.

He watched the crone flick between age and youth. She looked down at him with dark eyes and grinned. 'Soon, brother,' she whispered.

He nodded at her and smiled back. 'You're not my sister,' he whispered before sinking the dagger into the flesh of her thigh. It took a bit of pressure to get it through the muscle, but he kept on pushing. The warm gush of her blood flowing over his hand caused him to lose his grip, and he let go of the knife.

~~~~

Endellion inhaled sharply as the strength in her leg left her. The limb buckled beneath her, and she dropped both glimmers onto the throne room floor. Falling back on the glass throne, she looked down to see the cause of her pain. She was surprised to see a jewelled hilt protruding from her thigh and a thick gush of dark blood pouring from the wound, pooling on the glass throne.

She also registered two thuds as the glimmers hit the stone floor and rolled away from her possession.

The chanting stopped, and the purple mist began to recede, loosening its hold on her sacrifice. All she could do was watch as the boy rushed from her side. 'Red Glimmer,' she screeched as she leaned back on the glass throne, grasping her wounded leg. 'Come to me.'
~~~~

The red glass ball, which was resting before the men of the Glimm at the side of the throne, began to roll towards the old woman. It levitated, and a thin smile crept over her face as it rushed through the air into her grasp. She squeezed the orb, relishing its coolness within her fingers. She closed her eyes again. 'Blue Glimmer,' she said, her voice returning to its full strength. 'Come to me,' she hissed, holding out her hand to receive the orb.

The Glimmer didn't move.

'Blue Glimmer,' she repeated. 'Come to me!'

There was still no movement from the ball.

Everyone in the Throne Room watched as she attempted to stand on her wounded leg, then fell back onto the throne. 'Blue Glimmer,' she screamed. 'Come to me!'

Still, the orb did not move.

She tried to stand again, and again her leg buckled, causing her to fall, sprawling to the floor before the throne. 'To me!' she cried.

~~~~

The Glimm who had been Endellion's guide stepped forward. 'Neither Glimmer has dominion over the other, mistress,' he said in a hushed tone. A small smile peeped from beneath his long beard.

Endellion looked up at him from the stone floor. Her eyes narrowed, and her mouth moved as if she were issuing a curse. But no words escaped her.

The Glimm then turned towards Cassandra, who was also lying on the floor. 'Would you like us to do it now, mistress?' he asked, his smile growing.

Endellion screamed, the sound unmerciful, hideous. It was filled with anger, pain, and frustration. Every eye in the room turned towards the bleeding woman. Her teeth were gritted as she raised her orb. A flash of red streaked from it.

It hit the Glimm in the chest, and he dissipated in a cloud of purple smoke.

She closed her eyes and laughed. The roar could be heard around the whole room. 'You didn't expect that, did you, traitor?' she spat in-between laughs. 'I am still the custodian of the Glimmers; all the power is mine!'
~~~~

She turned to the other Glimmer lying close to Cassandra. 'Blue Glimmer, come to me,' she shouted the command again.

Once more, the orb didn't move.

She looked at Cassandra. *She is still sick,* she thought. *No match for me.*

Then, something happened that Endellion couldn't quite believe, something she had not been ready for. The red Glimmer, the one she held, began to glow. She looked at it and questioned what her eyes were telling her. She was no longer controlling it. She closed her eyes, reaching out to the power of the orb, but she could only sense it. Horrified, she realised that she no longer had control over it. Something with greater power than her was accessing it.

A bright flash of hot red shot from the orb, causing her to drop it.

She looked to where the flash had issued and shook her head.

The recently dissolved Glimm was returning.

She thought it was the same one but could not be sure, as they all looked the same to her. But something else happened to make her question herself.

The others she had killed were reappearing too.

'What's happening?' she whispered. 'You should all be gone.'

The reappeared Glimm ignored the shouts from the bleeding woman; he looked towards Cassandra and smiled.

'Mistress,' he addressed her, then repeated the earlier question. 'Shall we do it now?'

~~~~

Cassandra used what little strength she could muster to sit up. She shrugged the offer of help from Ambric; this was something she had to do for herself. The blue Glimmer, the parting gift from her brother, *so long ago,* was lying on the floor before her. It was within her grasp.

She could see Alexander. He was cowering in the corner of the room. He looked every day of his fourteen years. *That is a good thing,* she thought as she pondered briefly on the horrors he must have witnessed under the misguided guardianship of the witch. *I cannot blame him for anything,* she thought.
~~~~

She looked at Ambric, who was reaching for the blue orb himself. 'No, Ambric, it's not for you,' she whispered. 'You cannot influence any of this, remember. You are here to witness, nothing more.'

Ambric blinked. 'You truly are the Queen of Carnelia, Cassandra. I apologise if I ever misjudged you.'

'You are the bravest and most loyal servant either kingdom has ever seen,' she whispered. A sadness fell over her features. It was unexplained and unexpected, and she felt the need to look away from him. Her attentions returned to the bleeding woman on the floor before the Throne. Her ancient face was a rictus of hate, and madness held control within their obsidian depths.

'Sisters,' the witch shouted. 'Sisters, help another Sister of the Purple in her hour of need,' she pleaded. 'You led me here for this reason. I was willing to give back the power of life and dominion to your order. Help me now and I will be forever in your debt.'

Each of the wraiths looked at her. Their emotionless faces spoke to Cassandra.

The Sisterhood of the Purple had abandoned Endellion.

'Kill her,' Endellion shouted as she pointed at the unsteady Cassandra, who was now attempting to stand. 'I command you to kill her,' she screamed.

'Mistress, I think the time has come, don't you?' the Glimm who had helped Endellion said kindly to Cassandra.

Endellion snapped her head to glare at the old man, and then at Cassandra.

'Yes, please. Do it now,' Cassandra said, her voice calm, steady.

'As you wish, mistress.'

As one, the Glimm turned their heads towards the young girl and closed their eyes.

'Stop this!' Endellion screamed from the floor. 'Stop this now!' She scrambled towards her dropped Glimmer, which was just a little out of her reach. 'I will kill each and every one of Ambric's men,' she threatened.

Ambric and the men behind him unsheathed their weapons.

Cassandra held her hand out towards them.

Ambric's eyes were narrow, but he signalled the others to halt.

They all complied.

Endellion reached the red Glimmer and held it in the air. A flash ripped from it. As it passed through the air, it turned into a red mist. The mist dipped to the floor and tangled itself around Ambric's feet.

But nothing else happened.

Endellion's eyes were wild, and her face flushed pink. She turned to the lines of Glimm and the Sisterhood. 'What is the meaning of this? What is happening?'

The blue glow emanating from Cassandra caught her eye, and she turned to see what was happening.

~~~~

In Outpost Three and in Castle Azuria, the citizens watched, enraptured at what was happening. They had gathered around the floating portals, all of them in awe of what they were witnessing.

The Azurian people watched while their queen turned into an old crone and a younger girl, who looked strangely like their queen but bedraggled, stood up and began to glow a bright fluorescent blue.

They watched as the young girl began to levitate, as the light that seemed to come from inside her exited from her eyes, her mouth, her ears, and her fingertips. Bright beams of blue energy expelled from her; their target was the discarded blue ball lying on the floor.

There was a collective gasp in both Kingdoms as the orb began to glow and pulse, as if it had been asleep and was now awake.

Eventually, it exploded in a blue flash.

Everyone watching covered their eyes and ducked, as if to get away from the blinding light.

Then, the light was gone, leaving only darkness in its wake.

~~~~

The Throne room was silent.

Not even Endellion, lying bleeding in the centre of the room, said anything as the blue light from Cassandra was sucked back into the discarded Glimmer. All eyes were on it as it pulsed its cold blue light.

Only one person in the room moved.

They strode forward, bent down, and picked up the orb.

Everyone watched as they held it aloft.

The men of the Glimm bowed their heads, as did the Sisterhood.

Ambric's men bowed their heads too.

Endellion dropped the red Glimmer as she watched the blue orb pulse as it was held high in the air.

The men of the Glimm began to chant in unison. The red mist Endellion had commanded transferred itself back into the fallen Glimmer.

Then the person holding the blue orb picked the red one up too.

~~~~

For the first time in a long time, Endellion was powerless to control what was happening around her. The pain in her leg was intense and getting worse. Her head had begun to swim. The tips of her fingers were cold, and she felt she was losing strength in her aching hands, so much so that she could no longer hold onto her Glimmer. As it dropped to the floor, the thud rang in her ears.

Her red mist began to retreat into the orb, and she watched as the source of her power, her destiny, was picked up and held aloft by someone else.

Someone she deemed unworthy of the power they now wielded.

In her mind, she was back in the courtyard in Carnelia. She was naked, with her head and hands protruding through the stocks that held her, powerless to stop whoever from doing whatever they wanted to her. She had promised herself she would never feel so small, so pathetic, so vulnerable ever again.

Yet here she was.

She lunged herself at the new custodian, but there was little energy left in her body, and all she managed to do was to fall.

Her old, dark eyes narrowed as both Glimmers were held high in the rapidly darkening room.

~~~~

As Endellion fell, the Glimm and the Sisterhood continued their chants.

Every eye in the room was on the Glimmers as they pulsed blue and red in perfect harmony, the rhythm keeping perfect time with the chanting. The purple mist began to form again and it wrapped itself around the custodian of the Glimmers.

The Glimm, the one who had restored the power to the blue Glimmer, spoke. 'Who is the sacrifice?' he asked.

~~~~

'You tricked me,' Endellion cursed. 'You *all* tricked me!'

Her ex Glimm guide looked at her and smiled. 'Cassandra asked, when you took her from the tunnels, if the power of her Glimmer could be stored within her body. I told her it could, but only for a short period. You only ever held the illusion of the power of both Glimmers, Endellion. Your spirit was corrupt. Neither the Glimm nor the Sisterhood of the Purple could allow it to continue.'

She turned to look at the purple wraiths. 'You are supposed to look after your own,' she spat.

'You ceased to be one of our own,' the wraith, who Endellion recognised as Valaiden, said as she stepped forwards. 'When you became consumed with vengeance and hatred for what had happened to you, the real Endellion was gone. I feared she would never again come forth. My fears were founded.'

Endellion bared her teeth and hissed.

'Do you see me?' the wraith asked, her voice soft, almost comforting.

The face Endellion pulled told the wraith she thought this was a stupid question. 'Yes, of course I see you. Traitor!' she spat. 'I trusted you to help me, a sister, one of your own. But you chose to side with the men of the Glimm.'

'We didn't choose,' Valaiden said gently. 'We have always worked *with* the men of the Glimm. We drifted apart in life but were reunited in death. I asked if you see me for a reason, Endellion.'

'Well, state your stupid reason and allow me to die here in the Throne of Glimm, in what should have been my crowning glory.'

'I ask because you know me as Valaiden. But that is not my real name.'

'Why should I care?' Endellion asked.

'Because my name is Camarilla.'

'Is that supposed to mean anything to me?'
~~~~

'It is the name of your mother, Endellion. You asked me once before, and I had to conceal my identity, but I am your mother!'

Endellion's face softened. 'My mother?'

Camarilla nodded. 'I petitioned the Sisterhood to watch over you, even after the crimes you perpetrated on Thaddius and Cassandra's father. It was I who petitioned the Glimm to look over you and nurture your use of the Glimmer. I was there for you always. But you shamed me. Shamed me more than you could ever know.'

Endellion looked around the room, envious of the two raised Glimmers and the person holding them.

'I convinced the Sisterhood to lead you here. We needed the red Glimmer to be here for the transference. It was an ideal deception, the only way to stop you, my daughter. We had to trick you into thinking we were helping you. You were too consumed by hunger and power and the anger you carried within. Once the black rain was used, we knew then you could never hold the power of the Great Lord Glimm.'

'But *he* can?' she spat, pointing to the person holding the Glimmers.

'Yes, *he* can,' Camarilla replied.

Endellion turned her attention to Cassandra. The young girl was beaming towards the person holding the Glimmers. Her eyes flicked towards Endellion. Her smile faltered for just a moment.

'Is this true?' Endellion asked. Her voice little more than a harsh whisper. 'Did you hold the power of the blue within you all this time?'

Cassandra nodded.

'How?'

'It was all I had! You were winning. Your fireflies had decimated the Ferals and the Rebels; we were beaten. All I had was the Glimmer, but I was not as proficient with it as you were. I had to keep it from you. You were *not* to be the custodian of the Glimmers. Even if it killed me, *you* were not to be the one.'

Endellion snarled. 'Well, it seems you are not either,' she scoffed.

Cassandra smiled; her eyes looked past the sad old woman lying on the floor, bleeding from her leg. She shook her head. 'I never wanted it. It was never my … destiny!'

Endellion eyes moved on from her, settling on the person holding the Glimmers. The purple mist shrouded him as he reached towards the chanting Glimm and Sisterhood of the Purple.

The young boy's face was stoic as he held the orbs aloft.

'Who would have thought?' Endellion whispered as Alexander grew in stature before her.

With the last effort of her body, and with everything she had left in her, the injured woman lunged herself at the boy.

Alexander was taken by surprise, and the red glimmer was knocked from his hands.

With an athleticism that stretched almost every fibre of her being, she reached and caught the red ball as it fell. When it was secure in her hands, she closed her eyes.

Before anyone could react, before Ambric and his men could draw their swords, before the Glimm and the Sisterhood could stop what was happening, Endellion's body began to swell.

Her facial features distorted, elongated. Her legs began to shrivel and turn black, and then to multiply. Thin, gossamer wings sprouted from her back as she mutated from human into the form of a huge firefly.

A heavy thrum in the air, caused by her wings beating in rapid succession, heralded her curved, insectoid body rising from the floor. Her deadly sting was poised for attack and dripped with poison.

She flew into the air, high above where Alexander was now lying on the floor in her blood. She was once again custodian of the red Glimmer as she flew around the room, heading for the door.

It slammed shut just before she reached it, trapping the beast inside. The firefly swerved at the last moment, saving itself from crashing into it by inches. With a twist of its ugly body, it turned and flew back to the centre of the room.

Ambric had drawn his weapon and was watching every movement of the beast, as were Matthew, Carlos, and the others behind them.

Cassandra went to her stricken brother. He was covered in blood, but as she frantically wiped, it became apparent that none of it was his. She looked upwards to see the beast hovering directly above them. One of the firefly's legs was wounded and was hanging limply as the others flexed menacingly.

The red Glimmer was still in its grasp, and Cassandra worried what Endellion would command it to do as it began to pulse. The red glow flashed, faster and faster. Something was happening, but Cassandra was helpless to do anything about it. Ambric and his men were busying themselves looking for something, anything, to elevate them to be able to strike the horrific beast. Cassandra knew there was nothing they would be able to do in time to stop whatever Endellion's plan was.

She put her arms around her brother and hugged him tight. 'I'll never leave you again,' she whispered as she closed her eyes and awaited their fate.

The red pulse illuminated the room.

Cassandra pressed herself closer into the body of her brother.

A tear poured down her cheek as she waited for death.

It didn't come.

'What have you done?' Endellion's voice echoed around the room. It was the witches own voice, but there was a rasp to it as it came from the mouth of the insect.

Cassandra looked towards the Glimm. They were standing in a line, holding hands. Each of them was glowing red, each wore smiles on their faces. 'We can't do it all the time, but if we concentrate, we can null the power of an individual Glimmer, but only for short periods,' the Glimm at the front of the line said.

Cassandra heard the thud and the roll as the Glimmer slipped from the grasp of the firefly and hit the sone floor. As it rolled towards her brother, she heard the thrum of the beast's wings change pitch.

~~~~

Ambric watched as the firefly hovering above the throne room adjusted its position. The point of the sting at the bottom of its body was directed towards Cassandra and her brother. He looked at the size of it and then back at the young girl protecting her brother. He estimated the sting to be long enough to penetrate both their bodies. He also guessed that the same poison that killed Bernard was what was dripping from its tip now. His men were still looking for ways to attack the beast when he saw it flicker from firefly to Endellion and back to a firefly again. *The magic of the Glimmer is wearing thin,* he thought.

He didn't have time to wait for her to fall from the sky. He could see she was poised to strike, and he knew he couldn't, and wouldn't, allow it to happen.

The firefly tipped its sting towards the young couple on the floor and made its move. Its wings beat faster, and it accelerated, sting first, towards the defenceless queen and her brother.
~~~~

Without thinking, Ambric launched himself at the beast. He jumped, swinging his sword in a broad arch.

The swing was true.

There was resistance on his blade as the steel cut through the beast's body, opening it up, spilling glowing yellow poison over the stone floor. The beast screamed. It was a terrible sound. As the yellow slurry poured from its thorax, it flickered again between beast and Endellion. The scream changed too, an ugly hybrid of human and insect.

With another thrust, he pushed the whole of his sword into the beast until the warmth of its poison was slithering down his arm.

The thing flickered again.

The firefly visage melted away, leaving Endellion in her human form once again. Ambric's sword had ripped her torso from her chest to her stomach.

Her wide dark eyes were wild, shocked, and filled with wonder as they stared into Ambric's own. She lowered her head to look towards her wound as her intestines dripped down his sword. Her mouth twitched as if she was attempting to form words, or a question.

Ambric thought the question might have been … Why? Or how?

With another flicker, her human form melted away to be replaced once again by her firefly image.

Its wings drooped; its legs hung limp from its body.

The firefly died; Endellion died with a small shudder on the end of Ambric's sword. As she passed, the red glow from the Glimm passed back into the orb that lay on the blood strewn floor, next to Cassandra and Alexander.

~~~~

Cassandra watched as Ambric speared the firefly. It sickened her, but she couldn't look away as his blade tore through the thing's body.

Then she saw it turn.

It flickered from being a horrific monster, a thing of nightmares, into an old woman dying from the open wound in her chest, back to being an insect again, then it died.

She saw the flash of red as the Glimm transferred the power back into the red orb.

She also watched as the tide of blood began to surge towards her.
~~~~

Something was strange about it, something she couldn't put her finger on.

There was *too much* blood.

The wound in Endellion's chest was deep; it had caused her to bleed out, but there was more blood gushing towards her than could issue from just one person. She looked up from the crimson tide heading her way, and what she saw broke her heart.

The sting that had been heading towards her and Alexander never hit its intended targets because it hit an unexpected obstacle on its way.

That obstacle was Robert Ambric.

The sting pierced his stomach. She could see the sharp, bloody tip protruding from the old soldier's back.

The blood that was pouring towards her was Ambric's.

'The Glimmer,' he whispered, pink spittle flying from his mouth.

Cassandra didn't understand what he was talking about.

'The Glimmer,' he croaked. 'Take it. Do what needs to be done. Do it now.'

The pink foam from his mouth turned dark.

She looked to where he was gesturing and saw the red Glimmer. It was lying in a pool of blood. She reached and grasped for it. It was slick and slippery, but it felt familiar.

Alexander watched her pick it up.

He looked at the orb and offered her the blue one he was still holding. 'Here, sister. Take this one too. It's yours anyway. I gave it to you,' he smiled.

Cassandra looked to the blue orb and then to the red one in her hands. A feeling rose within her, a feeling she had never expected. She thought maybe she should be the one to hold the Glimmers, that she could stand in the place of Endellion. She knew she would be a fair and just ruler of the land.

But she didn't want it!

It was more than not wanting it; she was not destined for it.

It was someone else's destiny.

'No,' she said, handing them back to him. 'The Glimmers are yours. I watched you take ownership of them earlier. It's you who are chosen. You are the true, natural custodian of the Glimmers.'

He looked Cassandra in the eyes, and she saw it. He was truly regal. He *was* the bravest knight in all Azuria.

He was her brother.

He was Alexander.

He reached out and accepted the blood-soaked prizes from his sister.

The chanting from the Glimm and the Sisterhood continued as the lead Glimm and Camarilla stepped forward. Camarilla looked at the body of her daughter. She had died caught between firefly and human. The wraith's sad eyes paid respect to the broken body before her.

Ambric watched. His own broken body was tended to by his soldiers, Matthew at the fore, hoping to save his beloved general. The thick, dark blood pouring from the older man's mouth told him there was no saving Ambric this time.

'Alexander. You have presented the Glimmers before the Throne of Glimm. Do you accept the responsibility of the powers that come with the role of custodian?' the lead Glimm asked.

Alexander looked at the faces in the Throne Room. All of them were looking at him. His sister, the old men, the strange purple women, the soldiers, some he recognised from the castle, and the dying soldier beside the grotesquely twisted body of the old crone who was half firefly.

He looked at the Glimmers. They were glowing in his hands. He remembered the blue one from the last time he saw his true sister, and he remembered the red one, the one the witch had used. *The one she used to keep me in her thrall,* he thought.

'I am ready,' he said, his voice barely above a whisper. 'I am ready to wield this power for the good of the kingdoms and beyond. With the death of the witch Endellion, I release the falsehood that is the annexed kingdom. The City of the Fireflies will now, and forever, be known as the Kingdom of Carnelia.'

This brought a murmur of approval from the soldiers present, and he watched as Ambric attempted a pained smile.

'Now,' the boy, who had somehow grown into a man within the last few moments, continued. 'Allow the transference to begin.'

'In order for this to proceed, my Lord,' the lead Glimm said amid the chanting in the room, 'there requires a sacrifice. One who loves you and gives their life freely and of their own accord.'

The room was silent for a short while. Then Cassandra stepped forth. 'I'll do it,' she said aloud. 'For the love of my brother, I would give my life freely for him and for what he done for the kingdoms today.'

'Cassandra, no,' Alexander replied, his voice soft yet commanding. He shook his head. 'This is not your time.'

'It is not for you to say, brother. I give myself freely as sacrifice to Carnelia, Azuria, and for the many, many people who have suffered and died in my name.'

The Glimm looked at Alexander. 'Do you accept this sacrifice?' he asked.

Cassandra nodded as a tear fell down her brother's cheek.

'Ahem …' a voice behind them spoke up.

Both brother and sister turned to see who it was.

'Are you forgetting someone here?' Ambric's voice sounded like air being released from an old tyre. 'Do I not love you, Alexander?' he hissed, slowly. 'Do I not give myself to the cause of Carnelia, and to Azuria?'

Alexander watched as his sister dropped to her knees in the mixed blood of Endellion and Ambric.

'My dear Sir Ambric,' she whispered, 'you have already given so much to the cause. You are the true hero of both kingdoms. You cannot die here today; you are the symbol of everything that is worth fighting for.'

The old soldier smiled; his teeth were stained pink from the blood in his mouth. He laughed; it was an odd sound. 'Death is inevitable now, ma'am.' He raised his hand and touched the young girl's cheek. It left a bloody smear. 'I will continue to be a symbol. You have a lot of work to do, my queen. Mine is done. I *already am* the sacrifice.' He laughed again, coughing more blood as he did. 'Let me rest!'

The Glimm looked at Ambric and then at Alexander.

The youth nodded a small acknowledgement to the old man.

The Glimm closed his eyes, recognising the acceptance of the sacrifice. He turned his head and looked at Ambric. 'You, Robert Ambric, have accepted the role of sacrifice. Do you love this man before us unreservedly?'

Ambric swallowed hard. The taste of what he swallowed must not have been to his liking, as the face he pulled was almost comical. 'I do love him,' he manged. 'And I give myself freely.'

'Then I accept your word,' the Glimm said. He turned towards the stricken man and put his hand on his head. He leaned in, and Cassandra watched as he whispered something into his ear. The Glimm nodded at

Ambric's response before bending low and kissing him once on each check.

Ambric smiled, then closed his eyes.

The Glimm stood, his attention passed back to Alexander. 'It is done,' he said, his head bowed low. 'Sir Ambric of Carnelia is dead.'

The soldiers of Azuria, the Rebels, and the Ferals, all fell to their knees in reverence for what they had just witnessed.

Cassandra's tears were flowing freely. 'A true hero has passed today,' she whispered.

The Glimm looked at her and smiled. 'His passing is not insignificant,' he replied.

Cassandra nodded.

'He left a gift for you, and for both Kingdoms. He said it is something much needed.'

Alexander watched the conversation between his sister and the Glimm. He grinned as he closed his eyes. Both Glimmers began to glow.

A cold wind passed through the room, and the purple glow from both orbs filled the large room.

Then everything went black. It was silent. No one moved, no one spoke, no one breathed.

'What have I missed?' came the voice echoing from the darkness.

Cassandra recognised it at once, although she didn't quite believe it. The glow from the orbs resumed and illuminated the room once again. She turned her head and scanned for the owner of the voice.

He was standing behind the soldiers.

No one had noticed him. The men turned to see what the girl was looking at.

There was much shouting and dropping of swords. After many hugs and handshakes, the men, all of them, dropped to their knees again, this time before Bernard.

'My King!' Matthew announced.

Bernard shook his head and patted the man on the shoulder. 'How many times have I told you not to call me that?' he laughed as he pushed past him.

He had eyes for only one person in the room.

Cassandra!

The lovers stared at each other for what felt like an eternity.

'Is … is it really you?' she asked, her body shaking.

Bernard smiled. ‘I could ask the same of you,’ he replied.
Then, with no further ado, they took each other in their arms and kissed. The soldiers broke into spontaneous cheering.

~~~~

Those in the audience in Outpost Three were dancing in the courtyard as Cassandra and Bernard kissed.
Their king was back, and he had himself a queen.
Although, it didn’t quite feel that way. There was deep love for the young Bernard, but they knew in their hearts he was never destined to be their king.

~~~~

Castle Carnelia was stunned. They had seen the woman they thought of as their queen turn into a firefly. They had watched her attack and try to kill a young lady who also looked like their queen. Then they watched as their prince took custodian of the Glimmers.
It was a lot for everyone to take in.

~~~~

Cassandra looked at the Glimm, then at her brother. ‘Shall we do this? Sir Ambric was not one to be kept waiting.’ She smiled.
‘It is done, sister,’ Alexander said. ‘It was done the moment Bernard returned.’
‘The transference is complete,’ the lead Glimm announced as he regarded the boy with reverence.
‘The first thing I do with my power is to reopen the ways of the Glimm and the Sisterhood of the Purple to learning. I will open this castle and the Throne—’
‘Your castle and Throne,’ the Glimm interrupted him.
Alexander smiled and nodded. ‘I stand corrected,’ he laughed. ‘*My* castle and Throne. I will begin the teaching of the ways of the Great Lord Glimm once again. The Sisterhood and the Glimm will work towards a new millennium of peace, understanding, and knowledge.’
The Glimm and the Sisters all nodded their approval.
~~~~

'Bernard, you *will* be King of Carnelia, and Cassandra, you will be again be Queen of Azuria. A new era shall be ushered in. I will prove to be a fair and just custodian of the Glimmers, and I will bring balance back to our lands.'

Bernard shuffled his feet and looked at the young man with the Glimmers. 'Excuse me,' he whispered.

Alexander, and everyone else, looked to him.

Bernard shook his head. 'I … I can't take the crown.' He ignored the gasps from the soldiers as he turned towards Cassandra. 'All I want is you. I renounce my titles, my lands, and my throne. I believe in my heart they all belong to Matthew anyway.' He turned towards the gathered crowd and kneeled before the shocked knight, bowing his head. 'King Matthew and Queen Linda, the new king and queen of Carnelia.'

The other soldiers present all bowed their heads towards their new liege, as did Cassandra.

Part Six

1.

THERE WAS MUCH to do in both Kingdoms. Casandra was welcomed back into her home, along with her husband, Bernard. He steadfastly refused to be addressed as king, it was not a mantle he was comfortable with.

The men of the Rebels and Ferals worked closely with the armies of the Azure, led by Carlos, and the newly anointed King Matthew. They, along with Queen Linda, passed Carnelia's principal city and castle back to the control of the Carnelian people.

The two kingdoms vowed for peace, with healthy trade deals and a new and better understanding of how each Kingdom worked.

All disputes were to be brought before the royalty of each land. The good relations between them would bring forth a new tolerance for each, the likes of which had never been seen before.

All disputes they couldn't work out together would be taken before the Glimm and the Sisterhood of the Purple. Alexander presided over the newly opened University of Glimm, where students, both male and female, would study and work towards a better future under the tutelage of the Custodian of the Glimmers.

A new day had dawned, and a better future had been forged.

2.

THE NIGHT WAS dark, and the rains had come. The black sky was hidden by thick, murky clouds. Rumbles of thunder could be heard growling in the distance. It sounded like the crumbling of walls. The smell in the air told anyone with any understanding of the weather that the storm was getting closer instead of further away.

A purple streak of lighting illuminated Castle Carnelia.

People in their beds would hold their loved ones closer on nights like these. They would gather to tell tales of black rain, huge fireflies, and evil witches. Children would pretend to be brave, wanting to know more about Endellion and what she could do, but then they would sleep with illumination in their rooms after their parents had searched closets, under their beds, and anywhere shadows formed for signs of poisonous stings.

Tonight was one of those nights.

A scream tore through the corridors of the castle.

It was blood-thirsty and wet. It told of pain and suffering, and it sent shudders down the spines of any unfortunate soldier who found themselves within earshot.

The scream was followed by a cry.

It was a child's cry.

The child was screaming in protest of having been pulled cruelly from the comforts of its mother's womb, into a cold, frightening world filled with wonders and colours.

The child was a boy.

Bernard grasped Cassandra's hand. He squeezed hard as she pushed.

Both shed more than one tear that night.

A true heir of Carnelia, and of Azuria, was born.

In the dark hair on his head, a streak of purple was prominent.

The child was the joining of the two nations.

Prince Alexander Robert Philip Thaddius was presented to both nations the very next day. He was rightly seen by everyone as a symbol of the future.

It was a future filled with peace and prosperity, watched over by the purple glow of both Glimmers.

One was blue, one was red, both were powerful, but together, they were purple.

Author's Notes

Where do I start making notes for these three books? It's one long epic tale of bravery, magic, love, and sacrifice that has been a part of my life for a long, long time.

I think I started with the idea for this saga not long after I had finished writing *The Twelve*, my debut novel. That was at least five years ago. I think I started it because I wanted to write a book that my daughter could read when it was finished.

I wanted to have a strong female protagonist, but I wanted that character to be a bad-ass villain too. I don't know why, but I loved the idea of duality in a person. The idea came to me in a flash of inspiration about the villain of the piece impersonating the hero, and the Glimmers were born.

I am going to confess something here, something that might shock and put some people off, but I am not a huge fan of YA adventure books, and also, I am not a huge fan of fantasy books. Obviously, I have read *The Hobbit* and the Lord of the Rings saga, and I have devoured The Song of Ice and Fire books (hurry up with that last one), but not much else.

I enjoyed the latter a lot more than the former.

I can't even think if I have read any YA (*The Call*, by Peadar O Guilin is the only one I can recall). This will be remedied, as there are some fantastic YA books out there with strong, young protagonists.

Anyway, originally, this saga was just meant to be one book, just a battle against good and evil with a little bit of magic thrown in for good measure, but as these things tend to happen, more and more folklore about the Glimmers just kept on pouring out. I grew to love the Glimm, and I really enjoyed writing Endellion. She really needed a tragic background, and I hope I did her justice (as I really don't want her visiting me in my dreams).

Red against blue is a big thing in my family. Coming from Liverpool in the UK, there is a big football rivalry, with the red side being one of the most famous football clubs in the world and the blue side always seeming to be in their shadow. As a fan of the blue side, I had to make the red Glimmer the bad one … that was for my dad, Ted McCluskey, the strongest hero I have ever met in my whole life.

Many, many changes in my life have happened since I wrote the opening sentences for this book, and each scenario within this saga brings something back to the forefront of my mind when I have been editing and reiterating. That has been bittersweet, to put it lightly. One of the things that springs to mind was sitting and editing all three books, one after the other, while confined to my bed after being hit with COVID-19. I was lucky enough to only have a mild dose, but those ten days in bed really took it out of me.

But here it is, done, in its entirety. I am pretty stoked about how it turned out, and I really, really hope that you, the readers, can get behind Cassandra, Endellion, Bernard, Ambric, and the Glimm, and enjoy this saga for what it is … just a bit of fun.

~~~~

Now for the thank you section.

First and foremost, I have to thank Lauren Davies. She has put up with my mood swings for years as I journey along my writer's path, and these three books have been a challenge. As I write these notes, she hasn't read the books yet, as she is usually my final proof reader, but she has told me that after some of the horror I have *forced* her to read over the years, she is really looking forward to this one.

Next up, the rest of my family. Grace and Sian particularly. They have to put up with my day-to-day insanity too.

Tony Higginson, as always, is a writer's rock. He is a champion for indie authors everywhere, and I hope we can start up our business and make it a success, mostly because the effort he puts into the indie author scene in the Liverpool area is phenomenal.

Lisa Lee Tone, my editor. Once again, I have made her read some hideous stuff. But you know what? She loves the horrible stuff better than
~~~~

the nicer stuff. Ha … you want to see what's coming her way in the future.

The proof-readers for this series have been consistently fantastic. Kelly Rickard has turned out to be a real force of good (Blue Glimmer) for me and my books. She tells it as it is and always gives in-depth analysis of what she's thinking. Annmarie Barrell, Joanne Lewtas, and Tara Lane have also been fantastic.

Stephen, or is it Peter, Harper, as Forsaken Folklore did the fantastic artwork for these book. He is so easy to work with. If you haven't seen any of his other work (then where have you been as he's done most of my covers) then you seriously need to check his stuff out.

Most of all, and as always, I need to thank you guys, the readers. Without feedback, reviews, purchases, shoutouts on social media, readers groups, and just being there for me, this would all be a HUGE waste of time. So please accept this thanks and read the books.

So, all that is left for me to say is, PLEASE PLEASE PLEASE REVIEW THESE BOOKS once you have read them …

Thank you …

Dave McCluskey
Liverpool
January 2022

Printed in Great Britain
by Amazon

19199223R00129